Viktor Pavlov, code-named 'The Professional',
leads a unit of Soviet Jews whose mission is to kidnap
Vasily Yermakov, the Soviet leader. They
will demand in return the release to the West
of ten top Russian scientists. Each of 'The Zealots',
as they called themselves, is a specialist.
Each has fashioned a flawless mask of loyalty
to the U.S.S.R., but their true loyalty is to freedom
and as the Express slowly crosses the 5,800 miles
of Trans-Siberian Railway, each joins the train
with a carefully defined part to play in
The Yermakov Transfer.

The
Yermakov
Transfer

Derek Lambert

CORGI BOOKS
A DIVISION OF TRANSWORLD PUBLISHERS LTD

To Patrick, my son, an avid reader of Russian novels

THE YERMAKOV TRANSFER
A CORGI BOOK 0 552 09866 3

Originally published in Great Britain
by Arlington Books (Publishers) Ltd.

PRINTING HISTORY
Arlington edition published 1974
Corgi edition published 1975

Copyright © Derek Lambert 1974

This low-priced Corgi Book has been completely reset
in a type face designed for easy reading, and
was printed from new plates. It contains
the complete text of the original hard-cover edition.

Corgi Books are published by
Transworld Publishers Ltd.,
Cavendish House, 57-59 Uxbridge Road,
Ealing, London W.5.
Made and printed in the United States of America
by Arcata Graphics,
Buffalo, New York

'When the trains stop that will be the end'

—Lenin

Acknowledgements

Of the many books I have read during my research for this novel I should like, in particular, to acknowledge my debt to *To the Great Ocean* by Harmon Tupper, published by Secker and Warburg in Britain and Little, Brown and Co. in America; *A History of Russian Railways* by J. N. Westwood, published by George Allen and Unwin; *Romantic Railways* by Kenneth Westcott Jones, published by Arlington Books; *The Jews in Soviet Russia Since 1917* edited by Lionel Kochan, published by the Oxford University Press; *Between Hammer and Sickle* published by Signet Books.

DEPARTURE

Among those on board the Trans-Siberian Express leaving Moscow's Far Eastern station at 10:05 on Monday, October 1, 1973, was the most powerful man in the Soviet Union and the man who planned to kidnap him.

They sat four coaches apart: the Kremlin leader, Vasily Yermakov, in a special carriage surrounded by militia and KGB as thick as aphides; the kidnapper, Viktor Pavlov, in a soft-class sleeper with a Tartar general and his wife.

Yermakov, burly and jovial, sat at a desk in a black leather, wing-back chair smoking a cigarette with a cardboard filter and watching the KGB screen the last passengers boarding the train. The peasants with their samovars, blankets, punished suitcases, and live chickens looked apprehensive; but not as scared as the enemies of the state Yermakov had interrogated in the thirties. That was progress.

He stubbed out the cigarette as if he were squashing a cockroach. The abrupt movement alerted his two bodyguards and nervous secretary who hovered expectantly. Yermakov, as avuncular as Stalin, nodded approvingly: he liked disciplined obedience but not servility which he despised.

He said, "I think it's going to snow."

Now it *had* to snow.

"I think you're right, Comrade Yermakov," said the secretary, a pale man wearing gold-rimmed spectacles whose knowledge of Kremlin intrigue had given him neurasthenia.

The two bodyguards in gray suits with coathanger shoulders and pistol bulges at the chest, also voiced their agreement.

And outside it did smell of snow. The sky was gray and bruised, the faces of the crowds, marshaled for Yermakov's departure, stoic with the knowledge of the months ahead. The atmosphere was appropriate for the journey into Siberia, the journey into winter.

For Yermakov the journey had a magnificent symbolism. The historic Russian theme of pushing east—while the Americans pushed west; the freeing of the czars' manacled armies of slaves; the victorious pursuit of the White Russians; the new civilization the young Russians had built on foundations of permafrost as hard as concrete.

The trip had been his own idea, already much publicized. A series of rallies in the outposts of the Soviet Union with speeches warning the Chinese massed on the Siberian border, dissidents such as

Alexander Solzhenitsyn and Andrei Sakharov, and the Jews agitating to leave Russia for Israel.

He glanced at his wristwatch as big as a hand-cuff. Five minutes to go. He drank some Narzan mineral water.

On the platform two plainclothesmen hustled a passenger out of the station. A stocky, curly-haired man with a brown, Georgian complexion. He was bent double as if he had been kneed in the groin. Presumably his papers hadn't been in order; or his passport had been stamped with the word JEW.

Yesterday there had been a Zionist demonstration outside the Central Telegraph Office in Gorki Street. Privately, Yermakov thought: To hell with them. Let the troublemakers go, keep the brains.

He pointed at the prisoner being dragged along, his feet scuffing the ground. "Jew?"

His secretary nodded, polishing his spectacles. "Quite possibly. Security is very tight today."

"In Lubyanka he will have ample time to learn by heart the Universal Declaration of Human Rights. 'Everyone has the right to leave any country, including his own, and to return to his country.'"

"Article 13, Point 2," said the secretary, replacing his spectacles.

"The Universal Declaration of Human Treachery," Yermakov said.

Power flowed strongly in his veins. He stared at the wall map of Siberia with the railway wandering across it. Now he was Yermak the outlawed Cossack who, in 1581, began the conquest of Siberia for Ivan the Terrible and was rewarded with a breastplate of armor, a silver drinking chalice, and a fur cloak from Ivan's shoulders.

The train throbbed with life, the troops outside snapped to attention. The moment of departure was only partially spoiled by the completion of Yermakov's line of thought: Yermak's career was cut short by a band of Tartar warriors: he tried to swim to safety but was drowned by the weight of the breastplate.

Viktor Pavlov, who planned to hold Yermakov for ransom, lay on his bunk in the soft-class sleeper with his face close to the sandbag buttocks of the Tartar general's wife. He doubted at this moment whether the buttocks of Miss World would have aroused him.

From his East German briefcase he took a sheaf of papers covered with the figures and symbols of a scheme to automate the traffic system of Khabarovsk in the Far East of Siberia. To Pavlov, the computerized figures also gave the times agents would board the train, the distance out of Chita that the kidnap would be executed, the wavelengths of the radio messages to be transmitted from five European capitals, the long-range weather forecast and troop deployments east of Irkutsk.

But there were imponderables beyond the computer's electronic brainpower. For one—a jealous Tartar general who considered his elephantine wife to be irresistible; for another—the arrest of one operator before he had boarded the train (although they had made allowances for casualties); for yet another—the unknown occupant of the vacant bunk above Pavlov. The computer in his brain had allowed for six imponderables.

There were four bunks in the compartment, a small table and lamp, a dearth of space. Pavlov chose the bunk underneath the vacant berth in case he needed the advantage: he presumed the general had chosen the bunk above his wife in case of some frailty in the structure.

The general's wife was unpacking a suitcase. Flannel nightdress, striped pajamas, toilet bag, bottle of Stolichnya vodka, bottle of Armenian brandy, two loaves of black bread, goat's cheese, four onions, and a pistol.

The general, who was in civilian clothes, loosened his tie and said, "Nina, the vodka." He took a swig, wiped the neck of the bottle, and stared at Pavlov in case he had been sexually aroused by a movement of pectoral muscle, a creak of corset. Reassured, he handed the bottle to Pavlov.

Pavlov shook his head. "No thanks."

The general frowned, stroking his drooping moustache.

An enemy in the compartment, Pavlov decided, was an unnecessary complication, but so was liquor.

The general's wife began to peel an orange so that, with the vodka, the compartment smelled like a sweet liqueur. Juice spat in Pavlov's eyes.

He explained, "I've got work to do," waving the sheaf of papers. "I must have a clear head." He had learned the wisdom of telling lies which were also the truth.

The general took another swig. "A scientist?" His tone was hopeful because, of the two classes of citizens—the military and others—scientists ranked highest in the latter. "Nuclear, perhaps?"

"Let's just say I'm a scientist." The military appreciated secrecy.

Pavlov had been screened three times before getting his rail ticket. He had been cleared because he was the leading authority on computers, because he was married to a heroine of the Soviet Union waiting for him in Siberia, because there was no reference to his Jewishness on his papers.

He returned to his documents while the general unwrapped a mildewed cigar and his wife started eating sunflower seeds, blowing the husks on the floor. There were three agents already on the train, none with JEW on their passports; each with an irradicable strain of Jewishness in them; each a fanatic; each a possible martyr.

Martial music poured through the loudspeakers as the train picked up speed through the outskirts of Moscow. It became an anthem to which Pavlov supplied the words:

> *If I forget you, O Jerusalem*
> *Let my right hand wither away;*
> *Let my tongue cling to the roof of my mouth*
> *If I do not remember you,*
> *If I do not set Jerusalem*
> *Above my highest joy.*

The door opened and the missing passenger entered. A powerful man with polished cheeks, black hair thinning; built for the outdoors—hunting moose in the *taiga*, breath frosting the air; incongruous in his dark blue suit, uncomfortable beneath any roof. He breathed fresh air into the compartment, greeted them breezily, said his name was Yosif Gavralin, and swung himself into the berth above Pavlov.

Pavlov wondered what rank he held in the KGB. He thought he must feel vulnerable in the upper bunk. A single upward thrust of a knife.

The general sucked unsuccessfully at his cigar. Smoke dribbled from its fractured stem. "Cuban," he said with disgust, giving it to his wife who squashed it among her sunflower husks.

8

In the next compartment, Harry Bridges, an American journalist almost trusted by the Russians, read the carbon copy of the story he had filed that morning to New York via London. He read it without pride.

It was a description of the Communist party leader's departure for Siberia which a messenger had taken to their office in a penitentiary-style office block in Kutuzovsky Prospect to telex. It was uninspired, dull, and hackneyed. But it would be published because it announced that the paper's Moscow correspondent, Harold Bridges, was the only Western reporter—apart from correspondents of Communist journals like the *Morning Star*—permitted to cover the Siberian tour.

But at what cost?

From his upper berth Harry Bridges glanced speculatively at the English girl lying on the lower-berth bunk across the compartment. Somewhere on this train there was a story better than the speeches of which he had advance copies. Any story was better. The girl, perhaps—the only possibility in the compartment they shared with a train-spotter and an Intourist guide. Once Bridges would have looked for stories: these days they were handed to him. Once he would have instinctively asked himself: "What's a young English girl with a hyphen in her name and fear in her eyes crossing Siberia for?"

No more. There were a lot of answers Harry Bridges didn't want to find out; so he didn't ask himself the questions. Just the same, old instincts lurked so he smiled at her and asked, "Making the whole trip?"

Bridges's assessment of Libby Chandler was half right: she didn't possess a hyphen but she was scared.

She nodded. "But not as far as Vladivostock. No foreigners are allowed there, are they?"

"A few." Bridges didn't elaborate because he was one of the few allowed inside the port on the Bay of the Golden Horn, a closed city because of its naval installations.

Some said Harry Bridges had sold his soul. He didn't contradict them; merely reminded himself that his accusers were the correspondents harangued by their offices for missing his exclusives.

A girl attendant knocked on the door to see if they were settled. They said they were but she couldn't accept this. She tidied their luggage, tested the lamps and windows, distributed copies of Lenin's speeches. Through the open door came the smell of smoke from the samovar she tended.

Bridges clipped the carbon of his first dispatch into a springback file and consulted the advances. Yermakov attacked the dissidents at Novosibirsk, the Chinese at Irkutsk, the Jews at Khabarovsk.

They'll have to do better for me than that, Bridges decided. Not only would Tass give the speeches verbatim so that every paper in the States would have stories through AP and UPI, but the weary rhetoric wasn't worth publishing. He needed an interview with Yermakov.

He stuck the file under his pillow and lay with his head propped on one hand. In the old days he would have mentally recorded everything in the compartment including the names, occupations, and ages of his fellow travelers. He had always done this when flying in case the plane crashed and he was the sole survivor with the story: the names of the crew—in particular the stewardesses—and the credentials of the passenger next to him.

The train-spotter was filling his notebook with figures. The dark-haired Intourist girl with the heavy, sensuous figure was shuffling papers beneath him, rehearsing her recitation for a tour of a hydroelectric plant.

He caught the glance of the blonde English girl and they exchanged the special smile of travelers sharing experience. He passed his pack of cigarettes to her but she refused. He bracketed her as twenty-two years old, university graduate, the defender of several topical causes, apartment in Chelsea (shared?).

But what was she scared of?

Unsolicited, the professional instincts of Harry Bridges began to surface. "Are you breaking your journey?" he asked.

"Three times," she said. She didn't elaborate.

"Novosibirsk, Irkutsk, and Khabarovsk, I suppose. They usually offer you those. In fact they're the only places they'll let you off."

The Intourist girl made disapproving sounds.

Bridges said, "Anyway, you're traveling in distinguished company."

"I know. I didn't know anything about Yermakov being on the train."

"So we'll be together for at least a week."

She looked startled. "Why, are you breaking your journey as well?"

"Wherever *he* stops"—Bridges pointed in the direction of the special coach—"I stop."

"I see." She frowned. She should have asked why, Bridges thought. Her total lack of curiosity appalled him.

The train-spotter from Manchester joined in. "It's going to be difficult to know when to go to bed and when to get up. They keep Moscow time throughout the journey."

It was too much for the Intourist guide. "We sleep

when we're tired. We get up when we wake. We eat when we're hungry." She reminded Bridges of an air stewardess sulking because her affair with the pilot had run into turbulence.

"And we drink when we're thirsty?" Bridges added. He grinned at the girl. "Would you like a drink?"

"No thank you." She reacted as if he'd asked her to take her clothes off; it was out of character.

"Well, I'm going to have one." He slid off the bunk into the no-man's land between the berths. No one spoke.

He closed the door behind him and stood in the corridor hazed with smoke from the samovar. Frowning, he realized that he had set himself an assignment: to find out what the girl was scared of.

The serpent face of the pea-green electric locomotive of Train No. 2 with its yellow flashes, red star, and weather-proofed picture of Lenin nosed inquisitively through the fringes of Moscow. The driver, Boris Demurin, making his last journey, wished he was at the controls of an old locomotive for the occasion—a black giant with a red-hot furnace and a smokestack breathing smoke and cinders—not this sleek, electric snake.

For forty-three years Demurin had driven almost every type of engine on the Trans-Siberian. The old 2-4-4-0 Mallets built at Kolumna; S.O. classes from Ulan-Ude and Krasnoyarsk; towering P-36 steam locos, E classes now used for freight-switching; American lend-lease 2-8-0's built by Baldwin and ALCO for the United States Army which became the Soviet Sh (III); and then the eight-axle N-8 electrics renumbered VL-8's.

Time had now begun to lose its dimensions for Demurin. He was prematurely old with coal dust buried in the scars on his face and he lived in a capsule of experience in which he could reach out and touch the historic past as easily as the present.

The capsule embraced the slave labor that had helped to build the railway; the corrupt economies which had sent trains charging off frost-buckled track; the life and times of Czar Nicholas II who had baptized the railway only to die by the bullet beside it; the Czech Legion, which had converted the coaches into armored cars after the revolution; Lake Baikal which had contemptuously sucked an engine through its ice when the Russians tried to cross it to fight the Japanese.

The railway's heroes, its lovers and victims, peopled Demurin's capsule. At seventeen he had stood on the footplate of a butter train bound for Vladivostock carrying 150 exiles to the gold and silver mines, with soot and coals streaming past his face. Now, nearly half a century later, he was an attendant in a power house.

He scowled at his crew, bewildered by the fusion of time. "How are we doing for time?"

His second-in-command, a thirty-year-old Ukrainian with a neat, knowing face and a glossy hairstyle copied from a 1940 American movie still, said, "Don't worry, old-timer, we're on time."

The Ukrainian thought he should have been in charge. Demurin's rudimentary knowledge of electric power was notorious, and on this trip he was merely a symbol of heroic achievement. "Be kind to him," they had said. "Get him there on time on his last journey." If you fail, with Yermakov on board, they had implied, prepare yourself for a career shunting fish on Sakhalin island. The Ukrainian, whose ambition was to drive the prestige train between Moscow and Leningrad, intended to keep the Trans-Siberian on time.

Demurin wiped his hands with a cloth, a habit—no longer a necessity. "Steam was more reliable," he began. "I wonder . . . ."

The Ukrainian groaned theatrically. "What, old-timer, the line from St. Petersburg to the czar's summer palace at Tsarskoye Selo?" But, although he was half-smart, he wasn't unkind. He patted Demurin's shoulder, laughing to show that it was a joke. "What do you remember, Boris?"

"In 1936 I was on the footplate of an FD 2-10-2 which hauled a train of 568 axles weighing 11,310 tons, for 160 miles."

The item had surfaced like a nugget on sinking soil. He didn't know why he had repeated it. It bewildered him all the more.

The Ukrainian thought: That's what Siberia does for you.

"Did you know," Demurin rambled on, "that when Stalin and his comrades traveled on the Blue Express from Moscow to the Black Sea resorts they had the train sprayed with eau-de-cologne?"

The Ukrainian didn't reply. You could never tell what nuance could be inferred from any comment about a Soviet leader, dead, denounced, or reinstated. All the carriages were crawling with police: it was quite possible that the locomotive, as well as the coaches, was bugged. He stared uneasily at the darting fingers of the dials.

Demurin was silent for a few moments. Silver birches flickered past the windows. Time had overtaken him, the trains had overtaken him. Timber, coal, diesel, electric. What next? Nuclear power? He smelled the soot and steam of his youth, stared round a curve of track with snow plastering his face. He stayed there for a moment, a year, a lifetime, before returning to the electrified present.

"Mikhail," he said, "make sure we have a smooth journey. Make sure we keep to time. You understand, don't you?"

The Ukrainian said, "I understand." And momentarily the smartness which masked knowledge of his own inadequacies was nowhere visible on his neat, ambitious face.

It was 10:10. The train was gathering speed and it would average around 37 mph. It would traverse 5,778 miles to Vladivostok, pass through eight time zones, and, without interruptions, finish the journey in 7 days, 16½ hours. It would normally make 83 stops, spending 13 hours standing at stations. It would cross a land twice the size of Europe where temperatures touched $-38°F$ and trees exploded with the cold. It would circumvent Baikal, the deepest lake in the world, inhabited by freshwater seals and transparent fish that melt on contact with air. It would skirt the Sino-Soviet border where Chinese troops had shown their asses to the Soviets across the River Amur, where the threat of a holocaust still hovered, until it reached the forests near Khabarovsk where the Chinese once sought Gin-Seng, a root said to rejuvenate, where saber-toothed tigers still roam. At Khabarovsk, which claims 270 cloudless days a year—no more, no less—it would disgorge its foreigners who would change trains for Nakhodka and take the boat to Japan. The train had eighteen cars and thirty-six doors; the restaurant car boasted a fifteen-page menu in five languages and at least a few of the dishes were available.

In a small compartment at the rear of the special coach a KGB colonel and two junior officers occupied themselves with their own statistics: the records of every passenger and crew member. The colonel had marked red crosses against fourteen names; each of those fourteen was accompanied in his compartment by a KGB agent. As the last outposts of Moscow fled past the window the colonel, whose career and life were at stake, stood up, stretched, and addressed his two subordinates. "Now check out the whole train again. Every compartment, every lavatory, every passenger."

The officers walked respectively past Yermakov who stared at them closely, communicating apprehension which made them feel a little sick. He had just remembered that, in the old days, it was considered unlucky to travel on the Trans-Siberian on a Monday.

FIRST LEG

1.

The kidnap plot was first conceived by Viktor Pavlov in Room 48 of the Leningrad City Court at Fontanka on December 24, 1970.

On that day two Jews were sentenced to death and nine to long terms of imprisonment for attempting to hijack a twelve-seater AN-2 aircraft at Priozersk airport and fly it to Sweden en route to Israel.

At the back of the courtroom, which seated 200, Pavlov listened contemptuously to the details of the botched-up scheme. When he heard the evidence of one of the accused, Mendel Bodnya, revulsion burned inside him like acid.

Bodnya told the court that he had yielded to hostile influence and deeply regretted his mistake. He thanked the authorities for opening his eyes: he had only wanted to go to Israel to see his mother.

Bodnya got the lightest sentence: four years of camps with intensified regime, and confiscation of property.

Pavlov's contempt for the other amateurs was tempered by admiration for their brave, hopeless idealism.

The woman Silva Zalmanson, in her final statement: "Even now I do not doubt for a minute that some time I shall go after all and that I will live in Israel. . . . This dream, illuminated by two thousand years of hope, will never leave me."

Anatoly Altman: "Today, on the day when my fate is being decided, I feel wonderful and very sad. It is my hope that peace will come to Israel. I send my greetings today, my land. *Shalom Aleichem!* Peace unto you, land of Israel."

When the sentences were announced Pavlov joined the disciplined applause because he had cultivated the best cover there was—anti-Semitism. A woman relative of one of the defendants rounded on him, "Why applaud death?" He ignored her, controlling his emotion as he had controlled it so often before. He was a professional.

He watched impersonally as the relatives climbed onto the benches weeping and shouting. "Children, we shall be waiting for you in Israel. All the Jews are with you. The world is with you. Together we build our Jewish home. *Am Yisroel Khay.*"

With tears trickling down his cheeks, an old man began to sing *"Shma Yisroel."* The other relatives joined in, then some of the prisoners.

Viktor Pavlov sang it too, silently, with distilled feeling, while he continued to applaud the sentences. Then the local party secretary who had collected the obedient spectators realized that the hand-clapping had become part of the Zionist emotion.

Guiltily, he snapped, "Cease applause." Another amateur, Pavlov thought as he stopped clapping: each side had its share of them: the knowledge was encouraging.

At 11 A.M. on December 30, at the Moscow Supreme Court, after a sustained campaign of protest all over the world, the two death sentences were commuted to long sentences in strict regime camps and the sentences on three other defendants reduced.

While the collegium of the Supreme Court was deliberating the appeals, Pavlov waited outside noting the identity of a couple of demonstrators. With their permission he would later identify them to the KGB at their Lubyanka headquarters opposite the toy store. They would be locked up for a couple of weeks for hooliganism and his cover would be strengthened.

The Jewish poet, Iosif Kerler, was giving interviews to foreign correspondents. The Leningrad verdict, he told them, was a sentence on every Jew trying to get an exit visa for Israel. But Pavlov knew there was no point in laying information against Kerler: the police had a dossier on him and there was nothing poetic about it. Nor was there any point in informing on the Jewess from Kiev who was telling correspondents about her son dying in Jerusalem: the KGB had her number, too.

No, the information had to be new and comparatively harmless. Pavlov had an arrangement with a Jewish schoolteacher who didn't mind a two-week stretch during the school holidays. He wore a piece of white cloth pinned to his lapel bearing in Hebrew the slogan NO TO DEATH with a yellow, six-pointed Star of David beneath it. He meant well but he was overplaying his hand; it was like laying information against a man walking across Red Square with a smoking bomb in his hand. A pretty

Jewess had also agreed to serve a statutory two-week sentence. Pavlov would report that she had been chanting provocative Zionist slogans, although she had been doing nothing of the sort because, like Pavlov, she had little time for pleas and protests; Israel was strength and you didn't seek entry with a whine. Pavlov stared at her across the crowd; she stared back without recognition; she, too, was a professional.

Among the correspondents Pavlov noticed the American Harry Bridges. Tall, languid, watchful. He had the air of a man who had the story sewn up. He didn't bother interviewing the demonstrators and managed to patronize the other journalists. Pavlov admired him for that—at the same time he hoped he would rot in hell.

When the success of the appeals was announced the demonstrators sang and shouted their relief. Viktor Pavlov felt no relief; now the amateurs had even lost their martyrdom. They had perpetrated an abortion: he was conceiving a birth.

Viktor Pavlov belonged to that most virulent strain of revolutionaries: those who don't wholly belong to the cause they are fighting for. He was fighting for Soviet Jewry and he was only part Jewish.

Sometimes his motives scared him. Why, when so many full-blooded Jews advised "Caution, caution" did he, a mongrel, call for "Action, action"? What worried him most was the sincerity of his conviction. Was the scheming and inevitable brutality merely a heritage? A family tree planted in violence? And the right of the Jews to emigrate to Israel—was that merely a facile cause?

Passionately, Viktor Pavlov sought justification. He found it mostly in the richness of his Jewish strain of blood. So deeply did he feel it that it sometimes seemed to him that it had a different course from his gentile blood.

His great, great grandparents had been Jews born in the vast Pale of Settlement in European Russia where the czars confined the Jews. After the murder of Alexander II the Jews became scapegoats and Pavlov's ancestors were exiled to Siberia to one of the mines which produced 3,600 pounds of gold loot a year for Alexander III.

The persecution of the Jews continued and Viktor Pavlov found deep, bitter satisfaction in its history. Scapegoats; they were always the scapegoats. In 1905 gangs like the Black Hundreds carried out innumerable pogroms to distract attention from Russia's defeat—its debacle—at the hands of the Japanese. Followed in 1911 by the Beilis Case when a Jew in Kiev was accused, and subsequently acquitted, of the ritualistic murder of a child.

By this time the Jewish blood that was to flow in Viktor Pavlov's veins had been thinned. His grandmother, Katia, married a gentile, an ex-convict who helped to build the Great Siberian Railway and became a gold baron in the wild-east town of Irkutsk.

Here Pavlov's soul-searching got waylaid. His great grandfather lived in a palace—brawling, whoring, gambling, and using gold nuggets for ashtrays. He was a millionaire, a capitalist, and thus an enemy of the revolutionaries—a White Russian. Most of the Jews were Reds.

Pavlov allowed his great grandfather to retreat from his deliberations; across Eastern Siberia during the Civil War where he was finally shot by the American interventionists who were not always sure which Russians they were supporting—Reds or Whites.

Pavlov concentrated on World War I. Scapegoats again. The czarist government, trying to explain its shattering defeats by the Germans, blamed traitors in their midst. Jews, naturally.

Then, after the revolution, the Jews came into their own. The Star of David in ascendancy; but too brilliantly, too hopefully, a shooting star doomed to expire. The Jews were among the leaders of the October Revolution and, with an optimism which had no historical foundation—bolstered by the Balfour Declaration in November 1917—they anticipated the end of persecution. They were Russians, they were Bolsheviks, they were Jews.

Even V.I. Lenin lent his support in a speech in March 1919:

> Shame on accursed Tsarism which tortured and per-secuted the Jews. Shame on those who foment hatred towards the Jews, who foment hatred towards other nations.
> Long live the fraternal trust and fighting alliance of the workers of all nations in the struggle to over-throw capital.

Today, Viktor Pavlov thought, it was Leninism that he was fighting.

During the Civil War his grandfather, half-Jewish, a rabid Bolshevik, fell in love with a wild Jewish Muscovite who wore a red scarf and gold earrings. Illegitimately, they sired Pavlov's father.

According to Pavlov's father, Leonid, they had always intended to marry. But when the shooting star faded and Stalin, frightened of the Jewish power around him, began to turn on the Jews again with a ferocity unequaled by his aristocratic ene-mies, there came the 1 A.M. knock on the door. Pa-vlov's grandfather, who looked a little like Trotsky, was away addressing a meeting of railway workers; but his wife was at home and they took her away to one of the camps which history has always pro-

vided for Jews, and she died giving birth to Leonid
Pavlov.

There is my motive, Viktor Pavlov thought. The
origins of my hatred. More often than not, he believed it.

He was born in violence during the siege of
Leningrad in World War II, the son of a teen-ager,
Leonid Pavlov, and a peasant woman, possibly
wholly Jewish, possibly not, who had found time in
between dodging shells and eating stews made of
potato peelings and dog meat, to make love and get
married. She was killed by a German shell shortly
after giving birth to Viktor.

So many records were destroyed during the
siege that it was easy to register Viktor as a Russian. This groveling hypocrisy angered him in his
teens, but later it was to become his strength.

When he was ten Viktor Pavlov stopped some
bullies beating up a small boy with springy black
hair, rimless glasses, and a dark complexion, in the
school playground in Moscow.

"Why," he demanded, grabbing the arm of the
biggest bully, "are you picking on him?"

The bully, whose name was Ivanov, was astonished. "Why? Because he's a Yid, of course."

"So what?" Pavlov was an atheletic boy with
flints in his fists which commanded respect.

"So what? Where have you been? Everyone
knows about the Jews—it's in the papers. They've just
closed the synagogue down the road. It was the center
of the black market in gold rubles and Israeli spies."

"I didn't know you read the papers," Pavlov remarked. "I didn't know you could read."

A crowd had gathered round the two protagonists on the sunlit, asphalt playground. The original victim had vanished.

Ivanov, who had a pudding face and pale hair cut in a fringe, ignored the question. "My father's told me about the Yids. He was in the war. . . ."

"So was mine."

"He said the Jews wouldn't fight. He says he should finish off the job Hitler started."

"Then your father's an idiot. I was born in Leningrad. The Jews fought well. And what about the Jewish generals?"

Dodging logic, Ivanov searched for a diversion. He stared closely at Pavlov's intense dark features, his cap of black hair, his hawkish nose; he saw intelligence and good looks and it made him mad. "Are you a Yid?" he asked. "Are you *Abrashka?*"

The crowd of boys was silent. The question was a provocation, an insult; although they weren't sure why. Why was an *evrei*, so different from a Kazakh, a Kirghiz, a Uzbek?

Ivanov grinned when Pavlov didn't reply. "Prove you're not a Jew," he said.

A cold, dark anger froze inside Pavlov, like no anger he had experienced before. He wanted to batter Ivanov into insensibility; to kill him. "I'll prove it"—he put up his fists—"with these."

Ivanov was still trying to grin. "That's not proof."

"What proof do you want?"

"Show us your cock."

Recently, there had been a scandal in the suburb about Levin the circumciser. He had performed the small operation on the penis of a baby and then gone to Leningrad for a couple of days. But there had been bleeding, so the baby's parents took the baby to a clinic where a Jewish doctor dressed the cut and told the parents they needn't worry. But a male nurse reported the case to the police.

Three weeks later, after intensive interrogation, Levin made a public address renouncing his profession. It was, he announced in a beaten voice, a barbaric ritual. He appealed to Jews all over the Soviet Union to abandon it.

Pavlov advanced on Ivanov. Ivanov backed away appealing to the others, "I bet he's been cut." A few sniggered, the rest remained silent because there was ugliness here they couldn't comprehend.

Pavlov hit him first with his left, then with his right, dislodging a tooth. Ivanov fought back strongly but he couldn't match the inexorable determination of his opponent, his controlled ferocity. He got home with blows in the face and stomach but they had no visible effect on Pavlov who kept coming at him. Pavlov bloodied Ivanov's nose, closed one eye, buckled him with a punch in the solar plexus. Ivanov went down and stayed down whimpering.

Pavlov stood over him. "So you want to see my cock? Then you shall see it and lie there while I piss all over you."

Pavlov unbuttoned his fly and took out his penis, foreskin intact. But he was saved from degrading himself by the appearance of a teacher. He buttoned himself up, standing defiantly beside his fallen opponent.

They were both punished for fighting but no reference was made to the reason for the fight. The teacher seemed to understand Ivanov's attitude; likewise he understood Pavlov's reaction to the suggestion that he might be a Jew.

This was Pavlov's private shame: that he had taken the suggestion as an insult. He resolved to find out more about his mongrel heritage and asked his father, "Am I a Russian or a Jew?"

They were sitting in the small wooden house in the eastern suburbs of Moscow drinking *borscht* soup, mauve and curdled with dollops of cream, and black bread, which Viktor rolled into pellets. His father, although still a young man, was almost a recluse, hiding his Jewishness, earning a meager living doing odd jobs and keeping his nose clean. Although in his death throes, Stalin was still on the rampage.

His father stopped drinking his soup. "Why do you ask?"

Viktor told him what had happened in the playground.

His father looked worried. "Why fight about a thing like that?"

"I don't know. Why should I be so angry because he suggested I was a Jew?"

His father leaned across the table, prodding the air with his spoon. "Listen, boy, you are a Soviet citizen. You are registered as one. I am a Soviet citizen, too. Forget anything you may know about your ancestors." He paused. "About your mother even. This is a great country, perhaps the most powerful country in the world. Be proud to belong to it. Don't sacrifice your life for the sake of the martyrs."

Looking at his father's wasted features, Viktor knew that, although he spoke truths, he lied. Subsequently he wondered if the decision to fight for Zionism was made then. Out of perversity, out of contempt —not fully realized at the time—for paternal weakness; out of his own shame.

From the boy he had protected in the playground he learned about Israel. It was once called Palestine and it was populated by people who had come from Egypt thousands of years ago. They read the Bible, worshipped their own God, their land was destroyed by the Romans, and they spread all over the world. With them they took their traditions, their Bible, their customs, their diets, their suffering. Throughout history, the boy told his savior, the Jews had been persecuted and in the Holocaust they had been slaughtered by the millions by the Nazis.

Viktor envied the boy his birthright; but he couldn't understand his acceptance of his plight.

Pavlov's Jewishness continued to bother him in his early teens; but it was still only a needle, not the knife it was to become. There were summer camps and sports and girls to distract him; he was emerging as a scholar with a keen mathematical brain and the school had high hopes for him at university.

It wasn't till he reached the age when young men seek a cause—when, that is, he became a student—that Viktor Pavlov took the first steps that were to lead him on the path to high treason in the year 1973.

He was nineteen and sleeping with a passionate Jewish girl, a little older than himself, in the Black Sea resort of Sochi. He was at a Komsomol summer camp, she was staying in one of the town's 650 sanatoriums. Her passion and expertize gave him much pleasure; but her fervor had a long-term quality to it and he expected trouble if he broke up the affair, from her brother, a wiry young man with a lot of muscle adhering to his prominent bones, the face of a fanatic, and a premature bald patch which looked like a skull-cap.

One sleepy afternoon, with the sun throwing shoals of light on to the blue sea, Viktor and the girl, Olga Soliman, walked up the mountain road to Dagomys, the capital of Russian tea, 12 miles from Sochi. They drank tea on the porch of a log cabin, ate Kuban pies, then headed for the woods. Their lovemaking had a heightened lust to it on a bed of pineneedles with the sun casting leopard-spots of warmth on their bodies. Such was the aphrodisiac quality of the open air, the sun, the pinewoods, that Viktor was quicker than usual. But, anticipating him, so was Olga.

29

She pointed at his sex shrinking inside its little fleshy hood. "I shouldn't let you touch me with that," she said. "Why don't you have it cut off?"

It was a joke and Viktor laughed. But it was also the truth and a part of him hated the joke.

"Too late now," he said. "Perhaps I should have the whole thing cut off."

She nuzzled him, biting his ear. Her skirt was around her waist and her big, brown-nippled breasts were still free. She said, "Don't ever do that. I've got a lot of use for that." In the long years to come, she implied. And yet, Pavlov thought, with the sun dappling his skin, and the smell of her in his nostrils, I love her. Knowing at the same time that he didn't, not in the absolute, permanent sense. Love was an emotion he could control. He wasn't so sure about hate.

Arm in arm, they walked down the mountain road to Sochi where, it was claimed, the mineral waters of Matsesta could help patients suffering from heart diseases, neuroses, hypertension, skin diseases, and gynecological disorders. There wasn't much that Sochi couldn't alleviate and the brochures asserted that 95 percent of all those seeking treatment left the resort considerably improved or cured. But Viktor Pavlov wasn't among them. His disease went back centuries and no one had ever touched upon a cure.

When they arrived at the Kavkazskaya Riviera sanatorium which took Intourist guests and was therefore prestigious, Olga's brother, Lev, was waiting for them.

He looked at Viktor with fraternal menace. "Had a good time?" Olga's parents were also staying at the sanatorium and the view was that Viktor Pavlov was already one of the family and should make it legal.

"Pleasant," Olga said. "But exhausting." Allowing the implication to sink home before adding, "It

was a long walk." She smiled contentedly—posses-
sively, Viktor Pavlov thought.

They were standing in the lobby of the sanatorium, breathing cool, remedial air.

Lev said, "I have bad news for you." He held a
long manila envelope with the words Moscow University on it.

Olga took the envelope. "Why bad news?"

Lev Soliman grimaced. "Is it ever any other?"

They were all three at the university studying different subjects.

"You're a pessimist," Olga told her brother.

"I am a realist."

"To hell with your realism."

But her fingers shook as she ripped open the envelope with one decadent, pink-varnished fingernail.

She read the letter slowly. Then she began to
shiver.

"What is it?" Viktor asked.

"What's the good news?" her brother asked.

She refolded the letter, replacing it in the envelope. "I've been expelled from the university," she
said.

They were silent for a moment. Then Viktor demanded, "Why?" He paused because he knew the
answer. "You were doing well . . . your examination
marks were good."

Lev Soliman turned on him. "Don't pretend you
don't know. Don't be too much of a hypocrite, a half-
caste. She has been expelled because she is a Jew."

When they returned to Moscow, Viktor Pavlov
told Lev Soliman that he thought he should quit university.

They were walking through Gorky Park, filled

this late-summer day with guitar-strumming youths, picnicking families, lovers, soldiers, and sailors. Bands played, rowing boats patroled the mossy waters of the lake, the ferris wheel took shrieking girls to heaven and back again.

"Why?" Lev asked. "Your guilt again?"

"Perhaps." They stopped at a stall near a small theater and bought glasses of fizzy cherry cordial. They were close now, these two, close enough to exchange insults without malice. "I feel like a traitor."

"Don't," Lev Soliman said. "Feel like a hero."

"What the hell are you talking about?"

"I'll tell you." Lev pointed at the ferris wheel. "Let's take a ride. No one can overhear us up there. Not even the KGB."

The wheel stopped when they were at its zenith and they looked down on a Moscow glazed with heat; the gold cupolas of discarded religions, the drowsy river, the fingers of new apartment blocks. Lev Soliman pointed down at the pygmy people in the park. "Good people," he said. "A great country. Make no mistake about that."

"I don't," Viktor told him. "I was born in Leningrad. Any country that can come back after losing 20 million is a great country. But not so great if you're a Jew, eh?"

"But you're not."

A breeze sighed in the wheel's struts; the car perched in space, swayed slightly.

Pavlov said, "I *am* a Jew."

"That's not what it says on your papers."

"You can't blame me for that. There are thousands of Jews registered as Soviet citizens through mixed marriages."

Lev shrugged. "Maybe. But you're a more convincing case. All your family records destroyed in

Leningrad. Perhaps your mother was pure Russian."

"She was a Jewess."

"That's not what your father told the authorities. And he's registered as a Soviet citizen, too. So you see, your case is pretty clear-cut."

Viktor twisted round angrily, making the car lurch. "What are you getting at?"

"Simply this." Instinctively Lev looked around for eavesdroppers; but there were only the birds. "You can be far more useful to the movement than anyone with Jew stamped on his passport." He gripped Viktor's arm. "There is a movement within the government. That's where you belong."

One month later Lev Soliman was expelled from the university. His one-room apartment was searched under Article 64—"betrayal of the Motherland." He was taken to the Big House and interrogated. A fortnight later he was transferred to a mental institution. Viktor saw him once more two years later; by that time he was insane.

Lev Soliman left Viktor Pavlov with the embryo of an underground movement that had its origins in April 1942 when the Jewish Anti-Fascist Committee of the Soviet Union (JAC) was founded. In those days the Russians needed the Jews to help fight the Nazis and to spread propaganda to the four corners of the world to which the Diaspora had taken them.

For the first time since the Jewish sections of the Communist party, the *Yevsektsia*, were disbanded in 1930, Soviet Jewry had in JAC an officially sanctioned organization. Its journal was called *Unity* and Lev Soliman's parents were among its contributors.

JAC was, of course, another shooting star spluttering in the darkness of prejudice. The Jews thought that, by cooperating with the Soviets in defeating Hitler, they were also constructing a peaceful future in Russia. In 1943, when JAC emissaries Mikhoels and Feffer went on a tour of Jewish communities in the U.S.A., Britain, Canada, and Mexico, Joseph Stalin personally wished them well.

Such was the hope of a new understanding between Russians and Jews that Zionist leaders even suggested a meeting between Chaim Weizmann and Stalin. Churchill was asked to get them together at Yalta in 1945; but Churchill turned down the idea: Churchill knew better.

All this time the Solimans worked joyously for the cause and the future of their son, Lev.

The Allies finally beat the Nazis and the Soviet attitude toward JAC began to cool: the Black Years of Stalin's Jewish purges were beginning. On January 13, 1948, Solomon Mikhoels, director of the Moscow Yiddish State Theater and one of the two emissaries who had spread the word to the world in 1943, was murdered in Minsk. He was a personality and he was emerging as the leader of Russian Jewry.

The murder was followed by the liquidation of the committee. Lev Soliman's parents were charged under Articles 58/10, part 2, to ten years in strict regime camps on charges of "belonging to a Jewish nationalist organization and spreading nationalist propaganda." Lev was looked after by the state.

When Krushchev came to power the Solimans were pardoned and the family was reunited in Moscow. Lev continued his education, winning a place at Moscow University.

But JAC had left its scars on him. He despised naïveté, he trusted no one. Organized protest served a function, but to Lev, it had a whine about it, a recognition of Soviet supremacy. Caution, caution. Lev Soliman spat on caution.

He gathered around him half a dozen young fanatics who believed that violence was the only honorable solution. Like other extremists throughout the world they didn't necessarily represent the beliefs of those they fought for. But this didn't bother them; they regarded the patient resolve of Soviet Zionists as weakness and they operated clandestinely, treating both orthodox Zionists and Russians as the enemy.

This was the nucleus of subversion to which Lev Soliman introduced Viktor Pavlov. The nucleus of which Pavlov was soon to become leader.

In the autumn of 1962 Pavlov began to construct his cover. He already possessed Soviet nationality but he had to establish impeccable references. The secret police knew about his father; therefore they knew there was at least a strain of Jewish blood in him. So, with the approval of the KGB, he worked with the Jewish underground movement publishing *samizdat* newspapers, smuggling subversive literature out of the country—and informing on his colleagues.

Within a year he was an established *agent provocateur* in the student movement. He won a brilliant degree in mathematics and went to Leningrad to study computers to make himself invaluable to a country backward in such refinements.

There he met a girl who, at the age of eighteen, had been made a heroine of the Soviet Union. Viktor Pavlov welcomed her as the means to make his cover unassailable.

Anna Petrovna was the spirit of Russia, the rose of Siberia. Her bravery was the inspiration for a legion of Komsomols to head east, to build cities in the frost, to tap the hostile territories of their wealth.

As a student geologist, Anna Petrovna had flown to Arctic Siberia in an eight-seater AN-2 with two young men. To her, the snow-covered *taiga* of the north, inhabited by reindeer and primitive tribesmen, was a storehouse of precious stones—emeralds, amethysts, topaz, jasper, sapphires, garnets. But it was diamonds that fascinated her.

With a magnifying glass in one hand, she crawled beside a frozen river for two months, averaging a mile a day, searching for kimberlite, the blue-gray earth that advertises the presence of diamonds.

After the first month she couldn't stand up straight. Toward the end of the second, when the wilderness was briefly thawing and she was paddling on raw knees in slush, she was on the point of giving up. One day she reached a spine of hills and gazed down on a plain patched with snow beneath a mauve haze. Idly, she stooped and picked up a handful of mud, straightening up painfully. The mud was blue-gray.

For a week she and the two young men dug. One bright morning they gazed down the shaft and saw a shiny blue light at the bottom. It was the first diamond chimney in the area and they called it "Blue Flash."

Anna Petrovna and Viktor Pavlov met one evening at the White Nights club in Leningrad and fell in love; she unreservedly, he deeply and passionately but with a sliver of calculation in his soul, the chip of ice that never melted.

The marriage was popular. Such a fusion of talent; such a union of Russian beauty—he with his strong brown face and cap of glossy black hair, she the Siberian with her cool, glittering good looks—the sort of face that beckons from Aeroflot brochures. The wedding was honored with a photograph in *Komsomolskaya Pravda* and a story that speculated on the handsome geniuses the couple would produce.

They spent their honeymoon in Siberia beside Lake Baikal—the Holy Sea, the Northern Sea, the Rich Sea. So right for their union with all its bizarre superlatives. Here Genghis Khan once camped in the heart of the territory of Marco Polo, Strogonoff, Yermak, Godunov, Kuchum. The deepest lake in the world, 400 miles long and 50 miles wide in places, filled by 336 rivers and emptied by only one, the Angara. Populated by fresh-water seals, omul, and bright green sponges with which peasants clean their pots. Covered in winter by 9-foot deep ice which splits with a crack like thunder, tormented by storms and earthquakes which once, long ago, broke up the Gypsy Steppe on the eastern shore killing 1,300 people in the fissures, geysers, and flood waters.

But today the waters were becalmed with floating islands of blossomlike reflections of clouds and the only awesome sight was a ruff of white mountains in the distance.

They gazed upon it all from a rumpled bed in a guest house at Listvyanka. He very dark and hirsute beside her white body.

"Viktor Pavlov," she said, "I love you. I'll always love you."

"And I love you, Anna Petrovna, heroine of the Soviet Union."

"Does that bother you?" She stroked his chest, his flat belly, his sex.

"No, why should it?"

"It's bothered other men. . . ."

"To hell with other men."

"It upset them that I was made a heroine. That I crawled on my hands and knees for two months like some crazy cleaning woman."

"It doesn't bother me. They must have been very weak men."

"They were. Stupid men. You're the strongest man I've ever known. I felt your strength the first time we met." She kissed him. "Like some inner force. Like a secret."

"We all have secrets," he said. "You do—your lovers, your deepest thoughts. Even what you're thinking when you look out there." He pointed at a bed of pink blossom drifting past the window. "We even keep secrets from ourselves."

She shook her head so that her soft fair hair fell across her face. "I haven't any secrets. Just the silly ambitions of any girl. A few meaningless men before the right one, the only one." She pressed herself against him. "What's your secret, Viktor Pavlov?"

He didn't answer.

She held his arms down on the bed, staring at him with her blue eyes in which he could see sunlight and snow. "You frighten me a little."

"I can't imagine you being frightened of anyone."

"Promise me you'll always be faithful?" She thought about it. "Even when you go with other women—you'll be faithful?"

"I'll always be faithful," he lied.

"And there will be other women?"

"No other women," he told her, because that wasn't the nature of his infidelity. I shall betray everything you cherish, he thought. He pressed his face against her firm white breasts.

"I'm glad," she said, stroking his hair. "I was trying to be sophisticated. Men going with women and staying faithful to their wives. I wouldn't like that."

"Only you," he said.

"We'll go well together, you and I. We love the same things."

"Ah yes," he said. "The same things." Thinking that in a way it was true.

"Viktor?"

"Yes?"

"I'm right, aren't I?"

He kissed her, fondling her breasts, and, when he was hard again, made love with desperation.

When they were finished he glanced out of the window and saw a fishing boat drifting by, a breeze catching its sail. There was an illusory permanency about that moment and he always remembered it.

From 1962 to 1967 Viktor Pavlov consolidated his position. He worked hard and became Russia's leading authority on computers. He was given an apartment on Kutuzovsky Prospect in Moscow fit for a hero and heroine.

Before they left Leningrad he found, hidden in a book shop opposite the Gostiny Dvor, a slim booklet printed by the old Yiddish publishers, Der Emes, containing the Hebrew alphabet. He kept it locked in his desk; later he obtained a Hebrew textbook.

But it was a period of frustration. There were now twelve members of his group of revolutionaries calling themselves the Zealots. But, short of planting bombs and reviving the rabid anti-Semitism of the Black Years, they found nothing positive to do. Pavlov raged inwardly. Caution, caution! His marriage suffered and Anna, not understanding, not knowing that he was a Jew, found consolation in her work in the jewelled wastes of Siberia.

It wasn't until 1967 when, in six days, the Israelis routed the Arabs, and the desire to settle in the Promised Land flamed across the Soviet Union, that the ultimate plan began to take shape in the minds of Viktor Pavlov and the Zealots.

The Jews were on the rampage bombarding authority with appeals. The Presidium of the USSR Supreme Soviet, the secretary general of the United Nations, the International Red Cross, the Knesset, the Commission on Human Rights, UNO, premiers, editors, enemies, friends.

Viktor Pavlov, who had studied the fluctuating history of Zionism in Russia, regarded their efforts with good-natured cynicism.

The movement predated world Zionism. In 1884, fourteen Jews from Kharkov landed in Jaffa and, even before World War I, most of the forty settlements in Palestine were founded by Russian Jewry.

When the Bolsheviks came to power in October 1917, the movement seethed with excitement. But, as always, the excitement was short-lived. On September 1, 1919, the Cheka occupied the offices of the Zionist Central Committee in Leningrad, confiscated all documents and 120,000 roubles, arrested Committee members and banned the *Chronicle of Jewish Life*. Next day Zionist leaders were arrested in Moscow.

The harassment subsequently took a zig-zag course. Imprisoned Jews were released; others were arrested; seventy-five delegates to a convention in Moscow were accused of counterrevolutionary activities—peroxylin slabs of guncotton were said to have been found in the Zionist Central Committee offices —and thrown into Butirki jail.

In 1921 the pressure eased. In 1922 it stiffened again. Fifty-one members of the popular wing of the Zionists were arrested and accused of seeking help from reactionary elements ranging from Lloyd-George to the pope.

Arrests continued on a vast scale. The Russians wanted to get rid of a few expendable troublemakers and, in return for statements that their activities were anti-Soviet, some were allowed to go to Palestine.

By 1928 thousands of Jews were in prisons and camps. They were beaten, tortured, starved, thrown into a solitary confinement. By 1929 all the Hechalutz collective farms preparing Jews for conditions in Palestine had been liquidated. Between 1925 and 1926, 21,157 Jews managed to get out of Russia: between 1931 and 1936, only 1,848 made it to Palestine.

In 1934 the last outpost of underground Zionism, the Moscow Central Executive Committee of Tzeirei Zion and the Union of Zionist Youth, was destroyed. Its members were jailed and the government presumed Zionism dead.

It was reincarnated at the beginning of World War II when the Soviet Union annexed tracts of Eastern Europe, increasing its population by 2 million Jews, predominately Zionist. Hundreds of thousands of them were promptly sent to forced labor camps.

In June 1941, the Germans invaded Russia, slaughtering any Jews they encountered, and, years later, the Russians built a playground over the site of one of their massacres at Babi Yar.

Then came the formation of JAC. Hope followed inevitably by disillusion.

After the war Stalin supported the creation of the State of Israel because he thought it heralded the break-up of British power in the Middle East; Russia was one of the first powers to recognize the new country in 1948. But, after Stalin's death in 1953, the policy changed: the Americans held the influence in Israel and the Soviet Union decided to undermine Western power by supporting the Arabs.

Inside Russia, Khrushchev turned on the dead dictator Stalin, denouncing his butchery. Viktor Pavlov remembered the impact of the Khrushchev speech in his schoolroom. He also remembered that it made no mention of Stalin's persecution of the Jews.

During Khrushchev's reign the terror inside the Soviet Union relaxed. When he was deposed and Leonid Brezhnev and Alexei Kosygin finally came to power, Premier Kosygin announced in Paris on December 3, 1966, that "as far as the reunification of families is concerned, if some families wish to meet or if they want to leave the Soviet Union, the road is open to them and there is no problem in this. . . ." On December 5 his statement was published in *Izvestia*.

It launched a flood of applications for exit visas to the OVIR.

Between June 5 and 11, 1967, Israel smashed the Russian-equipped armies of Egypt, Syria, and Jordan and on June 10 the Soviet Union broke diplomatic relations with Israel; the Soviet attitude toward Jewish emigration hardened once more.

On August 5 Viktor Pavlov chanced upon a copy of *Sovietskaya Latvia* in which Zionism was likened to the Mafia. He liked the comparison.

The plot assembled in several phases. In 1967 it was merely concerned with getting the Jews out of Russia. At a party in 1969, one year before the Leningrad skyjack trial, it assumed a more definite shape.

The party was at Pavlov's Moscow apartment on Kutuzovsky Prospect in the complex of blocks where foreign diplomats and journalists lived, guarded at the gates by militiamen and bugged by the KGB. Many residents regarded the hidden microphones as a joke; about two committed suicide every year. The Pavlovs got the apartment because the complex was one of the best in town and it was salutory for foreigners to see the pride of Soviet man and womanhood crossing the shabby courtyard.

The Pavlovs' guests that evening included scientists, mathematicians, geologists, Yevtushenko the poet, a ballerina from the Bolshoi, and some of the staff of the prestige magazine *Novy Mir*.

Pavlov was talking to Professor David Gopnik, associate member, Ukrainian Academy of Sciences, department chief, Donetsk Computing Center. They talked in symbols and electrical pulses, boring other guests so that finally they were isolated in a corner of the lounge.

Gopnik, a thin, bespectacled man with a low forehead contradicting popular beliefs about intelligence, said casually: "I tried to get out again today."

Pavlov looked at him with surprise. "Get out of where?"

Gopnik looked equally surprised. "Out of Russia, of course. They turned me down again."

"I didn't realize you were a Jew."

Gopnik grinned. "Feed me back through a computer and you'd end up with Moses." He glanced around at the other guests, voluble with Soviet champagne and Stolichnaya vodka bought at the dollar shop on the first floor of the block. "And I'm not the only one here. A few of your guests are the products of mixed marriages. One or two have changed their names. Comrade Goldstein doesn't get very far in Soviet society."

"You've done all right," Pavlov commented.

"Only because they need my brains." Gopnik took a sliver of toast smeared with caviar and a glass of champagne from a tray carried by Pavlov's hired waitress. "My brains are my misfortune. Without them I might be in Jerusalem today." He stared at

Pavlov knowingly. "Is there, by any chance, any Jewish blood in you, Comrade Pavlov?"

Pavlov hadn't been asked the direct question since his student days. To deny it was treachery, blasphemy; like betraying your mother to the secret police. To confirm it was sticking a knife in the cover he had prepared for seven years. The KGB knew of the diluted Jewish strain through his father, nothing more. As far as they were concerned he had proved himself an exemplary Soviet citizen willing to rat on any Zionist.

Pavlov said: "Would you like to see my passport?"

Gopnik said: "That won't be necessary." He licked some black spawn from his fingers. "It was very brave of you to invite a Jew to such a distinguished gathering." He signaled to the waitress to bring him more champagne. "But, of course, you and your wife are somewhat privileged. And, of course, you didn't know I was a Jew."

His voice was loud with alcohol; Pavlov glanced around the lounge, with its comtemporary furniture, its glassware from Czechoslovakia, its new TV set, to see if anyone was listening. "Perhaps we could meet tomorrow?" he suggested.

"Why? So that you can tell me the truth without fear of being overheard?"

Which was precisely what Pavlov had in mind. "Just to have a chat," he said, listening to his own duplicity.

"What is there to talk about?"

"Perhaps I can help you."

"And perhaps you can put the KGB on to me."

Pavlov spoke quietly and intensely wanting to grip the man by his lapels. "The KGB already know everything about you. They've interrogated you, haven't they?"

Gopnik shrugged. "Perhaps you might like to tell them that I've been spreading seditious propaganda."

"Listen," Pavlov said. "Meet me tomorrow. I promise I'll tell no one."

"The promise," Gopnik asked, "of a Russian or a Jew?"

"A promise," Pavlov said.

Gopnik looked at him uncertainly, swaying slightly. "Where?"

Pavlov smiled at last. "Outside Lenin's tomb. Where else?"

Anna came across and took Viktor's arm. She looked pale and elegant in a black cocktail dress bought in London during a geological conference. "Come and join the party," she said. "Enough computerized conversation." To Viktor she whispered, "You are being very rude, darling." She led him away to a group of scientists and Pavlov wondered if any of them were Jews in disguise.

This phase of the plan, inspired unknowingly by David Gopnik, developed brilliantly during the evening and Pavlov became so elated that he hardly heard what anyone was saying. The guests put it down to vodka, which was probably a contributory factor.

"Don't you think you've had enough," his wife whispered as he tossed back a glass of firewater. "You're getting very flushed."

In reply he took another glass from the tray. Anna stalked angrily across the room to join Yevteshenko's audience.

Pavlov's first thought was: *If I could get the top Jewish brains to emigrate it would hit the Russians hard.*

He oiled the thought with more vodka.

Then he thought: *Why generalize? Why not deprive the Soviet Union of the nucleus of one branch of science?*

He was talking to an assistant editor of *Novy Mir* who, with a Molotov cocktail of champagne and vodka under his belt, was giving his personal opinion of the literary merits of Daniel and Synyevsky. "Just my opinion," the editor said, looking furtively around. "Just between you and me. Understand?" He prodded Pavlov in the ribs.

"Of course," Pavlov said conspiratorially. "I understand.

Supposing I could get all the Jewish nuclear physicists to emigrate?

Adrenalin and vodka raced in his veins.

" . . . and that's my opinion of Pasternak." The *Novy Mir* editor said challengingly.

Pavlov said: "I agree." With what? "I've been to his grave. No one looks after it. Did you know that?"

The editor looked bewildered. "Fancy that," he said.

What if I persuaded a team of Jewish nuclear physicists capable of making a hydrogen bomb to emigrate?

"Solzhenitzyn," the editor whispered. "A great writer."

Pavlov countered with: "What about Kuznetsov?"

But, of course, the Soviets would never grant nuclear physicists exit visas. The idea was crazy. Unless. . . .

The editor was still deliberating over Kuznetsov. His brain worked laboriously and his tongue was thick in his mouth. "Ah," he managed, "Kuznetsov, a fine writer but . . ."

Unless I found a way to force their hand.

His mind raced with the possibilities; but it got nowhere, not that night.

The *Novy Mir* editor abandoned the enigma Kuznetsov. The flushed guests began to leave.

Tomorrow, Pavlov thought as he shook their hands automatically, I must reaffirm my faith with David Gopnik.

His wife was lying in bed waiting for him. She wore a pink cotton nightdress. She looked warm and sleepy and unheroic.

"Viktor," she said, as he undressed clumsily, "you were very bad tonight."

"I know."

"I've never seen you drunk before."

He fumbled with his shoelaces, sitting on the edge of the bed. "It doesn't often happen."

"Why tonight? Was there a reason?"

"Not particularly. It doesn't matter. Everyone else was drunk."

He was naked, searching for his pajamas. "They're under the pillow," she told him. He climbed into bed, his legs heavy, and gazed at the spinning ceiling.

"Who was that man you were talking to?"

"Which man?"

"The man you were stuck with in the corner for nearly an hour."

"His name's Gopnik. He's one of the best men on computers in the Soviet Union." He closed his eyes but even the darkness lurched.

"Is he Jewish?"

He opened his eyes. "What if he is?"

She looked surprised. "Nothing. I just wondered if he was."

He knew the drink was talking and he knew he

must stop it. "You made it sound as if he was a leper."

She was bewildered. "I didn't mean to. I've nothing against the Jews. I just don't understand why they want to leave Russia."

The answers struggled to escape, but he fought them. He said: "Because they believe they have a land of their own."

"But they're more Russian than they're Jewish."

He wanted to shout "I'm a Jew" and see the shock on her face. "Not now," he managed. "I'm too tired. Too drunk." He reached for her. "Turn the other way. The smell of vodka must be foul."

Obediently, she turned and he slipped his arms around her. She felt warm and soft, still smelling faintly of perfume. He cupped one breast in his hand. We're good together, he thought. And yet I have to destroy our happiness.

"Viktor," she said, "I'm frightened."

But he was asleep.

The sky was pale blue this October morning with the sunlight finding the gold cupolas of the Kremlin and the sapphires in the frost on the cobblestones of Red Square.

The eternal queue was shuffling into the tomb, made of slabs of polished dark-red porphyry and black granite, to pay homage to Vladimir Ilyich Lenin, the man who gave them what they had.

Gopnik was waiting beside the queue wearing a shabby overcoat and a woolen scarf. He looked very vulnerable, Pavlov thought.

He greeted Pavlov almost shyly. "I believe I was rude last night. I'm sorry—I'm not used to alcohol. As you know *we* don't drink too much."

Pavlov patted him on the shoulder. "That's all right. You had just had a disappointment."

They walked beside the Kremlin walls, which enclosed so much beauty and so much intrigue, until they reached the Tomb of the Unknown Soldier in Alexander Gardens. The eternal flame was pale in the cold sunshine.

Gopnik pointed at it. "I, too, fought."

"For what?"

"I sometimes wonder," Gopnik said.

They drove in Pavlov's black Volga to the Exhibition of Economic Achievements. A vast park with 370 buildings, models of sputniks and space ships, industrial exhibits, shops and cafés. A few brown and yellow leaves still hung on the branches of the trees.

They toured the radio-electronics building first to give credence to their visit. Then they sat on a bench with dead leaves stirring at their feet.

Pavlov said: "You know why I wanted to see you?"

"To tell me you're a Jew. You didn't have to." Gopnik paused to light a cigarette. "Don't take any notice of what I said last night. You have more sense than me."

"Not necessarily. But I have my reasons. But I couldn't allow you to leave Moscow thinking I was a hypocrite." He smiled faintly. "A Judas." He dug his hands into the pockets of his gray Crombie. He was conscious of his clothes, the deep shine to his black shoes, the elegant cut of his trousers. He asked, "How long have you been trying to get out of Russia?"

Gopnik opened a cardboard case and consulted several sheets of paper headed Ukrainian Academy of Science. "Like most people," he said, "since June 1967."

"How many times have you tried?"

"Twenty." Gopnik ran his finger down the list.

"The director of the Department of Internal Affairs . . . the chairman of the Council of Ministers of the USSR . . . the prosecutor General of the USSR . . . the chairman of the Commission of Legal Provisions of the Council of Nationalities, Comrade Nishanov . . . the editor of *Literaturnaya Gazata*, Comrade Chakovsky. . . ."

He paused for breath. "You see, I've tried."

"Yes," Pavlov said, "you've tried."

"My story is the same as that of any Jew with brains. You can see the Russians' point—'Why give your brains to the enemy?' "

"Why do you want to go?" Pavlov asked.

"Why? You ask why?"

"Russia's a good country if you accept their laws, if you live as a Russian. There's not much anti-Semitism these days, only anti-Zionism. Jews are getting places at universities if they toe the line like everyone else."

"Perhaps," Gopnik said thoughtfully, "you're not a Jew at all. If you were you'd understand. The persecutions of the past, the attitudes of the present—they all count. But they're not the end-all of it. I want to go to Israel because it is my land." He paused. "Because it is written."

Pavlov stood up. "Then you shall go." He began to walk toward the car scuffing the leaves with his bright toecaps. Unconsciously, he was taking long strides, hands dug in the pockets of his coat.

Gopnik hurried beside him, scarf trailing. "What do you mean?" His voice was agitated. "I don't want any trouble. None of us want trouble."

Pavlov walked quicker as if deliberately trying to distress Gopnik. He spoke angrily. "You don't want trouble? What the hell do you expect to achieve without trouble? The Jews didn't want trouble in Germany. . . ."

Gopnik panted along beside him. "You don't understand. If we cause trouble we're lost. The pogroms would start again. Back to the Black Years. The way things are we're winning. More and more Jews are being allowed to leave. Soon, perhaps, we'll all go."

"All 3 million?"

"They don't all want to go. But the policy's changing. We're winning. . . ."

"Groveling," Pavlov snapped. "Forced to crawl for a character reference from your employer, permission from your parents—or even your divorced wife, suddenly given fourteen days to get out which is never long enough, body-searched before you leave, paying the government thousands of roubles blackmail money. Is that victory?"

"It's suffering," Gopnik said. "It's victory."

They passed some boys playing football, a couple of lovers arm in arm. A jet chalked a white line across the blue sky above the soaring Cosmonauts Obelisk. There didn't seem to be much oppression around this glittering day.

They reached the car. A militiaman in his blue winter overcoat was standing beside it. He pointed at the bodywork. "One rouble fine please," he said. "A very dirty car."

Pavlov let out the clutch savagely and headed back toward the Kremlin. "I'll get you out," he said. "Don't worry—I'll get you to Israel."

Gopnik said: "Please leave me alone. Let me find my own destiny."

"By crawling?"

"Don't you think we've been through enough without hotheads destroying everything we've worked for?" He wound down the window to let in the cold air, breathing deeply as if he felt faint. "Who are you anyway? What do you think you can do?"

"I'm a man," Pavlov said, "who thinks there is

more to be done than writing letters to the prime minister of England, the president of the United States and Mrs. Golda Meir."

"What can you do?"

The Volga swerved violently to avoid a taxi with a drunken driver.

"I can show the world," Pavlov said, "that we have balls."

They met mostly in the open air, on the Lenin Hills, or in the birch forests to the west of the city where Muscovites went swimming from the river-beaches in the summer and cross-country skiing in the long winter.

Sometimes they met in a small apartment near the junction of Sadovaya Samotetchnaya and Petrov-ka. While they talked about the Moscow Dynamo football team, mistresses, and money, they systematically searched the room for microphones. Delousing it, they called the process. So far no bugs had been found.

They only met three at a time to avoid arousing suspicion. On this evening there was Pavlov; Yury Mitin, poet and state prize winner; and Ivan Shiller, a journalist on *Pravda* specializing in Jewish affairs. Each had cultivated an anti-Zionist front; none had Jew on his passport.

Each was fierce in his belief, none more so than Shiller, his anger fomented by the daily betrayals he had to perpetrate in his newspaper. Yesterday he had finished rounding up fifty prominent Jews and ordering them to sign a letter condemning Israeli aggression in the Middle East.

The letter also referred to emigration. "We were born and bred in the Soviet Union. It is here that our ancestors of many centuries lived and died. There is no reason why we should go to Israel. And, anyway, how is it possible to 'return' to a place where one has never been?"

"And do you know," Shiller spoke with bitter contempt, "that some of them were quite happy to sign?"

Shiller was second-in-command of the Zealots who took their name from the 960 Jewish martyrs who killed themselves rather than surrender the citadel of Masada to the Romans. Death before dishonor. The Masada Complex symbolized the spirit of Israel: it symbolized the spirit of Russia's small band of Zealots.

To avoid detection they used code names, each having a trade beginning with the letter P in the English language. Pavlov was the Professional, Mitin the Poet, Shiller the Penman.

Shiller was a gaunt man with a muddy complexion, hollow cheeks, and bad teeth. His repressions were even stronger than Pavlov's because, unlike Pavlov, he was a practicing Jew. His greatest temptations came at such times as the New Year and the Atonement or the days when *Yizkor*, the prayer for the dead, was offered. Then he wanted to visit the synagogue, but if he did he would alert the police. Even to be *near* the synagogue on Arkhipova on the Sabbath was dangerous because it was under KGB surveillance. So Shiller prayed in private, ate his matzohs in secret, recited the Passover prayer "Next year in Jerusalem," and waited.

In one way Shiller was weaker than Pavlov: he was too religious to be a ruthless killer: Pavlov had no such inhibitions. But if there was ever to be any rift, any struggle for power, it would be between these two men.

The apartment belonged to Mitin the Poet. He made coffee while, on a rickety table covered with linoleum, under the benign gaze of Lenin framed on the wall, the other two men played chess. A get-together of old friends should the 1 A.M. knock on the door be heard.

Shiller said bitterly, "Last week I helped to arrange the publication of a statement from our religious leaders. 'Like citizens of other nationalities, Jews enjoy all the rights guaranteed by the Constitution, including the right to profess their own religion.' "

He knocked aside one of Pavlov's pawns with his bishop. "I got six so-called rabbis' signatures on that statement."

"Shit on the *Rabbi*," said the Poet. He was a slim young man with a pale face, a monkish fringe of hair, and a foul mouth. Whereas Shiller would have liked to smuggle Bibles into Russia, Mitin would have liked to smuggle Soviet literature out. His frustration found a small outlet in profanity, the brutalizing of his love-affair with words.

Pavlov said, "We mustn't get impatient. We're all making sacrifices. We are getting nearer our goal every day." He moved one of his own black bishops and called: "Check."

"What goal?" Shiller asked. He frowned at the wooden board and pieces made in a labor camp. "Since when have we had a goal."

"Piss on you," exclaimed the Poet. "We've had an ideal for years, a goal for months."

"Ah," Shiller muttered, "that goal. I apologize. I thought for a moment Pavlov meant we had a way of achieving it."

Shiller moved his knight and Pavlov said, "You're in check. Perhaps you misheard that as well."

Shiller took back the knight without apologizing. "How are we getting nearer our goal?"

Pavlov took a sheet of paper from his pocket. It

had eleven names on it. Pavlov read out the first name, adding the data from memory.

"Skolsky." He paused, thinking. "Yosef Skolsky, aged forty-two. Top physicist at the Scientific Institute of Nuclear Physics, Moscow. A pupil of Academician Andrei Sakharov, the father of the Soviet atom bomb, our leading dissident. Two applications for exit visas to Israel. Refused on the grounds that his relatives in Tel Aviv were too distant."

He read out another name, "Kremer, Yakov. Corresponding member of the USSR Academy of Sciences. Aged fifty. One application refused. Again—remoteness of kin."

The penultimate name was, "Zivz, Mikhail. Aged twenty-eight. Brilliant nuclear physicist working at the Scientific Research Center in Akademgorodok, fifteen miles from Novosibirsk. Permission refused once. Reason—still subject to army service."

The last name was Gopnik.

Shiller asked, "Who's he?"

Pavlov swooped with his queen. "Checkmate," he said.

"Who is Gopnik?"

"My conscience."

Mitin served the coffee. "Since when did you have a conscience?" he asked.

Pavlov sipped the sweet black coffee. "It doesn't matter." He ran his hand through his hair. "What matters is this: ten of those eleven names constitute the human components of one hydrogen bomb. Quite a gift for the Promised Land, eh?"

But how? Part of the answer came to Viktor Pavlov at the Leningrad skyjack trial. This skyjack had failed miserably, but even if it succeeded, it would

55

only have benefited a handful of nonentities. And, in any case, skyjacks were old-hat, bearing the hallmark of Arabs, Cubans, and maniacs. An old-fashioned kidnap had more panache.

Once again the adrenalin started to flow. What if they kidnapped a Kremlin leader and held him against the release of the ten nuclear physicists? The idea had a beautiful suicidal glory to it, the Masada Complex. Except that it was totally impracticable.

Or so it seemed until Viktor Pavlov heard that Vasily Yermakov was traveling on the Trans-Siberian Railway in October of 1973, the year of the twenty-fifth anniversary of the founding of the State of Israel.

2.

The first stop was Yaroslovl. Trans-Siberian No. 2 pulled in sharp at 2:02 P.M. Moscow time. But it wasn't until Sharia, which they reached on time at 8:22 P.M., that the first Zionist agent boarded the train.

He was a stocky man with a white face and a scar beside his mouth. He wore a black overcoat, fur boots and a sealskin hat.

He stood near a stall where blunt-faced women wearing blue scarves round their hair sold food from a canvas-covered pushcart. Meat pastries, fried chicken and fish, ice cream and beer.

As the train slid into the station the agent whose name was Semenov clapped his gloved hands together. Cold or nerves or both.

The Trans-Siberian hadn't yet reached the snow. But the air was sharp with frost glittering on the platform. It was almost dark.

In the lighted window of the special coach he saw Yermakov's face. The glass had misted up so that the outlines were blurred; it reminded Semenov of a face masked with a stocking.

Framed in a window of coach 1251, Semenov saw the face of Viktor Pavlov. He shivered inside his warm overcoat and took a white handkerchief from his pocket. Pavlov's face faded.

Before the train stopped, KGB officers dropped off like commuters late for work. They lined up the waiting passengers and began to check their papers. Local militia who had already done the job protested but they were pushed aside; it reminded Semenov of the airport scene at the time of the abortive skyjack when Moscow and Leningrad security officers fought each other.

Semenov was fourth in line. He handed his papers to a brusque KGB man. The KGB officer glanced at them, smiled slightly, and said softly, "Welcome aboard, Comrade."

Semenov the Policeman, a member of the KGB with the best cover of all the Zealots, nodded and climbed into a carriage. The cover also enabled him to carry a gun.

Standing beside Pavlov in the corridor was Stanley Wagstaff, the train-spotter from Manchester. His mind was a filing cabinet of railway statistics and trains were his substitute for the hungers that affected other men; if his wife ever wanted to divorce him she would have to cite a locomotive.

For twenty years Stanley Wagstaff had saved

for this trip. He knew the Trans-Siberian's history, every station, every class of locomotive.

He pointed into the gathering darkness and said to Pavlov, "See those over there?"

Pavlov looked, dimly seeing the silhouettes of old black steam engines with coal cars; they looked like a herd of elephants shouldered close to each other.

"There's fifty of them," Stanley Wagstaff informed him. "Sad, isn't it? A graveyard."

"Very," said Pavlov. He saw Semenov signal with the handkerchief and leaned back against the wall.

"Did you know," Stanley asked, "that Russia has the widest gauge in the world?"

Pavlov shook his head; Stanley thought he detected a man eager to have his ignorance repaired.

"Yes," Stanley continued, his voice assuming authority and importance, "it's 5 feet, unlike the standard gauge of 4 feet 8½ inches used in Europe and America. Whistler—you know, the painter's father—recommended it. A lot of people reckoned they had a bigger gauge to stop trains being used by invading armies." He paused, waiting for reaction; but there was none. "In fact it worked the other way. It's much easier for an enemy to re-lay one line on a broad gauge than it is for the Russians to widen an enemy gauge. They found that out when they attacked the Poles in the Civil War."

The train began to move out of the station. Stanley spotted a stationary engine, whipped out his notebook, and recorded its number, JI 4526. "An old L class freight locomotive," he said. "I wonder what it's doing here."

The stranger didn't seem to care. He was staring out of the window at the dark countryside moving by. A strong, dark man filled with some inner intensity. But not for trains. Stanley Wagstaff persevered a little longer.

"Next stop Svecha," he informed the stranger. "We arrive at 10:14 and leave at 10:30." His earnest face broke into a grin and he said in his North Country voice, "And I bet it'll be on time with his nibs back there."

"Who?"

"His nibs. The bloke from the Kremlin."

"Ah," the stranger said. "Yes, we'll be on time all right." He spoke good English with a slight accent.

"Perhaps," Stanley Wagstaff suggested, "you'd care to join me in the restaurant car? I could tell you quite a lot of history about the Trans-Siberian."

The stranger shook his head. "Some other time." He squeezed past Stanley. "This could be quite an historic trip," he said, tapping Stanley's notebook. "Keep that handy." He opened the door of his compartment and went in.

Stanley sighed. The alternatives were the American journalist who didn't look a likely candidate for swapping railway stories, the English girl—women were usually frigid on the subject of trains, regarding them as rivals—and the Intourist woman with whom he had already crossed swords.

Stanley had been telling the three of them how much the Trans-Siberian owed to the Americans and British. He had started with the American railroad engineer Whistler, then progressed to Perry McDonough Collins, from New York, the first foreigner to propose a steam railway across Siberia. "He arrived with red pepper in his socks to keep out the cold and changed horses 210 times crossing Siberia. He offered to raise $20 million by subscription but the Russians turned it down."

The Intourist girl said. "Soon the lights will be going off. We must prepare for bed."

Stanley then recalled Prince Khilkov, minister of communications during the construction of the line. "Did you know he was called *The American* because he learned all his stuff in Philadelphia?"

The Intourist girl stood up. "Perhaps the Americans have a lot to thank the Soviet people for."

Harry Bridges said from his top bunk, "They have—they bought Alaska from Russia for one cent an acre."

The Intourist girl said, "Tomorrow we reach Sverdlovsk where a Soviet ground-to-air missile shot down the American U-2 spy plane piloted by Gary Powers."

"We get there at two in the afternoon." Stanley Wagstaff chipped in. "Named after Jacob Sverdlov who arranged the execution of Nicholas II and his family on July 17, 1918. In those days it was called Ekaterinburg. . . ."

"Mr. Wagstaff," said the girl, "it is my job to explain the route. . . ."

"Then you're lucky I'm in your compartment," Stanley said. "I can help you quite a bit." He consulted a pamphlet. "We leave Sverdlovsk at 2:18. It's 1,127 miles from Moscow," he added.

"It's time to get undressed," the girl said.

It was the moment Libby Chandler had been anticipating with some trepidation. She wasn't happy about undressing in front of three strangers; but, oddly, it was the thought of the Russian girl that worried her more than the men.

Bridges said, "Okay, Stanley and I will wait in the corridor while you girls get changed."

Libby Chandler took out her pajamas. The Russian girl was already stripped down to her brassiere and panties. Her body was on the thick side, but voluptuous. Libby thought she might put on a nightdress and remove her underwear beneath it. She didn't. She unhooked the brassiere revealing big, firm breasts; then the panties came off showing a thatch of black pubic hair.

She glanced down at Libby and smiled. "Hurry up," she said, "or the men will be back while you're undressed." She seemed completely unconcerned about her nakedness. She stood there for a few moments and Libby smelled her cologne—all Russian cologne smelled the same.

"Perhaps," Libby Chandler said, "there would be more room if you got into bed first."

The girl shrugged. "As you wish." She pulled on a pink cotton nightdress, climbed into her bunk, and lay watching Libby as she maneuvered herself into her pajamas feeling as if she were undressing in the convent where she had been educated, where one's anatomy was not supposed to be visible to anyone—even God.

When Viktor Pavlov entered his compartment after meeting Stanley Wagstaff in the corridor, he found that the breezy stranger, Yosif Gavralin, who had arrived last, had occupied his berth. He looked up as Pavlov came in and said, "Hope you don't mind. It was difficult climbing up there." He slapped his thigh under the bedclothes. "A hunting accident." Pavlov, who knew there was nothing he could do, said he didn't mind, but during the night he dreamed a knife was coming through the mattress, sliding between spine and shoulder blade.

By 10:00 P.M. on the first day, the two KGB officers had searched the next three cars to the special coach attached to the end of the train. They had reexamined the papers of every passenger and attendant, they had removed and replaced panelling, checked luggage and taken two Russians into custody in a compartment like a cell guarded by armed militia. The Russians had committed no real crime; but there were slight irregularities in their papers and the police couldn't afford to take chances; they would be put off the train at Kirov.

They started on the fourth coach. They took their time, apologizing for getting passengers out of their beds, knowing that this was the best time to interrogate and search. They were very thorough and, although they were in civilian clothes, they looked as if they were in uniform—charcoal gray suits with shoulders filled with muscle, light gray ties almost transparent, and wide trousers which had become fashionable in the West. One had a schoolboyish face, the other was shorter with slightly Mongolian features.

"Quite trendy," said a young Englishman on his way to Hong Kong, pointing at their trousers.

"Your papers, please," said the officer with the schoolboy features. He stared at the young man's passport photograph, "Is that you?"

"Of course it's me. Who do you think it is? Mark Phillips?"

The other policeman examined the photograph. "It doesn't look like you."

Fear edged the young man's voice. All he had ever read and ridiculed was coming true. "I've got my driving license," he said. He looked suddenly frail in his Kings Road nightshirt, his long hair falling across his eyes.

The first officer said, "We're on a train not in a car. When did you have this photograph taken?"

"When I left school."

"How long ago was that?"

"Two years."

The one with the Mongolian face stared hard at the photograph. Finally he said, "You weren't quite so trendy—is that the word?—in those days." He handed the passport back to the young man.

Outside in the corridor the two officers smiled at each other.

Before they entered the next compartment they were overtaken by Colonel Yury Razin who was in charge of the whole security operation. He was a big man, a benevolent family man, a professional survivor who had once been close to Beria and retained his rank even after Stalin and his stooges had been discredited; to maintain his survival record he allowed none of his paternal benevolence to affect his work.

The two junior officers stopped smiling and straightened up. One of them made a small salute.

The colonel was holding the list of names marked with red crosses. "Any luck?"

"Two doubtfuls," said the shorter of the two. "We wouldn't have bothered with them normally. Minor irregularities in their papers."

Col. Razin nodded. He had soft brown eyes, a big head, and a blue chin which he shaved often. During the Stalin era he had been involved in fabricating charges against nine physicians—the infamous "Doctors' Plot" exposed in *Pravda* on January 13, 1953. Six of the accused were Jews and they were charged with conspiring not only with American and British agents but with "Zionist spies." One month after Stalin's death Moscow Radio announced that

64

the charges against the doctors were false. Col. Razin, the survivor, who didn't see himself as anti-Semitic—merely as an obedient policeman—helped indict those who had fabricated the plot.

He rubbed the cleft in his chin, which was difficult to shave, and prodded the list. "Leave the next compartment to me."

The two officers nodded. They didn't expect an explanation, but they got one.

The colonel said, "This man Pavlov. I know him. He's given information against Jewish agitators in the past. A brilliant mathematician. Married to Anna Petrovna, heroine of the Soviet Union. Odd to find him on the train today?"

The two officers looked at each other. Finally one of them asked, "Why's that, sir?"

The other said respectfully, "He's got authorization from the very top—from Comrade Baranov—and a letter from the State Committee of Ministers for Science and Technology."

Razin silenced them. "I know all that. And he's going to meet his wife in Khabarovsk." He lit a cigarette and inhaled deeply. "He and I are old friends. I'll talk to him." He blew out a lot of smoke. "But it's odd just the same." He didn't enlighten them any more.

He opened the door and switched on the light.

Pavlov wasn't surprised to see him: he wouldn't have been surprised to see anyone. He shaded his eyes and said: "Good evening, Comrade Razin."

"Good evening," Razin said. "A pleasant surprise."

"Pleasant," Pavlov said. "But surely no surprise?"

The Tartar general glared down from the top bunk. "What now? What the hell's going on?"

Razin said, "You must excuse me, general. I

am only doing my duty. We have a very important guest on board."

The general's wife stuck her head out from beneath her husband's berth. Her hair was in curlers and there was cream on her face. Her chest looked formidable. She said, "You're surely not suggesting. . . ."

Col. Razin held up his hand. "I wouldn't dream of suggesting anything. You and your husband are well-known to us. But there are others in the compartment."

The general and his wife stared at the breezy stranger and Pavlov knew that a small charade was about to be acted.

Col. Razin said: "Can I see your papers, please?"

The stranger sighed and reached for his wallet. A smell of embrocation reached Pavlov: the stranger had been working on his cover—but he had forgotten to limp when he first arrived.

Col. Razin thumbed through the papers while he addressed Pavlov: "I understand you're meeting your wife in Khabarovsk."

Pavlov, head on his hand, nodded. "First I have some business in Novosibirsk and Irkutsk."

"You're not the only one."

"I know," Pavlov said. "I hope to hear the speeches."

"Do you, Comrade Pavlov? Do you indeed?" He handed the stranger's papers back to him with a perfunctory "Thank you." To Pavlov he said, "We must meet and have a drink for old-time's sake. In the restaurant car, perhaps, at eleven tomorrow morning?"

"That would be fine," Pavlov said.

"Are you making the whole journey?"

"I'm leaving the train at Khabarovsk. I presumed you knew that, colonel."

Razin looked annoyed: he didn't like to hear his rank used. Particularly in the presence of a general. Even if his status was superior when the chips were down.

Pavlov asked, "Don't you want to see my papers?"

"It won't be necessary. The husband of a heroine of the Soviet Union shouldn't suffer the indignity."

He bowed as if he were in uniform, a Prussian officer's bow. "Good-night, ladies and gentlemen. Pleasant dreams."

After he had closed the door the general's wife asked, "Is it true that your wife's a heroine . . . ?" Her voice sounded as if her mouth was full of food.

Pavlov said, "I'll tell you in the morning."

He lay quietly listening to the soporific sound of wheels on rails—the 5-foot gauge! Could anything go wrong before the plan was actually put into action? With the appearance of Col. Razin one more imponderable had been used. He worried about it for an hour, then fell asleep. By that time it was 1:13 A.M. Moscow time and they were just leaving Kirov at the beginning of the second day of the journey.

The special coach was a mixture of styles. A functional office, two soft-class sleeping compartments for guards and staff, a KGB control room with radio and receiving equipment for the microphones planted on the train, a cell, a larder, and two compartments knocked into a large deluxe sleeper with mahogany paneling, thick pink drapes, a chair made of buttoned red satin, a Chinese carpet, washbasin and mirror with frosted patterns round the edge, a mahogany table and chair, and a bed with pink plush curtains controlled by a gold cord with a tassel.

Despite the luxury, the Kremlin leader couldn't sleep. He lay alone, guarded in the corridor by two armed militia. It was always at night that the power left him to be replaced by doubt. He was sixty-six, entering the period of self-appraisal when the past presents itself for assessment. He saw the faces of those whom he had executed; he remembered the way he had hacked his way to absolute power. And he tried to equate it all with achievement: the prestige of the Soviet Union, the fear it struck into the bowels of other powers; the standard of living of the people. When he concentrated—when he recalled the tyranny of czarist days, the 20 million lost in World War II, the massive injustices of the Stalin era—the equation sometimes worked.

It was for these searching reasons—and the fact that a younger man was snapping at his heels in the Kremlin hierarchy—that he had decided to make the journey across Siberia. To see for himself the "heroic achievements" which his writers monotonously inserted into speeches until they had no impact at all and to reaffirm his popularity. But tonight he wasn't so sure that it had been a good idea. He felt as if the train was plunging him into bloodshed and oppression. He thought of the camps on the steppes where enemies of the state still languished; he felt that when he looked out of the windows at the dark shadows that he was seeing his conscience drift past.

He turned to the diminishing future. He wished there was a God who would understand; but he had helped to banish Him from the land.

He reached toward the table, a bulky figure in

striped pajamas, not impressive now during the naked small hours of the morning, and found his sleeping pills. He took one, held it on his tongue and
washed it down with a draught of Narzan water. It
burned for a moment in his stomach; then he slept
to awake a leader once more.

The train nosed through the night, an express
only in name, but inexorable with its steady speed,
bumping a little but hardly swaying.

Soon it would reach the Urals, the gateway to
Siberia. Near the Chusovaya River it passed a
striped post, the boundary between Europe and
Asia; on this boundary, at a point known as the
Monument of Tears, the exiles used to bid farewell
to their families before marching, manacled, into Siberia where the law was the three-flonged *plet,*
where home was a sod hut, and work was a mine
sunk in permafrost. They had died by the thousands
but millions had survived, the Russian way. And,
with commuted sentences as the incentive, they
helped to build the great railway carrying Train
No. 2.

In the 1890's, 5 million were estimated to have
traveled east to start new lives. There was another
exodus between 1927 and 1939; then, during World
War II, as the Germans drove deep into European
Russia, another 10.5 million—the greatest evacuation
in history.

When dawn broke the train was burrowing
through valleys over which, it was said, there wasn't
a patch of blue sky without its own eagle.

3.

After queuing for half an hour Harry Bridges took his place for breakfast in the dining car. He sat opposite Libby Chandler and smiled at her.

"Look," he said, "we might as well be friends."

She smiled back. "Why not? I was tired yesterday."

His professional instincts took over again. "And nervous?" She didn't look so frightened this blue-and-gold morning; but he knew the fear was still there.

"Just excited," she said.

He ordered a hard-boiled egg, coffee, and toast. The waitress, wearing a tiara of paper lace, brought him a soft-boiled egg, tea, and bread.

She laughed. "They're not very efficient, are they?"

He jumped to the defense. "You're not in Highgate Village now."

She flushed. "I wasn't ridiculing them. I've always admired the Russians."

"You have? You're one of the few. Most tourists see the Kremlin, the Winter Palace and GUM and go home complaining that there wasn't a plug in their bath."

"I'm not one of those, Mr. Bridges."

"Harry," he said. He dipped his spoon into his liquid egg. "It's fear really," he said. "People make fun of things they're scared of. They made fun of the kaiser and Hitler," he added.

She ordered more coffee. "Do you live in Moscow, Harry?"

He nodded. "I have an apartment there. I'm a journalist in case you're wondering."

"I guessed as much. Do you find it difficult? I mean with the restrictions and everything?"

He was silent for a moment, thinking that this beautiful girl with her long blonde hair and blue eyes was very perceptive. Unconsciously, perhaps, but with an unerring knack of asking the pertinent question—sensing that he had a special status. He also thought she was tough, like one of those pioneering Englishwomen who had traversed the steppes and taiga at the turn of the century; therefore her fear had a formidable source.

He dodged the answer by saying: "It's usually me who asks the questions. What are you doing crossing Siberia?" he asked.

"Escaping," she said, staring out of the window.

"We're all doing that," Harry Bridges said. "Escaping from what? The police? A jealous lover?"

"Just escaping." She pointed at a railway siding called Naked Boy Halt. "It looks as if I've made it."

"The Wild East," Harry Bridges said. "Wilder than the West ever was. Especially farther east. Escaped convicts, Cossacks, gold barons, bandits. In Irkutsk they used to have six murders a week until the whole town was burned down because the firemen were all drunk."

"Look," she said. They gazed at gentle hills covered with birch and red pine, running with streams. Beside the railway stood a log-cutter's hut with red and blue fretworked eaves. An old woman with a hard, ancient face was feeding geese beside a pool tissued with ice.

"Your first Siberian," Bridges told her.

"Let's take a walk down the train and see some more. They got on at the last stop. They're traveling hard class."

"You make them sound like animals."

"I didn't mean to." She was through his defenses again. "They're the toughest people in the world. And the most honest. Do you know what they say in Siberia?"

She shook her head.

"They say that in the taiga only bears steal." He decided that he sounded naïve so he added: "And to get over that in the old days they used to put food out for the escaped convicts—the *brodyagi*—so that they didn't have to steal."

She looked at him over the top of her coffee cup. "Are you an honest man, Harry?"

Hell! he thought. "As honest as most. More than some, less than others."

She nodded without belief, without disbelief.

"What about you?" he asked.

"I think so."

"Then tell me what you're doing on this train."

"I'm an adventuress," she said.

"I guess dishonesty isn't just a question of telling lies," Bridges said. "It's also a question of evading the truth."

"I suppose you're right," Libby Chandler said, lighting a cigarette with a gold Dunhill.

They were joined by Viktor Pavlov who ordered lemon tea and toast and said to Bridges, "I think we've met before."

Bridges said, "Have we? I don't remember."

"You're a journalist, aren't you?"

Bridges said he was.

"An American?"

"This morning," Bridges said, "people seem to be asking a lot of questions."

"I've read your stuff and we both live on Kutuzovsky. Maybe we haven't actually met. You've written some . . . some glowing reports." He chose his words carefully.

Bridges seemed to take exception to the remark, although Libby Chandler couldn't see why. She felt the hostility between these two men; and yet they hardly knew each other. If there had been time for anything but her own crisis it would have worried her.

Bridges said, "You mean I've written some good assessments of Soviet policy?"

Pavlov shrugged, squeezing lemon into his tea. "I said glowing reports. That's a compliment, surely?"

"Then you've missed the critical aspects."

"No," Pavlov told him, "I haven't. I thought they were inserted by your editors in America." He smiled. "I must have been wrong." He sipped his tea. "Are you covering the tour, Mr. Bridges?"

"That's the general idea."

"And you?" Pavlov turned to Libby Chandler.

"A holiday," she lied.

"You've chosen an auspicious occasion."

"So has Comrade Yermakov," Libby Chandler said.

"Why do you say that?"

She looked at him in surprise. "Because I'm on the train. Just a joke."

Harry Bridges said, "Now it's your turn. What are you doing on the train, Comrade Pavlov?"

"Then you do know me."

"By reputation. The finest mathematical brain in the Soviet Union. A living computer."

"I'm honored."

Bridges paused before asking, "So what brings you on the Trans-Siberian. Just your work?"

Pavlov hesitated. "You've had your ear to the ground, Mr. Bridges. I congratulate you."

"I don't know what the hell you mean."

"You are referring to my wife and myself?"

"I wasn't," Bridges said. "But I'll buy it."

Pavlov looked confused. "About my wife and myself. Don't tell me, Mr. Bridges, that a man like yourself who attends two Moscow cocktail parties a night didn't know that the greatest mathematical brain in the Soviet Union and his wife, a heroine of the Soviet Union, had parted? That our marriage, as you say in America, was on the rocks?" He smiled bleakly. "An apt description for a geologist?"

"I didn't know," Bridges said.

"You surprise me. I should have thought it was the sort of gossip that would appeal to the bourgeois capitalist press."

"It's not that important," Bridges said.

"It would have appealed to me," Libby Chandler said. "I love gossip." No one smiled and she decided to keep her mouth shut.

"In that case I can tell you the main reason for

my journey across Siberia. I'm going to be reunited with my wife."

Libby put her hand on his arm. "I'm glad," she said.

"Thank you," Pavlov said stiffly. "Now I must return to my compartment. I've got work to do." He made his way through the dining car, holding onto chairs as the carriage bounced slightly, an intense, hawkish man with a face that might have contained humor if things had been different.

The door at the opposite end of the car opened and the first Siberian diners came in. Four of them —two bearded men in faded-blue shirts and trousers, peaked caps, and fur boots. The women wore black shawls, thick skirts, and darned woollen jumpers. They were ageless, with brown skin tight on expressionless faces, eyes the color of ice beneath a blue sky.

They went up to the glass-cabinet, beside the abacus and cash register, pointing at the cigarettes, preserves, sweet bottles of Russian champagne, and Georgian brandy.

One of them asked the girl in the paper tiara for a bottle of vodka. She shook her head. The man swore a pungent, Siberian oath.

"Why no vodka?" Libby asked Bridges.

"Because it's cheap and might lead to undignified behavior in front of foreigners. They figure that people who can afford the brandy and champagne know how to hold their liquor." He stood up. "Come on— let's go and see how the other half live."

The other half lived in hard-class dormitories with fifty-seven bunks arranged in tiers. They made communities of them with samovars steaming in the aisle, babies taking their feed at the breast, blankets spread with meals of black bread, cheese, and vodka smuggled onto the train from the steppes. The floor was sprinkled with the husks of sunflower seeds and pine-nut shells and a couple of ropes dripping with clothes were strung across the aisle.

"Which do you prefer?" Bridges asked, "soft class or this?"

"I shouldn't think it's changed in fifty years," Libby Chandler replied, ignoring the question.

"Probably not. But it's still an improvement on the 8:30 commuter to Charing Cross or Pennsylvania Station. Or the New York subway," he added. "At least you don't get mugged here."

In the center of the aisle a group of men had gathered around two chess players. One was young and sharp; the other was in his sixties with a wise, ravaged face.

Bridges spoke to a man wearing striped flannel pajamas with war medals pinned on his chest.

"Who's winning?" Libby asked.

"The young guy. It seems that the old fellow was once the champion of Perm. A grandmaster or a master. Apparently he once played Botvinnik and beat him. It must have been one of Botvinnik's off days. But the old boy must have been good."

"And he isn't any more?"

"He got old. He started to drink. Now he's trying to prove something." Like Yermakov, Bridges thought. "Just one win. He's played seven games on the train and lost them all."

"How terrible for him," Libby said. There were tears in her eyes and she brushed them away irritably. "I hope he wins. Couldn't the young one throw the game?"

"He'd know," Bridges said. "And that would be worse for him, wouldn't it?"

"I suppose so. If only he'd stop drinking."

The old man took a swig from a bottle of vodka and moved his queen. The spectators sighed.

"I'm afraid he's going to lose this one," Bridges said.

The sleek young man made a quick move. The former champion said something and they set up the pieces again.

"He lost," Bridges said. The train was slowing down. "We're coming into Shalia. Let's go back and see if the Intourist lady has strangled Mr. Wagstaff yet."

"I wonder what her name is?" Libby said.

"Larissa. It has to be."

Punctually at 11:31 the Trans-Siberian slid into the platform at Shalia.

But it wasn't until five hours later, when the train was waiting at Sverdlovsk, 1,127 miles from Moscow, that another imponderable in Viktor Pavlov's scheme of things occurred and a man was shot.

From the railway Sverdlovsk looks a dreary place. A city of 1 million inhabitants contained in a cocoon of railway tracks and wire drooping, like abandoned fairy lights, from pylons. It is like Baltimore from the highway or Stockport from anywhere. It is a coal and steel metropolis and it seems to have assumed industrial drabness to distract memory from the bloodletting in the cellar of a modest house on July 17, 1918.

In this cellar (although it has subsequently been disputed) Czar Nicholas II, victim of events and an assumption of divine right, was murdered with his wife and family.

But history didn't allow Sverdlovsk—or Ekaterinburg as it was once called—to escape the limelight. In May 1960 the U-2 spy plane piloted by Francis Gary Powers was brought down by a ground-to-air missile.

The rocket battery was commanded by a Jew, Lieut. Feldman.

No tourists are allowed to alight at Sverdlovsk.

Boris Demurin took over the controls as the locomotive nosed into the station. "Are we on time?" he asked the Ukrainian.

"Of course," the Ukrainian replied indulgently.

"Good," Demurin said. "We don't want anything to go wrong. I remember. . . ."

"Just remember the brakes," the Ukrainian said.

The train stopped. It was due to leave in eighteen minutes.

As at the previous stops, the KGB alighted before the wheels had stopped. The embarking passengers were lined up for questioning. Among those who alighted was Semenov the Policeman. He waited at a bookstall flipping through copies of the London *Morning Star* and the Paris *L'Humanité* while the secret police went about their work. He noted that the representative of the Zealots, the Peasant, was fifth in line.

The two examining KGB officers took their time with him. Then one of them waved to the window where Razin stood watching. Razin hurried over. He examined the papers while the Peasant, wearing a peaked cap and blue denims, protested. One of the officers snapped at him and he shut up.

Semenov saw Razin point to a waiting room taken over by the militia and local KGB.

The Peasant hesitated, turned and headed for the

waiting room with Razin behind him. Semenov followed at a discreet distance.

At the entrance to the waiting room he heard Razin say: "Get him into the car. We don't want any trouble here."

Semenov sauntered through the booking hall to the outside of the station where a black Chaika, the limousine used by the Kremlin, was ticking over.

The Peasant decided to make a run for it as he emerged from the station.

He wrenched himself free from his captors and ran toward Semenov. The KGB men drew pistols but the Peasant was ducking and weaving between startled pedestrians.

Semenov heard Razin shout, "Don't kill him."

As the Peasant approached Semenov he veered away. Semenov didn't know whether he recognized him. But he knew what he would prefer if he were in the Peasant's place: a bullet through the heart rather than interrogation by the KGB.

Semenov knew they always talk. No matter how tough, they always talk. A lot of nonsense was written about man's resilience to torture. An electric current through the testicles and they talked.

"Stop him," someone shouted; maybe Razin.

Semenov took his pistol from his shoulder holster. As he did so he heard the thick, phlegmy thud of a pistol equipped with a silencer. The Peasant ran on and the KGB officer aimed again; but the Peasant was behind a line of Moskvich and Volga cars. But he was still in Semenov's line of fire.

Militia were running in all directions, boots thudding on the ground. Men, women, and children lay on the ground terrified.

The Peasant slipped on the frosty ground. The militia were gaining. Semenov took careful aim and fired. The Peasant reared up, spun round staring at Semenov—in gratitude or disbelief?—and fell to the ground.

Razin pushed the body with his foot. "Good shooting," he said to Semenov. "But he won't talk to us now."

"I didn't mean to kill him," Semenov said.

"No?" Razin rubbed his chin. "But I was led to understand that you were a crack shot." He pointed to the body. "Take it to the mortuary. Check him out and call me at Novosibirsk tomorrow." He glanced at his watch. "Time to be off." He took Semenov's arm. "Come, Comrade, you and I must have a talk."

For once the Trans-Siberian pulled out of Sverdlovsk two minutes early, at 2:16. No more passengers were allowed on board to spread alarm. Eyewitnesses at the station were told that the Peasant was a rapist trying to escape to Khabarovsk; they were advised not to talk about the incident; the local offices of *Izvestia*, *Pravda*, and Tass were instructed not to report it.

Viktor Pavlov didn't hear about the killing until they reached Tiumen. He was standing on the platform buying a paper cone of red currants, deep-frozen from the summer, from one of the girls patrolling the waiting train with buckets of baked potatoes, pies, and fruit.

He was joined by Semenov who bought some currants and, as he turned to go back to the train, said, lips hardly moving, "The Peasant's dead."

Pavlov went on munching, a trickle of juice like blood dribbling from the corner of his mouth. He tossed the cone on the platform and headed back to his carriage. The girl selling the currants called after him. He turned to see her pointing at the cone. She scowled, scolded him, and threw the cone into a refuse basket.

Pavlov went to the dining car and ordered himself a brandy. This was the fourth imponderable. Excluding the presence of the Tartar general and his wife, which was inconsequential, the imponderables were the agents arrested at Moscow's Far Eastern station, the KGB man taking the bunk below him, Col. Razin on the train, the death of the Peasant. How many more? He drank some brandy, feeling it burn his stomach, and fed the plan through the computer that was his brain. The gray cells received the messages, assimilated them, and came back with the answer: success with the reservation—only three imponderables left.

He watched a forest of silver birch, ghostly in the evening light, flit past the window. The death of the Peasant had been the worst setback. It was he who had known the exact location of the Kalashnikov semiautomatic assault rifles—a version of the Soviet army's AK-47's—the grenades and the submachine guns. Now, with the death of the Peasant, he had to work on Variation 1. How to find out the location of the weapons. Simple: he would have to get a message from Novosibirsk to one of the Zealots in Irkutsk.

Pavlov relaxed a little and ordered another brandy. This morning's encounter with Col. Razin hadn't been too bad.

A table had been reserved for them. Razin sat down, ordered a coffee and said: "You're a Jew, aren't you, Comrade Pavlov?"

Pavlov had been expecting it. The KGB, and the NKVD before them, must have checked him out exhaustively back to his birth in the devastated city of Leningrad. But there was no positive check on his

81

mother. He had always known that the KGB knew he was a mongrel; but they were only certain of some Jewish blood on his father's side.

Pavlov said, as he always said, "Do you want to see my papers?"

"No need, Comrade Pavlov. I know perfectly well what's on them."

"Why do you ask then? You know I've got a strain of Jewish blood. So have millions of Soviet citizens."

Razin's brown eyes were gentle as he agreed. "Perhaps even myself if I checked back far enough." He reached across the table and touched Pavlov's arm. "Don't be alarmed, I was only making conversation. It's pleasant to see a familiar face on the train. It relieves the tension a little. I have a terrible responsibility," he confided. "You must forgive me if I seemed . . . abrupt." He offered Pavlov a pack of American cigarettes obtained on the diplomatic circuit, but Pavlov refused. "A bad habit. Undoubtedly injurious to health. But it soothes the nerves in positions like this."

"You don't look nervous," Pavlov said, studying Razin's big features, the deep cleft in the chin where the razor had missed a few bristles.

Razin shrugged. "I've nothing against the Jews," he said. "They constitute some of the finest brains in the Soviet Union. Too many, perhaps. That's why we have to put certain obstacles in their way in the schools and universities otherwise they'd grab *all* the places. Wasn't it Madame Furtseva, the Minister of Culture who, when asked to comment on the situation, replied, 'It would do no harm if there was one Jewish miner for every Jewish student'?"

"I thought Khrushchev said it. Anyway it's highly complimentary to the Jews."

"Indeed." Razin inhaled deeply; he smoked a cigarette with great deliberation, as he did everything. He went on: "Look at you, Comrade Pavlov. The greatest mathematical brain in Russia today. And that's only with a thin strain of Jewish blood. What would you be like if you were totally Jewish? You're a genius now so there's only one logical answer." He paused. "You'd be a madman."

The waitress, a dark-skinned Georgian with glossy hair tied in braids, hovered nervously near the table. She felt the undercurrent of power and she was frightened to go too near to it.

Razin beckoned her over; she approached as if she were stepping over an electric cable. "More coffee," he said. He favored her with his gentle smile and his big head turned as she walked away. "Attractive, eh? A good figure. But her backside's a bit on the small side. We Russians like a good rump."

"I'm a Russian," Pavlov reminded him. "You seem to forget."

"Ah, yes." Razin leaned forward waiting for the hard sugar to melt in his coffee. "If only they were all like you." He prodded at the lump of Cuban sugar with his teaspoon. "The majority are, of course. They're good Russians and they want to stay here. And why not? There are fantastic opportunities in the Soviet Union." He pointed out of the window, past a village of gingerbread houses with blue and yellow jig-saw eaves, past the pine and birch and larch to the steppes. "Siberia," Razin said. "It could supply the world with coal for 2,000 years and still have some left over. It could release enough diamonds to make them as valueless as pebbles on the beach."

Razin conquered the sugar. "No," he continued, "the majority of Jews have the right idea. It's the

83

minority that causes the trouble. The troublemakers the world hears about. The Zionists." He spat out the word. "I have nothing against Jews"—Pavlov thought he was over-emphatic—"I have no time for Zionists. They're traitors," he finished, his eyes searching Pavlov's face.

Pavlov said, "I agree." The lie didn't trouble him because with this man, an associate of the butcher Beria, it was merely a defensive weapon; it only hurt when he had to deny his heritage to another Jew, to Gopnik.

"One thing puzzles me," Razin said, sawing at the cleft in his chin with his forefinger. "How did you get authority at such a high level to travel on this particular train?" He waved aside Pavlov's explanation. "I know about your wife, I know about your work. But it seems remarkable to me that a man of known Jewish origins should have been allowed to travel on the same train as Comrade Yermakov."

Pavlov said, "Perhaps you didn't know, Comrade colonel, that Comrade Yermakov has made it known that he wants to meet my wife in Khabarovsk. Publicly. A great opportunity for glamorous publicity. The photographers have already been warned. Can't you see the photographs now? The flower of Siberian womanhood and the might of the Soviet Union with garlands round their necks?" Beauty and the beast, he thought.

"I hadn't heard about it," Razin said. "I suppose I should have. Someone slipped up."

Pavlov felt sorry for the official who had slipped up.

"So you see," Pavlov went on, "it was considered important that I should be on the train. Apparently my wife was unwilling to participate if I wasn't there."

"I see," Razin said thoughtfully. He stared out of the window fingering the cleft in his chin, his brown eyes troubled.

One foreigner on board the train did know about the shooting at Sverdlovsk. He was Harry Bridges and, with his special pass, he had been wandering around the back of the station when he saw a man in peasant dress wrench himself away from two plainclothes police and run toward a line of parked cars. He also saw another man in plainclothes with a white face and a scar at the corner of his mouth draw a pistol.

The man with the scar seemed to hesitate, even though he was patently KGB. Then he raised the pistol and gunned down the man in peasant clothes. The peasant spun round and, or so it seemed to Harry Bridges, looked at the man with the scar with recognition as he fell dying. Bridge's professional eye switched back to his killer. Fleetingly, there seemed to be an expression of anguish on his pale face.

Bridges retreated into the station building and climbed back on to the train: eyewitnesses of a police killing were never welcome. He stood for a while in the corridor, noting that the train pulled out two minutes early, wondering what he had witnessed.

Every instinct screamed: Story. Even the legendary reporter assigned to cover a speech who didn't file a story because the town hall was burned down, would have been alerted. Even if it was routine cops-and-robbers it was worth filing when it happened within 100 yards of Vasily Yermakov.

But Bridges suspected that the shooting was more than routine. The black Chaika waiting outside, Razin taking charge, the glances between killer and victim, the Trans-Siberian departing two minutes early.

But it wasn't the sort of story the Russians would want him to file. If I break faith, he thought, the exclusive stories will stop; if I break faith I'll be deported. He lit a cigarette and blew the smoke against the window watching it flatten against the glass. If I break faith it's the end of the great experiment.

But there were other faiths. The unwritten law to report the truth; suppression of news was merely a by-law of that premise. But have I already broken that law? Bridges wondered, knowing the answer. He hadn't yet suppressed a story, he hadn't yet filed a deliberately false story. But there were degrees of journalistic dishonesty. Had he ever tracked down a story that might be detrimental to the Soviet Union? Had he ever pursued a breath of Kremlin scandal?

Bridges walked along the corridor toward the special coach. But who had filed the most exclusives from Moscow in the past two years? Harry Bridges. While the rest of the American pack got the routine stories from the United States Embassy—swapping them with British correspondents with contacts at their own embassy—Bridges got the big ones from the Kremlin.

As he approached the two guards at the door of the special coach Bridges had the uneasy feeling that the train was inexorably propelling him toward the biggest story of his life. So now he made a gesture to the professional pride he had once cherished: he made an approach to Col. Yury Razin.

He showed his pass to the first guard, a vast man with a shaven skull and a tick in one eye.

The guard shook his head. "No good."

Bridges said, "I want to see Colonel Razin."

The name stopped the tick for a moment. "What for? No one is allowed in there."

"Tell him to come out here."

"*Tell* him?" The tick was frozen.

"For your own good tell him. If you don't want to end up here, that is." Bridges pointed out at Siberia.

The guard hesitated, then conferred with his companion. Beyond these two stood two uniformed militia, the holsters of the pistols at their hips unbuttoned.

The first guard turned to Bridges. "Very well. What shall I say you want?"

Bridges said, "Tell him it's about the peasant."

"The peasant?"

"Just tell him."

Col. Razin looked benign enough, but there was a tautness about him—a muscle leaping on his jaw as he clenched and unclenched his teeth. "Mr. Bridges," he said, extending his hand, "what can I do for you?"

Bridges said bluntly: "There was a man shot dead at Sverdlovsk."

"Was there?" The colonel seemed uninterested. "Let's go in here." He gestured toward the small bathroom-lavatory. "My hands are filthy. You'd think it would be different with electric trains, wouldn't you?"

Inside, Col. Razin carefully locked the door. Then he turned on the hot tap and began to wash his hands with the tiny bar of carbolic soap. Looking at Bridges in the mirror above the washbasin, he asked: "What's all this about a shooting?"

Bridges said, "Let's not waste words. I was in the station. I saw a peasant make a break and get shot. What was it all about?"

Razin rinsed his hands under the cold tap. They were big hands, covered with mats of hair. Finally, he said, "You're very good at your job, Mr. Bridges. Always there at the right time. I've heard quite a lot about you from my friends at *Novosti* and Tass. Your reports have always been very . . . reasonable." He turned off the water and reached for a coarse paper towel. "I believe that we, in our turn, have been cooperative with you. Isn't that so?"

"Sure you have," Bridges agreed.

Col. Razin turned, drying his hands. "And, of course, we shall continue to cooperate. . . ."

"If I forget the shooting?"

Razin tossed the sodden towel into a basket. "The shooting isn't even worth forgetting." There was a blade in his voice now, although his face was still bland. "It certainly isn't worth reporting."

"Surely I should be the judge of that?" Bridges said.

"Would your newspaper really be interested in the death in the middle of Siberia of a criminal accused of raping a little girl of ten? I don't think so, Mr. Bridges. I really don't think so." He inspected his hands and found them clean. "Let's put it this way: your newspaper would hardly thank you for jeopardizing their flow of exclusive news." He moved closer to Bridges. "They would hardly thank you for being forced to leave the Trans-Siberian in the middle of Siberia." He smiled. "A good story for your rivals, eh? Nor would they thank you for terminating their accreditation in Moscow." He turned the handle of the door. "You must assess your values. Is the story of the shooting of one child rapist worth all that?"

Bridges was grateful to him in a way. It wasn't worth it. Any journalist would agree. It was a question of mature appraisal, of responsibility.

And it wasn't till he got back to his compartment and lay on his bunk above the Intourist girl that he thought: Harry Bridges, you hypocritical bastard.

4.

Harry Bridges was born at the end of World War II in a hamlet in upstate New York overlooking a fat curve of the Hudson River somewhere between Yonkers and Sing Sing.

It was a sweet village of white, clapboard houses tucked into the hills dropping down to the river. It contained a lot of people of the same name, a general store that smelled of most things you can eat or smoke, a liquor store, a couple of bars, a neat church, and a spooky mansion. In those days its roads were clean of plastic bottles and worn-out tires, it had its share of loonies, and up the road at Bear Mountain the bears had returned in the absence of hunters who had gone to war—or so the children were told.

Harry's father hadn't gone to war. He wrote a syndicated column and, suffering from such occupational ailments as ulcers and high blood pressure, had been exempted from military service. In any case he was almost too old and he was doing a good job boosting morale.

Harry was happy in his village and never had any doubt that he would become a journalist like his father. On the weekends, when his father brought boozy friends back with him from New York, he hung around listening to their talk which sounded just like movie newspapermen except that his father's friends didn't wear snap-brimmed hats and, instead of dames, they brought their wives with them.

Harry's mother wasn't so keen on him becoming a journalist. She talked a lot about a decent profession and at night, when he was in bed, Harry heard her questioning his future. She said things like, "You don't want him to grow up like you, do you?" and made reference to his father's rough friends, his long absences from home, his lifelong friendship with Old Grandad, his ulcers. "Leave it to the kid," said his father. And, because she was that sort of wife and mother, she did; even though she still hoped he might one day study medicine.

His father wanted Harry to go to college. "Get a degree in journalism," he said. "That's the way it's going to be. Don't claw your way up the way I did. It takes too much out of you."

But Harry had to claw his way up because some time after the war America found that, having helped to beat fascism, they now had to beat communism. Eagerly and masochistically—like a husband hoping to catch his wife being unfaithful—they searched within themselves for The Red Menace. Under the leadership of Senator McCarthy, the witch-hunters sniffed out anyone from dedicated, self-confessed

Communists to junk-dealers with an old print of Lenin in the attic.

Among those indicted was Harry's father. He was found to have knowingly sought the company of Communists—"How the hell else do you get stories?" he demanded—and to have published articles propagating communism which turned out to be two columns giving both sides of an industrial dispute in Detroit. Forgotten were the columns once described as "the inspiration behind the United States' war effort."

Harry's father was one of McCarthy's first victims and the execution was thorough. He lost his column, hit the bottle, and died eighteen months later leaving his wife and son with a mortgaged house and a few thousand dollars. They moved to a dingy tenement on upper Park Avenue and Harry got a job as a messenger boy on the New York *Daily News* while his mother cleaned apartments.

He also went to night school and one evening on the way home he witnessed an armed robbery—which, in those days, was still news—and took pictures with his box camera. It transpired that the victim was an old-time movie star and the *Daily News* published Harry's pictures and eyewitness account and put his name above the whole spread. Harry took home six copies and kept one clipping all his life.

Throughout this period he was never too sure of what communism was: he was merely aware that it was the opposing force to capitalism, which was responsible for his father's humiliation and death.

When his mother died from overwork—just as much a victim of McCarthyism as his father—he quit his job, paid the rent, and took the copy of the *Daily News* with his story and pictures and headed south to Florida where he found a job as a junior reporter in Orlando. His ultimate destination was always the *New York Times*.

When he finished his Army service, he heard about a vacancy in the Miami bureau of the Associated Press and, campaigning with his Florida experience of swamp fires, orange harvests, and crooked real estate, he landed the job.

He was twenty-one, tall, deceptively languid, a little on the skinny side, handsome but not pretty, with brown hair that took on a bleach in the sun. He was popular with the blue rinses and one or two claimed they could get him into pictures; but Harry Bridges wasn't interested; his father and his boozy friends had set the pattern and, whereas other young men with his looks would have slept with a Florida alligator to get their name in lights, Harry only wanted his at the top of a column in the *Times*.

He enjoyed the sun and the girls but Miami wasn't his town; not with upstate New York and upper Park Avenue so close behind him. The opposite poles of the American Dream disturbed him; but not too much because he had his job and Carol Ralston, a dark and beautiful girl with Spanish ancestry way back, who was content to go on dreary assignments with him, wait for him while he banged out stories on a decrepit portable, feed him when he turned up starving after a day chasing hunches, and making passionate but unconsummated love in the back of his second-hand Chevy.

Her father was in his late fifties, an executive with a Chicago company trying to undercut the contractors tendering for the high-rise hotels and apartment blocks creeping along the beach as if they were trying to keep out the sea. Harry thought the family had it made, that their house with its Spanish arches and drapes of bourgainvillea was permanent; that the ice in the cocktail-hour drinks would tinkle forever.

He hadn't learned that happiness and security is on a mortgage; nor did he know that Carol Ralston's father despised the mean work he was doing and would have quit if it hadn't been for his debts.

One sweltering day a half-built apartment block for which John Ralston's company had submitted the lowest tender collapsed killing two workmen. Files in Chicago containing records of Ralston's opposition to the deal were destroyed and he took the blame.

One month later John Ralston shot himself through the roof of his mouth with a Smith & Wesson.

The subsequent family pattern was similar to that followed by Bridges and his mother; the combination of the two was to affect his values deeply for the rest of his life. Miami is no place for the impoverished widow of a suicide branded a homicidal racketeer and Mrs. Ralston departed with her daughter to the Chicago suburb where she had once embarked on a glittering future with her young and ambitious husband.

If Carol Ralston had stayed in Miami, Harry might have married her and one day moved to an apartment in Manhattan. But lasting devotion owes much to circumstances and, although the letters continued for more than a year, and although Harry managed one visit to Chicago, their passion didn't survive.

Meanwhile Harry returned to night school, learned French and German, and plagued his head office with requests to join the foreign staff. Finally they capitulated after he had filed two exclusive political stories said to be the source of acute embarrassment in Washington—the acme of journalistic distinction. And, as is the way with the house decisions of the press, they dispatched him to a South

American bureau where neither French nor German was of much use. So he learned Spanish.

From there he went to South Africa and then to the Middle East where he assaulted the Arabic language.

From Beirut he was frequently taken to areas devastated by Israeli jets and commandos. Conscientiously, he filed factual reports of what he saw without attempting to interpret or moralize because he knew the A.P. would be receiving reports from the Israeli side and could circulate balanced versions of the conflict.

Then he got the newspaper job; the paper had a style of its own and Bridges had to comply. Thus he described more emotionally the victims of war, realizing again that everything he filed would be equated with reports from Israel. If he had been in Israel he would have acted the same way describing the Palestinian attacks and bomb outrages. Harry Bridges was a noninvolved professional.

But there was a persistent query in his life. He wasn't sure whether it was a strength or a weakness. He wanted to see how communism worked. When he presented it to himself as a strength he told himself: Any self-respecting foreign correspondent operating in a world dominated by capitalism and communism should see both sides of the coin. When he suspected weakness he confessed that, in the light of his experience, equality and common endeavor had a certain allure.

One day, when heat was bouncing off the concrete and splintering on the sea, he was joined on the verandah of a Beirut hotel, where he was drinking arak, by a Russian correspondent. They had talked before and Harry had expressed a desire to visit the Soviet Union.

The Russian, named Suslov, ordered a vodka,

uncharacteristically made a long drink out of it with tonic and ice, and said, "How are things, Harry?" Like many of his kind he spoke English with an American accent.

"So so," Bridges told him. "I'm getting bored with Beirut. It's too much like Miami."

"You'd prefer a more Spartan life?"

"Maybe. Not too Spartan. I'm growing soft."

Suslov, a pale man with soft brown hair whose skin peeled in the sun, considered this. He drank thirstily and said, "No, not too Spartan. Moscow isn't too Spartan. At least not for the correspondents of Western newspapers."

"Great," Bridges said. "Except that my paper hasn't asked me to go to Moscow."

"Not yet," Suslov remarked, ordering another vodka tonic and an arak for Bridges.

"You know something that I don't?"

"Perhaps." Suslov peeled a little skin from his nose. "I do know that your representative in Moscow has been recalled."

"The hell he has. Are you sure? He was doing pretty well."

"Quite sure. Perhaps he was doing too well."

"You mean the Russians have told him he can't stay, not that his paper's recalled him?"

"Something like that. I'm not in full possession of the facts."

Suslov examined his fingernails while Bridges absorbed the information. Bridges stared across the Mediterranean where the Soviet and Western navies were chasing each other around.

After a while he asked, "What makes you think my paper will want me to go to Russia? I don't even speak Russian," he added.

"Let's put it this way," Suslov said. "As is well known, no Western journalist can get accreditation in Moscow without the consent of the Soviet authorities. Now your paper hasn't made itself too popular in Kremlin circles. Supposing every name put forward was rejected until yours came up?"

Bridges gazed at Suslov in astonishment. "Why should your people want me in Moscow?"

Suslov said, "Perhaps because your reporting has been objective. It has been noted." He fished the lemon from his drink and bit it daintily. "Believe it or not, that's all we seek."

"Except, of course, that objective reporting is open to several interpretations."

Suslov shrugged. "If your name was submitted, would you take the job?"

"I wouldn't have any choice," Bridges said. He gazed around the rich, somnolent city; it reminded him of a gorged millionaire who has dined heavily, belched, and gone to sleep. He had a vision of a snow-clean city free of graft and corruption; of pine-covered hills on which skis sang a lonely song.

Two months later he was in Moscow.

He took over a big apartment in Kutuzovsky with a maid, interpreter, telex, and an incoming Tass machine stuttering monotonously in the office.

He toured the Western cocktail circuit and soon got bored with the scared, stuffy diplomats who talked as though the olive in every vodka martini was bugged. He was handed an exclusive by the Russians —an interview with a defector from the States— and earned the hostility of the other Western correspondents.

Out of perversity he broke Rule No. 1 and had an affair with a Russian girl. He waited fatalistically to be compromised but nothing happened. No photographs, no accusation that the girl was under age, no police bursting into the bedroom. In fact, he and the girl spent a delightful summer on the river beaches of Moscow and in his bed.

Out of perversity he traveled out of limits waiting for the roar of motorcycles behind his green Lincoln. But, as far as he could see, he could have driven to Archangel without being stopped.

His presence was requested at the American Embassy where, in a small room with the radio playing "to drown the bugs," he was warned by a CIA agent thinly disguised as a first secretary, "They're setting you up for something."

"Good for them," Bridges said.

Flirting with communism, wasn't it called? At night in his apartment, drinking Scotch at $1.50 a bottle, listening to jazz on his hi-fi imported from New York, Harry Bridges wondered about his motives. Sheer perversity seemed favorite. But, at the same time, he remembered his father who had died because of bigotry toward socialism and, in his mind, he linked it with a man called Ralston blowing his brains out on the terrace of a fine Spanish-style house.

Give it time, Bridges decided. Time to see both sides of the coin.

Then he gave himself extensions of time and was never quite sure at what stage he realized he was being trapped—if, that is, he wanted to escape.

He traveled extensively and saw all the "heroic achievements." He admired them and was angered by Western derision born of fear; equally he was angered by the plodding Soviet criticism of Western progress. In shadowy form, aided by a few slugs of Scotch, Bridges sometimes saw himself as an instrument for improving East-West communications; a sort of global PRO.

And all the time he kept his paper happy with a steady flow of exclusives. He liked seeing his by-line; he liked reigning over the other correspondents; he liked the hard winters and the soft life.

There was a lot he disliked in Moscow, in particular the company of the defectors, lonely fugitives living in limbo; they were his steadying influence, his warning light; although he persuaded himself that they had come over because of character flaws whereas he was merely staying to get the balanced view. Staying and staying.

He was, of course, depressed by the lack of freedom, the power of the secret police, the treatment of the Jews, the blind obedience of the people. "But," he wrote to friends in the States, "you've got to equate all this against their achievements, their fundamental happiness, their indomitable spirit." And he was fond of pointing out in his letters that you could still walk the streets of Moscow without fear of being mugged and that he had never come across a drug problem.

Back in America his friends asked, "What the hell's with Harry Bridges? Has he gone over to the other side?"

Bridges wasn't sure. Nor was he sure what sort of journalist he was any more. He decided to allow himself one more assignment before making his final decision. That assignment was Yermakov's Trans-Siberian tour. He had seen both sides of the coin for long enough. Somewhere on the train journey he would have to toss the coin and see on which side it came down.

5.

They reached Novosibirsk, the Chicago of Siberia, at 10:31 on the morning of the third day. They were on the edge of winter and the first wisps of snow were falling hesitantly.

As always, the police alighted first followed by Yermakov, jovial and menacing in a bulky black over-coat, scarf and seal-skin hat. His eyes were pouchy beneath the thick eyebrows and his skin looked tired. He shook hands with local party officials and the stationmaster beaming nervously and accepted a bouquet of red orchids grown in the city's green-houses from a little girl. Then, with a military band playing, he inspected the jack-booted troops in their long coats drawn up outside the station.

It wasn't until he had been driven away, in a

black Chaika, waving to the crowds, that the rest of the passengers were allowed to disembark. Among those staying overnight were the driver, Boris Demurin, who was taking the special coach all the way to Vladivostok; Harry Bridges and his fellow passengers; Viktor Pavlov and his fellow passengers.

All except Demurin and his crew went by cab to the Grand Hotel.

Pavlov stayed in his room for two hours. The room was functional with pink satin over the bed, pillows covered with towels, pink curtains, and strips of white paper sealing the windows against the cold that was to come. He checked it methodically and, after fifty minutes, found a tiny black microphone concealed in the head of the brass bedstead. Not very original, he thought: the traditional hiding place for untaxed loot.

He didn't think the bug had been installed for him; it was probably one of the rooms reserved for Western visitors. But you couldn't take chances. He left the microphone intact and primed the tape recorder which had been left for him at reception. Then he knocked on his own door, opened it, and said, "Why, hello Vladimir, come in. We've got a lot to talk about." He closed the door, switched on the tape and listened for a few moments to himself talking to a man called Vladimir about computers. The machine had been adapted and the tape would play for two hours.

He glanced at his wrist watch. It was 12:45. Between 12:45 and 12:50 the female watchdog installed on each floor to discourage hooliganism and fornication went downstairs to fetch her lunch of borscht, black bread, lemon tea, and chocolate cake. The timing, like the meal, he had been advised, never changed. Gently, he opened the door and gazed down the corridor; it was empty. Instead of turning left toward the stairs which would take him down to the marble hall with its Corinthian columns he turned right toward a small service door. He opened it and ran down the stairs, through a yard cluttered with garbage cans into the street behind the hotel.

Harry Bridges who, throughout his career, had made a point of surveying the rear aspects of hotels, much favored by publicity-shy celebrities and call-girls visiting politicians, saw him leave from the end of the street. Again every instinct bristled. Viktor Pavlov, mathematical genius and husband of a hero-ine, leaving as furtively as a jewel thief? Just as he had once followed fire engines and ambulances, Bridges followed Pavlov.

The snow was falling more thickly now, set-tling on the sidewalks, laying fingers on window ledges. At the end of the street Pavlov struck out to the left. It was then that Bridges realized that there was someone else who knew about the rear aspects of hotels. From a doorway a figure detached itself and set out after Pavlov.

The snow blurred his outline but, if Bridges wasn't mistaken, it was Gavralin, Pavlov's healthy-looking companion on the train. He had been walking on the train with a limp: there was no limp now. He moved cautiously but confidently; a trained shadow, allow-ing Pavlov a good lead, using doorways and phone kiosks if he sensed that he was about to look round, accelerating whenever he turned a corner.

Bridges adopted the same tactics. He had an advantage: it was unlikely that Gavralin would sus-pect that he himself was being followed.

Pavlov turned into a main thoroughfare near the Institute of Applied Chemistry. Gavralin ran to the corner, waited a few moments before rounding it. Bridges did likewise. They proceeded along the main street, each separated by about 100 yards.

The snow fell steadily to the level of the big gray blocks of offices and apartments, then went mad in the wind tunnel created by the blocks. The snow muffled sound and the red tramcars were as bright as holly berries against the white. Pedestrians bowed their heads, lurching fatalistically into interminable winter, and only the little, long-haired horses trotting beside the trams looked unconcerned—Christmas pantomime ponies with the snow mantling their coats.

Pavlov now made pursuit more difficult by turning into the municipal park. There were few people here and the only cover was the trees. A few children played, rolling this first snow into dirty snowballs. One hit Pavlov; he turned and his shadow slid behind a wooden hut. Bridges, who hadn't entered the park, waited beside a couple of vacuum snowcleaners brought out from summer hibernation and an assembling army of old women with broad shovels.

Pavlov strode on, a tall, lonely figure in dark coat and fur hat. Gavralin let him get a couple of hundred yards along the path before following. Bridges entered the park, seeing only the man between him and Pavlov. There were only two sets of footprints on the snow; occasionally they crossed each other.

At the far side of the park Pavlov crossed the road, making for the wooden city. He dodged a boy on a sledge, its runners scraping on the sidewalk, and walked briskly down a narrow street of houses with carved eaves, their roofs already looking like white envelopes. He stopped at No. 43, a neat house with birch saplings in the garden and a row of dead, decapitated sunflowers. The wooden gate was carved in the shape of two huge rose blossoms.

Pavlov glanced around, went up the pathway, and rang the bell. The door opened, Pavlov stamped, shook the snow off his coat and went inside. Gavralin took up a position behind a tree fifty yards away, Bridges waited fifty yards further down the street.

The snow fell thickly and the cold slipped inside Bridges's overcoat.

Pavlov said, "The Peasant's dead."

The Prospector asked, "How?"

"Shot at Sverdlovsk."

"Who by?"

"The Policeman," Pavlov said. Before the Prospector could express shock Pavlov explained what he thought had happened. "They had got the Peasant. There was nothing else he could do. He saved us." He shivered despite the warmth from the red-hot stove in the middle of the room. "Give me a brandy. The cold's got inside me."

"Cold? This isn't cold. You should go to the Cold Pole at Indigirka. Minus 38 Fahrenheit. It takes the skin off you like peeling an apple."

The Prospector was a big shaggy man who had spent all his life prospecting in the northern wastes of Siberia. He wore a cap made of mink, boots of wolf skin. He had found gas and petroleum for the Soviet Union; he had been marooned on an iceberg; he had existed for two months on wild mares' milk; he had lived with Tungu tribesmen—once said to be the dirtiest people in the world. There wasn't much that the Prospector hadn't done and one day he had found gold. But, anticipating his reward, he had taken a few large nuggets for himself. His final reward was four years in a strict regime camp with confiscation of property. The camp was close to the Siberian Railway—so that reinforcements could be mobilized in the event of a break—and he knew well the stretch of railroad east of Irkutsk where the kidnap was to take place.

The Prospector was thirty-eight, a gentile. But four years' imprisonment had affected him more savagely than it would most people: it had warped his adventurous soul. Now he wanted revenge. He didn't care how he got it, and in 1970, he was recruited by the Zealots. They trusted him completely.

He had one disadvantage: he had a criminal record and therefore automatically attracted suspicion. The plan was that he should take the night train to Irkutsk and then a helicopter for the rest of the journey. Since his release from the camp he had joined the helicopter service hunting wolves and he was due to go on patrol.

He handed Pavlov a tumberful of brandy and poured himself a large vodka from a bottle he kept in the garden so that, in deep winter, the colorless liquid was as thick as oil. In the kitchen the wolf he kept as a pet snuffled at the door.

"So what do we do now?" the Prospector asked.

"It hasn't changed anything."

"The Peasant knew where the guns were. He put them there."

"The Priest knows where they are," Pavlov said. "I thought of phoning him in Irkutsk. But all the clergy are under surveillance. It would be too dangerous."

"So?"

"You'll have to see him when you reach Irkutsk."

The Prospector shook his shaggy head: he had let all his hair grow in the old days to keep out the cold and had kept the style; his beard was long and thick but the hair on his scalp had never grown properly after the attentions of the camp barber.

He said, "I won't have time."

"You'll have to make time. The Priest won't go where the action is. You can't have priests running around in the middle of battlefields."

"Battlefields?"

Pavlov gulped his brandy. "It could happen."

"All right," the Prospector said. "I'll make time." He lit a cardboard-tipped cigarette and poured himself more vodka. "To success." He drained the vodka and smashed the glass against the incandescent stove.

Bridges, who looked and felt like a snowman, watched Gavralin flit across the road into a glass phone booth and, still watching the house, make a phone call. He guessed the purpose of the call. To police headquarters: "Give me the identity of the occupant of No. 43."

Bridges watched Gavralin speaking, waiting, dusting the snow from his *shapka,* stamping his feet, then nodding vigorously. He hung up the receiver slowly, as if he had heard momentous news. Then he slid his hand inside his coat, took out a pistol, checked it, and slipped it back.

He came out of the booth and stood stamping his feet for a moment. He seemed to be making a decision. He reached it and headed for No. 43, keeping close to the wooden fences on the same side so that anyone looking out of a window wouldn't see him unless they craned their necks.

Bridges thought: You are a stupid glory-seeker trying to go it alone.

As Gavralin climbed over the fence, approaching No. 43 along the line of dead sunflowers, Bridges heard barking. Gavralin drew his pistol and knocked on the front door.

From inside came a growling voice: "Who is it?"

"Police," Gavralin shouted.

Bridges moved closer observing Gavralin move to one side to make sure no one left by the back door.

The front door opened and Gavralin went straight in, kicking the door aside, ramming the pistol in the ribs of the bearded man who answered it. The door shut. Bridges went to the window and peered in.

The Prospector said, "What the hell. . . ."

"Where is he?" Gavralin snapped.

"Where's who?"

"Viktor Pavlov."

"I don't know any Viktor Pavlov."

Gavralin stood back, the pistol an extension of his arm. "You've already done four years. This could get you another twenty. Or," he said, "you could be shot or sent down a cobalt mine where the death is slower. We usually give people the choice. Most of them prefer the cobalt mines. They wouldn't if they saw the way men die. . . ." He jerked the pistol. "Where is he?"

The Prospector wavered. "In there," he said, pointing at the kitchen.

"All right, you go first."

The Prospector shrugged and turned, fumbling for a moment in the breast pocket of his faded blue blouse.

Gavralin thrust the pistol into his spine. "Open the door."

"Just as you please."

The Prospector opened the door, standing aside as the wolf went for Gavralin's throat. The pistol fired once, the bullet punching a hole in the wall. Then the wolf had him down, white teeth deep in his throat. The man struggled for a moment, making small bubbling cries.

The Prospector blew again on the soundless dog whistle he had taken from his breast pocket and the wolf stood back. Gavralin struggled feebly at the blood spurting from a savaged artery, then died.

Pavlov came down the stairs. "Is he dead?"

The Prospector nodded. "He"—pointing at the wolf—"doesn't play games."

"So I see." Pavlov indicated the corpse. "We'll have to get rid of that somehow."

"How do you suggest?"

"You've got your truck here?"

"It's at the back."

"Then you'll have to take the body and dump it in the river." Pavlov sat down near the stove. "Lock that thing up," he said, pointing at the wolf. "I've got to think."

The Prospector patted the wolf and led it into the kitchen.

Thinking aloud, Pavlov said, "You can never come back here now. Gavralin must have checked with the local police to see who lived here. Otherwise he wouldn't have rushed you with a gun. The question is, did he tell them I was here?" Pavlov poured himself some brandy. "Another imponderable. . . ."

"Imponderable? That's a big word, my friend. What does it mean?" The Prospector stepped over the body and sat opposite Pavlov.

"If he did we're finished. But I don't think he did. If he had they'd have sent a whole posse of police here headed by Razin."

"Then you're safe?"

"Probably. But you're not. Get the body into a sack. Dump it in the truck." He stood up suddenly and adjusted the curtains. "Tell the neighbors that you're going away on your usual patrol. Dump the body and get to Irkutsk as fast as you can."

The Prospector stroked his beard. "What about the shot? Someone may have heard it. And another thing—they'll be waiting for me at the helicopter."

Pavlov said: "Forget about the helicopter. Go by road—no one suspects what you're really up to."

"And the shot?"

"You can't take the wolf with you. Tell the neighbors you had to shoot it because it attacked you."

The Prospector stared hard at Pavlov. "And what do you suggest I do with the dog?" He never called it a wolf.

"Cut its throat," Pavlov said.

The Prospector wrapped the body in sacking and, in broad daylight, with the falling snow veiling him, dumped it in the back of his truck. Then he returned to the kitchen and talked to the wolf. "He wanted me to cut your throat." He patted the wolf's lean gray back. "I'd rather cut my own." He snapped a lead on the animal's collar and, as the wolf opened its jaws, said, "Just keep your mouth shut."

He took the wolf with him, sitting him in the seat beside the wheel. Then he drove to the banks of the Ob and, as dusk thickened, dumped the body. But it hit a boulder, lodging on the brink of the dark water. The Prospector cursed. He was about to go after it when he heard the sound of a vehicle coming up behind him. He drove a hundred yards along the road and waited.

The vehicle was a snow-cleaner which had come to disgorge its first load of the winter. The snow gushed into the air and fell on the blurred shape on the river-bank. Soon snow covered the body.

The Prospector grinned. The body wouldn't be found until the spring. A hundred years ago, when escaped convicts collapsed in a blizzard to be found perfectly preserved in the spring, they called the bodies snow flowers.

The first instinct of Harry Bridges, who left the garden of No. 43 when Pavlov came down the stairs, was to sprint to the telephone kiosk and phone a story.

But as he walked rapidly down the street of wooden houses he took a hold on himself. Phoning such a story in Russia was merely fanciful. But what *should* he do?

He knew now that he was on to a big story, the biggest of his life. If he didn't tell Razin he was condoning murder and, if his premonitions were right, high treason. It could also be argued that he was an accessory.

He hailed a cab and told the driver to take him to the Grand Hotel.

I have to toss a coin, he told himself; the decision was being forced upon him. Then it occurred to him that, if he told Razin what he knew, he would be instrumental in foiling the plot. Not only would there be no more bloodshed but he would have an exclusive spread all over the front page and his future in the Soviet Union would be assured. Surely that was journalistic good sense?

In the lobby of the hotel he met Razin.

Razin said, "Good evening, Mr. Bridges. Have you been exploring Chicago?"

Bridges hesitated. "Yes," he said, "it's a fine city."

He walked up the stairs to his room and stared through the window. It had stopped snowing and, through the glass, he could feel the muffled quiet.

Libby Chandler shivered in the hot bedroom. This was the city, the appointment was in half an hour and she was scared.

She put on her coat, fur hat, and Kings-road, knee-length leather boots which retained the cold. She put an Intourist guide to Novosibirsk in her sling bag and her Pentax camera over her shoulder. The complete tourist.

She opened the door, handed the key to the watchdog who had taken a liking to her and put hot-house dahlias in her room and went downstairs to the Corinthian columns.

On the way she passed Harry Bridges. She greeted him but he answered abruptly and ran up the stairs.

In the lobby she found the Intourist guide from the train, Stanley Wagstaff, and a couple of Australians.

The Intourist girl greeted her enthusiastically. "I was just coming to find you. In five minutes we shall make a tour of the city." She paused for effect. "This evening we shall visit a typical Siberian restaurant where there will be music and laughter."

She was in her blue uniform, a little shiny around the rump, but Libby remembered her naked in the train compartment. It gave her an advantage, talking to a naked woman.

Libby said: "I'm sorry. I shan't be coming with you. I like to see cities by myself."

The girl's expression hardened. "But you must come with me. I know everything about this city, the capital of Western Siberia. . . ."

"One million inhabitants," Stanley Wagstaff cut in. "Famous for machine tools, perfumes. . . . Got the biggest opera house in Russia."

The Intourist girl said, "Please, Mr. Wagstaff, I am the guide." There was an edge to her voice.

"Miss Chandler, it is my duty to see that you enjoy this beautiful city."

"I'm sorry," Libby said. "I really do want to see it by myself." She started for the door.

"Miss Chandler, I insist."

Oh no, Libby Chandler thought, don't let her stop me. Please God, don't let her call the police. She hesitated and turned, trying to see the girl naked again; but she saw only the uniform. "Don't worry," she said. "You won't get into trouble. I'll explain."

One of the Australians, who looked like a life-guard, cut in. "Perhaps you'd like an escort."

"I could show you as much as her," Stanley Wag-staff said.

The composure of the Intourist girl was begin-ning to crumble. "Please," she said, "let's all go to-gether."

"Next time," Libby said. "At Irkutsk maybe. But not here." She realized it was a stupid thing to say.

The big Australian said: "What about it, Libby?"

She attacked him because she was becoming sorry for the Intourist girl. "I'm going alone. Can't you understand English?"

The Australian shrugged cheerfully. "Out of ev-ery three you win one."

The Intourist girl said: "Please, this is my first assignment. . . ."

The Australian put his arm round her. "We'll look after you, Sheila," he said.

"Tell me," Libby said, "is your name Larissa?"

The girl nodded. "How did you know?"

"I just knew," Libby said, making for the doors, feeling that she had scored.

Outside, the gray sky had a sheen to it and the snow was wet. The streets resounded to the rhyth-mic scrape of the babushkas' shovels. Libby walked quickly, her feet crunching in the snow. She felt exposed, as if every militiaman staring at her *knew*. She remembered her instructions and took the second on the left past the Central Post Office.

She glanced at her watch. Three minutes to go. She stared desperately up and down the narrow street, wondering if she had remembered the instructions properly:

A bookshop. There is only one in the street. Next to the pharmacy, opposite the linen shop.

She couldn't see a pharmacy. Dear God, what have I got myself into? Suddenly, she saw her parents sitting down to tea in the farmhouse in Devon. She tasted honey and new bread. Libby Chandler, emancipated adventuress, felt the buildings closing in on her. On the opposite side of the road a middle-aged man in a gray overcoat stopped and stared at her. He crossed the street.

I mustn't panic, she told herself. Mustn't panic. Despite the cold, she felt sweat trickling down her body.

She remembered the gold brooch shaped like a coiled serpent with amethysts for its eyes and pinned it on the lapel of her coat.

The man in the gray overcoat said, "Excuse me, are you looking for something?" He smiled apologetically. "You are obviously a stranger—from the West?—and you look lost." He spoke English with a slight lisp.

"A pharmacy," Libby said. "I was looking for a pharmacy. I was told it had a prominent sign."

"Ah, they always say that, don't they." He gave a curious, high-pitched laugh. "In this case they were right. Except"—he paused—"that the pharmacy was closed down three days ago. Something to do with the black market. You know how it is. . . ."

One minute to go.

"Thank you," Libby said.

She turned to go but he laid his hand gently on her arm. "You have dollars, pounds?"

"No," Libby said, "no money."

"I have plenty of roubles. I could give you a very good rate. Far better than you'll get with anyone else." He fingered the material of Libby's coat. "Enough to buy good furs. There are plenty of them in Novosibirsk."

Libby disengaged his hand. "Find another customer," she said. She walked away, feet slipping a little on the melting snow.

As she turned his expression changed. "Sensible girl," he murmured. "What a very sensible young lady."

He shrugged and headed for the main thoroughfare.

The bookshop was there beside the empty shop which until recently had been a pharmacy. She was exactly on time. The young man was standing behind the fourth row of bookshelves. He glanced up as she entered and she fingered the gold brooch. He nodded as if approving something in the book he was reading.

The bookshop was empty except for the two of them and the proprietor, an old man reading a thin vellum book through an eyeglass. Outside, she could hear snow flopping from the roofs.

Libby went around the fourth bookshelf so that she could see part of his face above a row of books. Just a pair of pale blue eyes, like the eyes in a mask. But the eyes spoke to her. He replaced the volume he had been reading and slipped the package across the tops of the books. She thought the eyes smiled; then he was gone.

Shielding the package with a book, she slipped it into her pocket. It was much smaller than she had imagined it would be; later she realized that it was a microfilm.

She took the book she had selected and paid for it without looking at the title. Once outside, she discovered that it was *War and Peace*.

Libby Chandler's plan was drawn up in a boulevard café on the Champs Élysées with two members of Amnesty International one hot, sullen afternoon in August 1973.

But her rebellion began much earlier.

She was born in the White Highlands of Kenya, the only daughter of a farmer and his wife. The house was casually opulent, white with a big terrace, skins on the floors, and glass-eyed trophies on the walls; its sounds were the tinkle of ice in drinks as the day faded in lemon light and the slap of servants' bare feet on stone floors. Libby loved animals, rode a lot, and had grown into a beautiful, brown-limbed girl of ten when her father decided to sell out and return to England.

The farmhouse in Devon was big and white and the earth was red like Kenya earth. Her parents spent most of their time regretting their departure from Kenya and irritating locals by comparing Devon with East Africa. The sun-downer drinking hour extended; gardeners, farm-hands and cooks came and went; the Chandlers retreated into moody isolation.

Libby went to a convent, then to Exeter University where the rebellion got underway. She campaigned for the homeless, for criminal law reform, for curbs on pollution, and still managed to get a good degree in geography. She was a warm and loving girl and slept with a few boys; but most of them bored her with their self-importance. She didn't smoke pot, she liked to go riding by herself, she sought achievement beyond conventional boundaries. She returned less and less to the farmhouse where parents still addressed Devonian servants in kitchen Swahili and searched the horizon for the peak of Mount Kilimanjaro.

When she left the university she was liberated, but not overpermissive. Tall, with long, fair hair which she pinned up with sunglasses, and the hauteur which a lot of male admiration breeds. When she went to Paris for the summer she was still in search of fulfillment.

She had a brief affair with a professional Frenchman until she found the weakness beneath his virile assurance. She left him and rented a one-room studio where she cooked and slept and read a lot; sitting in front of the open window, smelling coffee and Gauloises and the honey from the lime trees, listening to the lovers, brawlers and children in the narrow street below, wondering what to do before she started to think about security.

This was the period when she started to read modern Russian novels. Only Pasternak and Solzhenitsyn at that time; she didn't realize it but they were her tickets to Siberia.

One day, when she was drinking a glass of white wine and reading *Cancer Ward,* she was joined by a tall, fair-haired young Englishman who said, "Do you mind if I join you?"

Libby said: "I don't own the table," and went on reading.

He ordered a beer and asked, "Have you read his other books?"

"Yes," Libby Chandler replied, turning a page. She considered paying her bill and moving on; but it was pleasant in the boulevard café with the sun throwing coins of light on the tables through the leaves of the plane tree, and the Englishman wasn't a nuisance, not yet. She glanced at him—blue jeans, faded blue shirt, a shark's tooth on a gold chain round his neck, languidly assured.

"Have you read *Sequel to a Legend?*"

"No," she said, trying to think who wrote it.

He answered her. "Kuznetsov. All about a disillusioned young man who leaves Moscow for Siberia. I'll lend it to you if you like."

"Don't bother." She closed her book and searched her handbag for change.

He said, "How was Africa?"

She looked at him with surprise. "How did you know I was in Africa?"

He pointed at her elephant-hair bracelet.

She smiled and gave up because the sunlight was pleasant and she sensed he wasn't on the make. Or, if he was, he was at least subtle about it.

He ordered a carafe of white wine and they drank it; soon their table was an oasis amid the bullying traffic and all the people in a hurry.

He explained that he was a member of the Amnesty which concerned itself with the plight of prisoners but that he had a private crusade which he would tell her about later that evening. Libby said she would look forward to hearing about it.

The young man whose name was Richard Harrison looked at her wisely and Libby wondered where all the wisdom had come from because he was only twenty-four.

That evening, he introduced her to a couple of his friends from Amnesty and they drank more wine in another open-air café. They didn't impress her because they talked hysterically about countries they had never visited, because they were as dogmatic as the regimes they abused, because their generalizations were often naïve.

But Richard Harrison was different. When his

two friends had left they went back to her studio to drink coffee and discuss his own crusade.

She cooked steaks, tossed salad, and found his presence easy. He was, he told her, working for an Italian publishing company which specialized in printing literature smuggled out of Russia. "I used to get the stuff out myself but they rumbled me. No visa— no reasons given. All of us in the organization are in the same boat."

"I see." She looked at him carefully across the empty plates. "Why are you telling me all this?"

He said bluntly, "Because they wouldn't suspect a girl." He hurried on. "And because you look the sort of girl who could do it. You remind me of a girl called Annette Meakin."

"Do I?" Despite herself, she asked, "Who was Annette Meakin?"

"She and her mother were the first Englishwomen to cross Siberia by water and rail in 1900. They took the Trans-Siberian Railway. She was a girl of great spirit." He grinned. "Just like you except that she was older and not half as pretty."

"Flattery," Libby said, "will get you everywhere."

"A little on the obvious side?"

"A little. But I can take it." She poured more coffee and put a record on. "Lara's Theme." "It has to be, doesn't it?"

"Annette Meakin," Harrison told her, "also became a great travel writer and an authority on Schiller and Goethe." He handed her one of the books he had been carrying. "Here, read this." It was a book about Siberia with colored photographs in white, gold, and blue; eagles and reindeer, hoarfrost and hardship.

"I'll see you again tomorrow," he told her. "See what you think. If you agree then we'll make some plans."

He knows he's made it, she thought. And he

hasn't even tried to get me into bed. Vaguely, this annoyed her because she knew that Richard Harrison was a man who always got what he wanted.

Next day all she wanted to do was to get to Siberia. He knew this when they met in the same, sun-dappled café. "You're very sure of yourself," she said.

He shrugged. "I know quality when I see it. I know you'll succeed."

They had some coffee while he explained that a book was to be smuggled out of a hard-regime camp 124 miles north of Novosibirsk in the autumn. It would be brought to the city where she would pick it up. All she had to do then was continue her journey across Siberia and mail the package from Japan to Rome.

"And if I get caught?"

"Annette Meakin wouldn't have got caught."

"You're quite ruthless, aren't you?"

"For the sake of literature."

They met a couple of times more and the final arrangements were made in the middle of September. He never tried to make love to her and Libby Chandler often wondered about him. He held no particular sexual attraction for her; but she admired him and she wasn't lavish with admiration.

On their last meeting at the café he told her about the bookshop and gave her the brooch with the amethyst eyes. Then he grinned and said, "Take a tip from Miss Meakin's writings. If you don't want your mail stolen send it in an envelope with black borders. They're still very superstitious in Siberia."

He kissed her and was gone.

When she got back to her room in the Grand Hotel with the microfilm in her pocket, Col. Yury Razin was waiting for her.

"How did you get in?" she asked.

"Through the door," he said, introducing himself.

She took off her coat and hung it on the door. Razin, who, she presumed, was KGB, stood within three feet of the microfilm. She felt sick and her lips were trembling. "What do you want? Do you usually break into women's bedrooms when they're out?"

Razin smiled apologetically. "Only when the women have been misbehaving."

Libby remembered the man with the lisp. I should have known, she thought. I should have gone back some other time. Instead I've been caught like some clumsy tourist trying to smuggle perfume through customs.

Razin sat on the edge of the bed, his big head bowed, his face taut with responsibility, a razor-nick on his dark chin. He lit an American cigarette. He said: "It was the girl from Intourist who told me."

"Told you?"

"That you had gone out by yourself," Razin answered impatiently.

Libby recovered quickly, relief like a drug. She wanted to laugh; instead she said, "Surely there's no harm in that. You've nothing to hide in Novosibirsk have you?"

Razin seemed to be apologizing for national incompetence. "I don't think so. But others. . . . You know how it is. People are too sensitive and they don't like photographs of our wooden houses, women in shabby clothes. That's why we try to keep tourists on one, well-trodden path."

"I think the wooden houses are beautiful," Libby said. She could feel the menace of the man beneath his manners.

Razin said, "It's a matter of taste. To these people"—gesturing to the peasants in the city outside—

"anything old-fashioned is a sign of failure. They haven't kept up with the Western world."

Libby wondered if he were laughing at her. She said, "You should see some parts of London. But why," she asked, "has a man of your importance come to warn a girl tourist who may have wandered by mistake into your wooden city?"

"A man of importance?"

"You're obviously not a traffic warden."

"Please?"

"You have presence, importance."

"You are a girl of perception," Razin said, not displeased. He drew on his cigarette. "It's like this. Through no fault of your own you have come on the Trans-Siberian with a very important passenger. I know you didn't intend to."

"How did you know that?"

"Because your booking was made before Comrade Yermakov decided to make the journey. We are very thorough, you see. We have checked everyone. And we have to check every little irregularity. Like a pretty English girl defying an Intourist request and wandering abroad by herself. That's why I came here. To *ask* you not to do it again." He smiled at her. "It would help me greatly. You see, my future depends on the outcome of this journey."

Libby smiled back because you couldn't help liking him.

"Tonight," Razin said, "I believe you're dining with Mr. Harry Bridges."

"Am I?" She was surprised. "I didn't know I was. He passed me on the stairs a little while back, as if he hardly noticed me."

"Did he?" Razin examined this as he examined everything that didn't fit. "I wonder why?" He paused and then went on, "Anyway he's taking you to dinner.

I have a record of the booking he made at a restaurant. Happily the restaurant is approved by Intourist."

Razin stood up to leave. He said, "Please stay with Intourist, Miss Chandler, at least until we get to Khabarovsk where we go our separate ways."

As he went out he fingered the pocket containing the microfilm. "A nice piece of cloth," he remarked. "I wish I could buy my wife a coat like that in Moscow."

He couldn't explain the apprehension; usually it came to him in the early hours of the morning to be quietened with sleeping pills. These days, since he set out across Siberia, it had been arriving earlier. It was something to do with this vast land; the frosty arrogance that had never been tamed. This isn't my Russia, he thought. They don't give a damn about the Kremlin here. In the cities, perhaps, but not on the steppes, in the taiga.

And Yermakov thought suddenly: This is a place to die.

He poured himself a shot of vodka, swallowed it neatly, and called to his secretary waiting in the office outside his suite in the mansion on the outskirts of Novosibirsk. "Get me Razin," he said, when the young man came in, mouth trembling.

"I'll try," the secretary said. "But I don't know where he is."

"Get him," Yermakov said.

He poured himself another vodka, took off his jacket and tie, and went to the bathroom to shave.

Outside in the grounds dogs prowled and sentries were posted round the walls. Not enough protection, he thought, skimming the cut-throat razor down his cheeks, staring at the pouchy face looking back at him.

A place to die—and thousands had as the victorious Red Army chased the Whites toward the Pacific. When the Reds crossed the Ob in mid-December 1919, they found 30,000 dead in Novonikolayevsk as it was then called. Four months later 60,000 had died from typhus.

The leader tried to find some glory in these victories which were his roots. Instead he saw women and children abandoned in the snow to die of cold, starvation, and disease.

He carefully shaved his neck where the tired skin bled easily. You are thinking like an old man tottering toward death, scared of what lies ahead, scared of the punishments for your crimes, he told himself; but the razor was still unsteady in his hand.

Think what you have achieved, he argued to himself; think of the power and prosperity; instead he thought of the Jew kicked in the groin on the platform at Moscow and of the years between 1936 and 38 when 1 million people had been imprisoned and executed in Siberia. I'm returning to the graveyard I helped to dig, he thought.

Razin knocked at the door and came in. They were alike, these two survivors, the price of survival showing on their faces.

Yermakov said, "Is everything all right, Comrade Razin?"

Razin looked surprised. "Everything's fine. The crowds are waiting for you in the square."

"I meant security. Have there been any incidents? With the Jews or anyone?"

"Not that I know of."

Yermakov turned round. "If there had been you would know, Comrade Razin?"

"Of course."

Yermakov said, "I want the guards doubled.

Have you checked every window and rooftop in the square?"

"You are quite safe," Razin answered, his voice losing a little of its respect.

"I'd better be, Comrade Razin," Yermakov said.

He dismissed Razin with a wave of his hand. The city's a graveyard, he murmured to himself. He shivered despite the central heating.

The speech was a success as usual, the crowds packed into the floodlit square cheering the predictable exhortations and promises. But, because it was a fine night deep with stars and the moon, a curved knife, hanging among them, the rally was endowed with a pagan majesty: Yermakov's voice echoing through loudspeakers planted throughout the city, marksmen with high velocity rifles on the rooftops, winged with snow, searching the floodlit faces.

Harry Bridges and Libby Chandler walked with the crowd after the speech, their shoes crunching on the slush that had frozen at dusk.

"I get the impression you expected me to ask you out," Bridges said, guiding her through a bunch of children celebrating the public holiday declared by Yermakov.

"I did."

"That was very presumptuous of you."

"A man called Razin said you were taking me out."

Bridges tightened his grip on her arm. "Razin? How did he come to say that?"

Libby told him about Razin's warning.

Bridges said, "They're very worried."

"With any reason?"

Bridges shrugged. "How should I know?"

"You're a journalist."

"I *was* a journalist."

Libby said, "Why did you pass me on the stairs like that?"

"I'm sorry," Bridges said.

They went into a restaurant, sporting a gold-braided doorman, where Bridges had booked a table. They sat near a small band playing Glen Miller.

Bridges ordered them 100 grams of vodka each —"You're not allowed any more," he explained— borscht, jelly-fish salad, and *pilmeni*.

She felt the vodka burn and smiled at him. Now that she had carried out her assignment she was more relaxed and she liked this tall American with the languid ways; there was a maturity about him and a suppressed quality which she couldn't analyze. He was wasting, she thought, and she didn't know why.

Bridges pointed at the band wearing punished tuxedos playing "Moonlight Serenade" and said, "We could be back in the forties. I guess a lot of Russia's like Europe was in the last war. The clothes, the queues." He stopped as if he were betraying something. "But in a hundred years time Russia, with the help of Siberia, will be the richest country in the world."

"Are you going to stay?" She poured some more vodka from her carafe.

"I don't know yet."

"You can't spend the rest of your life here."

"Why not?"

"Because it's not for us. We've grown up with freedom."

"You may have," Bridges said. He told her about his father, about John Ralston who had blown his brains out in Miami.

"You can't dismiss freedom because of personal experience," she said. "You're looking for an escape and cultivating two injustices as an excuse."

Bridges said, "I'm a journalist operating in one of the most exciting countries in the world. It's about time Western journalists gave Russia a break."

"And it's about time Russian journalists gave the West a break."

"Sure," Bridges said. "Both ways. And I can do it this end."

The waiter brought them *blini* pancakes covered with jam.

"Why can you do it better than anyone else?" Libby asked. "Do you have some sort of influence with the Kremlin?"

"I tell you what I'll do," Bridges told her. "I'll get you a job on my paper. You haven't stopped interviewing me since we sat down."

She put down her spoon as the band swung into "Tuxedo Junction." "Are you a Communist, Harry?"

"Goddam," he said.

"Are you?"

"No. At least, I don't think so."

They were silent for a few moments then Harry Bridges took over the questioning. "What's happened to you since we got here? On the train you were scared. You aren't any more."

The microfilm was in her room hidden inside a wooden Russian doll with fat red cheeks and yellow painted hair.

She looked at him candidly. "It was just the train, coming to Siberia. . . . Annette Meakin probably felt the same way."

"Annette Meakin?"

She told him about her pioneering counterpart. Bridges shook his head. "It was more than that. You're not the sort of girl who scares easily." He put his hand over hers. "Before the journey's over I'll find out. I used to be a good reporter."

Outside her hotel room she thought he might kiss

her. He hesitated, glanced along the corridor, saw the implacable watchdog staring grimly at them, squeezed her arm and went to his own room.

Next day the streets were running with water and the wooden city steamed in the sunshine.

The overnight passengers took cabs to the station to pick up the Trans-Siberian due at 10:31. The special coach was hitched on and at 10:46 the train moved out.

On the banks of the Ob the snow spewed out by the vacuum-cleaner was melting and the shape of a body in a sack was becoming discernible.

6.

From the locomotive Boris Demurin watched the taiga gently rotating past the windows under a lavender-blue sky. To most passengers the impression was one of emptiness; but not to Demurin making his last trip.

When he climbed from the footplate for the last time at Vladivostock—where, on May 31, 1891, His Imperial Highness Czarevich Nicholas dug the first shovelful of clay soil to inaugurate the railway—Demurin would start to write his history of the Great Siberian Railway.

The gleaming rails and the Siberian jungle on either side were peopled with its characters. This was the Mid-Siberian sector and it had been one of the toughest to build. Started in 1893 by a plump engineer with an arrogant little beard called Nicholas P. Mezheninov, it had been cut through jungle so thick that, in places, the sun never reached the ground. And nature had fought the metal road every inch of the way: the granite permafrost lingered till July, then thawed dramatically leaving the construction crews paddling in mud; the local timber was too feeble for sleepers and bridges; great conifers, weakened by excavations, crashed across the newly laid line; once an avalanche of sand buried the line; when a flintstone hill was found to be impassable an engineer called O.K. Sidorov diverted a river and laid the rails on its bed, his crews working in waist-high water and quicksand. But not one life was lost.

Along the track Boris Demurin saw the convicts shipped from Irkutsk felling trees and building bridges. Murderers, thugs and innocents, they slept in sod huts and worked in 32- below temperatures to get their sentences cut and earn 12 ½ cents a day to buy tobacco and illegal vodka.

The other enemies of the constructors were the crooked contractors who swindled the Government and the manufacturers who supplied shoddy goods. Demurin wasn't sure whether he would refer to them in his book: it was always difficult to assess what episodes of history were acceptable.

On August 18, 1898, two years ahead of schedule, Mezheninov completed the Mid-Siberian and the first engine steamed into Irkutsk.

Demurin's thoughts were interrupted by a loudspeaker announcement:

"The identity of our illustrious passenger is well known to all of us." The man's voice had a tremor in it because Yermakov would be listening. "What is not so well-known is the identity of the heroic driver. His name is Comrade Boris Demurin and he is making his last journey as leader of the crew of this train which he has served loyally for forty years."

"Forty-three," Demurin said.

"He was chosen specially for this auspicious occasion. We salute you, Comrade Demurin, loyal servant of the Soviet Union. May this train speed you to a long and happy retirement." There was a sharp click and the voice was replaced by martial music.

Tears misted Demurin's eyes. He smelled smoke and steam and heard the clank of hammers driving home bolts. He was Nicholas P. Mezheninov hacking his way through birch and pine and larch. He was a father of Siberia, The Sleeping Land which he had helped to awaken.

Viktor Pavlov was another who wasn't fooled by the emptiness. He was saddened by what lay beneath and beyond it: it was the storehouse of which his wife was queen and he was betraying her. He was returning to her throne, not because she had demanded his presence but because of a heritage: the Masada Complex.

The taiga twirled past, a spinning top returning the same bunches of trees, the same small stations, the same women drawing boiled water from taps, the same men parading the platform in striped pajamas or blue track suits, the same peasant women in faded blue standing beside the track waving on the train with gold batons. "The Siberians love their cold," he had read somewhere. And so did Anna. Her country—where the people watched each other's faces for frostbite, where they loved flowers so much that they would pay two roubles for a lily or a rose.

Often she had bored him with Siberia's awesome statistics. An oil field at Tyumen which, in two years, would produce 130 million tons; a gas field at Nadym containing three-quarters of all American reserves.

Pavlov tried not to think about Anna. He picked up a copy of the European *Herald Tribune* which a tourist had managed to get past customs on the Soviet border—more reassuring evidence of incompetence.

It contained an article referring to an Israeli commando raid in April into the center of Beirut to liquidate Palestinian leaders. That's the way we have to fight, he thought. Direct, cold-blooded, brilliantly executed. Caution, caution—to hell with caution.

Col. Yury Razin said, "I see you read the decadent imperialist press."

Startled, Pavlov put the paper on the restaurant car table. "It was lying there," he said, and was immediately angry with his defensive attitude.

"I've no doubt," Razin said. He leaned over the table and Pavlov noticed a slight tick in one eye. He looked exhausted. "There's a new passenger in your compartment now," he said.

Pavlov said, "I noticed. What happened to Gavralin?"

"I thought you might be able to tell me."

"I've no idea. I presume he left the train at Novosibirsk."

"Please." Razin touched the pouches of tender skin under his eyes. "Let's not pretend with each other. You know perfectly well he was one of my men making the whole journey. I want to know what happened to him."

A Yak 40 minijet overtook them in the pale sky. Pavlov wondered if the Prospector had reached Irkutsk.

"I'm afraid I can't help you," Pavlov said.

The same crew had been retained and the plump-breasted girl with the glossy hair hovered unhappily behind Razin.

Razin waved his hand to dismiss her. "It's very odd," he murmured, "that he should disappear from *your* compartment."

Pavlov shrugged. "It's not my fault if one of your men is missing."

Razin straightened up. "If you can think of anything that might help. . . ." He walked away without smiling: the benevolent exterior under strain. He paused for a moment to glance at the girl's backside. He shook his heavy head as though remembering his youth and walked slowly back toward the special coach.

Pavlov waited a few moments before returning to his compartment. The Tartar general was there lying on his bunk in his wool vest; he had been eating a raw onion and reading *Red Star,* the army newspaper which had once been so critical of the Arab League; but its contents had sent him to sleep and he was snoring contentedly, refighting old battles. Beneath him, his wife was starting her third orange of the morning, the peel scattered around her like fallen petals.

The new occupant was another man from the outdoors with a Red Indian face, deep brown eyes, and a lean body. When Pavlov opened the door his eyes opened and his hand slid to the hunting rifle lying beside him on the bunk. He apologized, smiling. "A natural reaction," he explained. "You've got to be awake when you're asleep when there are bears around."

He told Pavlov and the general's wife that his business was soft gold—furs; that he was a hunter and a trapper. Pavlov sat beside the window, half-listening. The trapper explained that it was a release to talk after months alone in the taiga.

Once, he said, he had shot tigers—the shaggy Siberian tigers that used to prowl the forests of the Far East killing Chinese coolies working on the Trans-Siberian for supper. These days he trapped them; but not very often because they were becoming scarce.

The general snarled in his sleep as his belea-guered infantry drove back the enemy. His wife peeled another orange.

"We still trap them the same way they did a hundred years ago," the hunter continued. "At dawn, with dogs, when the sun throws bars of light through the trees like the tiger's stripes." He became lyrical. "Sometimes in the autumn, before the snow, the ground is covered with blueberries. When the dogs pick up the tiger's trail we suddenly see the slats of light move because this time they're the stripes of old *felis tigris*. The dogs surround him and we lasso him. One man, usually me"—the trapper swung his legs off the bunk and sat on the edge, fists bunched—"gets him by the neck. I get a muz-zle round his jaws, then, when he's finally beaten, we rope his legs to a pole and carry him away up-side down. It's sad in a way," he said, "such a no-ble animal. But I'd rather trap a tiger than a bear. Funny animals, bears. Our national image. Very friendly when they're happy, bastards when they're mad. I've seen them dance to a mouth organ and I've seen them kill a tiger with one blow. Part of our heritage, bears," he said.

"Where are you heading for?" Pavlov asked.

"East," the trapper said. He picked up his rifle and stroked it with love. "They want me to go north-west of Baikal to help out with the barguzin—a pure black sable," he explained. "But it's going brown and they want me to help put it right. Catch the blackest I can find and mate them. I might smoke out some ermine while I'm at it. There's money in ermine but I don't like killing them. You just squeeze them till they die." He put down the rifle. "Then I'll go back east. That's my territory. Tigers, leopards, wolves, elk, sable, glutton, mink, squirrel. You name them," said the trapper, "and you can find them in the east. We clothe Hollywood."

The general went on snoring and his wife joined him in a duet. They had both turned on their sides, away from Pavlov and the trapper.

Pavlov nodded at the trapper. "Good hunting," he said. The trapper smiled because they both knew that this time the prey was a man and that in the hierarchy of the Zealots the trapper was known as the Poacher.

The Poacher patted his rifle. "No more use than a walking stick," he said. "They took all my ammunition off me when I got on the train."

In the next compartment the duel between Larissa from Intourist and Stanley Wagstaff continued. Stanley was writing in his notebook while the girl recited facts about the railway.

"Soon," she said, "the whole line will be electrified." She stared hard at the little bespectacled man who reminded Libby Chandler of a bird trapped in the compartment. "I believe," Larissa said distinctly, "that the last type of steam locomotive to be built in the Soviet Union was the E Class."

Without looking up from his notes Stanley Wagstaff said, "I'm afraid you're wrong there." He had a North Country accent with a rasp of coal dust in it. But he was kind. "It's a mistake anyone could make. The E Class was the most numerous in the world. The last steam passenger loco to be made over here was the P 36."

"No," the girl said, "the E Class."

"Sorry," Stanley said, closing his notebook and polishing his spectacles. "The P 36." He delved into his suitcase and brought out a book, thumbed through it and stabbed his finger at a photograph of an engine. "There. It says so."

The girl glanced at the book with disdain. "It's by an American," she said. "What would he know about our railways?"

Stanley heard a train coming from the opposite direction. He opened his notebook and peered out of the window. There were twenty-five cars on the train, each loaded with howitzers covered with olive tarpaulin. Stanley noted the number of the engine and closed his book again.

A girl arrived to vacuum the compartment—the second time that day. She was followed by the two KGB officers searching the train.

"Again?" Harry Bridges asked.

"Again, Comrade Bridges," the one with the Mongolian features said.

"What is it this time?"

"Just routine."

"Uh-huh," said Bridges guessing they were looking for a lead to the disappearance of Gavralin.

He glanced at Libby Chandler sitting on the edge of her bunk thumbing through a volume of *War and Peace* in Russian. He noticed that the fear had returned.

The KGB officer with the boyish face looked cursorily through Bridges's luggage. They knew all about him: he was tame.

They checked out Stanley Wagstaff and asked Libby Chandler to open her bags. Bridges watched fascinated at her reactions. It was as if she was going through customs with a bar of gold, the studied nonchalance that every customs officer looks for. Christ, he thought, I hope they don't find whatever she's hiding.

The "Mongolian" consulted a notebook. "Miss Chandler," he said, "I believe you went out in Novosibirsk alone."

"That's right," she said.

Larissa glared at her.

"Did you buy anything?"

"This," Libby said handing him *War and Peace*.

The officer ignored it. "Please," he said, "your cases."

She put her two cases on her bunk. One made of faded white leather with the stickers of famous old liners on it; the other a smart gray holdall by Favo of Paris. In the two cases Bridges, the professional, saw the life she had told him about: the colonial upbringing, the boredom, the escape. She bent over the cases, unlocking them. Bridges hoped she hadn't got anything—but he knew she had. He noticed her hands fumbling with the keys and prayed for her.

The cases opened exposing her belongings. It was humiliating and Harry Bridges knew he shouldn't be looking. Clothes, minute underwear, skirts and sweaters, books, toiletries, some pills.

The boyish officer rummaged through the contents. "That's fine," he said. "Sorry we had to trouble you."

Libby attempted a smile, but it was a failure. There was sweat above her lip.

The other officer stopped the descending lid of the white suitcase and took out a wooden doll with

136

rosy cheeks and painted hair. He shook it and it rattled. Bridges saw the color leave Libby Chandler's face, the sweat spreading to her forehead.

The officer said, "Pretty, eh? And inside are several other little wooden dolls?"

Libby nodded.

"Good. They will like those back in England. I have a set back home." He popped the doll back into the suitcase.

The two officers saluted and left the compartment.

Bridges thought: Before we get to Irkutsk I've got to find out what's inside that doll.

At 2:01 the train pulled into Taiga, where passengers for Tomsk changed to a branch line. According to legend, the Trans-Siberian should have passed through Tomsk which, in the 1890's, had many gold millionaires and forty distilleries. The railway surveyors demanded bribes to bring the track to Tomsk but the millionaires turned them down because they believed the railroad would have to come to such a prosperous metropolis as Tomsk. So the surveyors returned to Moscow and reported impenetrable terrain on the approaches to Tomsk—and the track by-passed the city fifty-four miles to the south.

There was a fourteen-minute stop here so Viktor Pavlov jumped onto the platform where he bought half a roasted hare and a bottle of beer. He was joined by Bridges.

One Zealot was due to board the train here, the Painter. Pavlov searched the queue of peasants and workers from Tomsk being frisked by the KGB. Halfway down the line he spotted the house-painter in blue, paint-flecked blouse and trousers and fur hat. He was the son of a mixed marriage and the word JEW was missing from his papers. But, with one Jewish parent, the Painter was a risk and they were relying on the lack of enthusiasm of the local KGB who resented orders from their masters at the Lubyanka in Moscow. Siberians were like that.

Bridges said, "They're pretty worried, aren't they."

"The KGB have a great responsibility."

"It would be a hell of a thing if something happened to Yermakov." Bridges tilted his brown bottle with a barley-sugar pattern on it and drank some beer.

Pavlov stared at him speculatively. Was it possible that Bridges knew something? Had he started to sniff round for a story? Pavlov drank his own beer from a paper cup. No, the man had abandoned all his principles; he was a pathetic puppet like all the dreary Western sympathizers in Moscow. Just the same, Pavlov thought, letting the beer fizz in his mouth, if he does start to interfere I shall have to kill him.

The Painter passed the checkpoint and boarded the train.

The engine gave a blast from its compressed air whistle warning passengers to get back. Pavlov and Bridges strolled back together, two tall, striking men, one distinguished by purposefulness, the other by thoughtfulness.

Razin watched them from the window. They made him uneasy. There was a threat there somewhere. He felt it most with Pavlov, to a lesser degree with Bridges. Seeing them together compounded his unease. He sawed at the cleft in his chin with his forefinger. The difficulty was that he wasn't sure these days when his suspicions were justified. He had lived his whole life with betrayal and deceit and he could no longer identify other qualities. Except in his own family—his wife and his two teen-age sons. It's for them that I live like this, he thought. It's for them that I survive.

Pavlov and Bridges boarded the train. Both men, Razin thought, could make trouble if he acted against them too hastily. He then made a decision, possibly born of fatigue: he decided to consult Vasily Yermakov about Pavlov.

Yermakov looked up and saw Razin standing beside him. He respected and distrusted Razin because he knew his mind intimately: it was the same as his. "Yes, Comrade colonel, what is it?"

"Could you spare a few moments?"

Yermakov dismissed his secretary who retired gratefully with a copy of the Irkutsk speech which they had been working on.

Razin sat down. They might have been twins, these two men, each hunched warily as if a stiletto had been poised behind their backs all their lives.

"Well?"

"I'm not happy about one of the passengers."

"Only one? That's quite a tribute to my popularity." The harsh voice was sardonic. "Which one, Comrade Razin?"

"The Jew," Razin said, hoping to shock.

He failed. "You mean Viktor Pavlov?"

Razin nodded.

"Hardly a Jew. Just a drop of blood, a splash of semen, a long time ago." His knowledge of Pavlov's antecedents disturbed Razin; it was as if he had police informants other than himself. Yermakov went on: "We can't indict every loyal Soviet citizen who has the misfortune to have a trace of ancient Jewish blood in him." He smiled—the airport smile which visiting heads of state knew so well. "If we did we'd lose half our brainpower." Yermakov paused. "What's worrying you, Comrade Razin? Is it the disappearance of one of your men in Novosibirsk?"

This jolted Razin but nothing showed on his face. He had made a point of keeping the disappearance from Yermakov: someone had made a point of telling him.

"He and Pavlov shared the same compartment," Razin said.

"He was watching Pavlov, I presume."

"He was," Razin said, "and now he's disappeared. It may be a coincidence."

"Is anyone with Pavlov now?"

Razin shook his heavy head. "I'm watching him and he's got a Tartar general and his wife in there. If he tried anything the wife would crush him to death."

"I see." Yermakov gazed out at the countryside dotted with small thick-set pines spinning past the window. "And what do you propose to do about Pavlov?"

Razin didn't make decisions in Yermakov's presence. He rolled the responsibility adroitly back across the table. "I just thought I would communicate my feelings about him."

Yermakov lit a cigarette. "That was very sensible of you, Comrade Razin." He appraised the KGB colonel. "But I don't think we need worry too much about Viktor Pavlov. The man is a genius and he has done superb work for the Soviet Union. He is also married to Anna Petrovna. He will be meeting her at Khabarovsk. They are a handsome and heroic couple and the three of us will look very well together on the platform."

Tentatively, Razin continued to play his defensive hand. "You know, of course, that there's been a quarrel. That they've been parted for several months."

The Leader smiled benevolently, enjoying a small triumph. "Oh yes, Comrade Razin, I know all about that. And I shall enjoy being the instrument of reconciliation."

Razin went back to his compartment in the special carriage looking meditatively at his two aides. One of them was feeding information to Yermakov. You're too young to be double-crossing Yury Razin, he thought.

He said to the boyish-faced assistant: "Do you have reports on everyone on this train?"

"Yes, Comrade Razin. Dossiers on the names with red crosses beside them. Page reports on all others."

Razin sat down. "Good, good," he said. "I want to see two reports."

"Which two?" the other assistant officer asked.

Razin raised his big head and stared at them. "On you two," he said.

He enjoyed their expressions before lighting one of his American cigarettes and relaxing a little, like a man with a liqueur after dinner, happy that Yermakov had accepted responsibility for keeping Pavlov on the train. The euphoria didn't last because, halfway through his cigarette he realized that, if anything went wrong, the responsibility would be denied.

For dinner that night, as the train ran smoothly between Chernorechenskaya and Krasnoyarsk, Harry

Bridges and Libby Chandler ate cabbage soup floating with meat and curdled with cream, saddle-hard steak and French fries, fruit salad, and drank half a liter each of strong, red Georgian wine.

Opposite them sat the Tartar general and his wife who didn't speak while they ate. Vodka from the general's own supplies, red wine, two plates each of cabbage soup, marrows stuffed with mincemeat, goat's cheese and black bread, Ghanain bananas, Georgian oranges, Armenian brandy and coffee. They ate for two hours, then synchronized their belches.

At last the general spoke. He said to Bridges, "Were you in the army?"

Bridges nodded. "I did my stint."

The general looked pleased. He said to his wife: "He was in the American army."

"I know," she said. "I speak English too."

Her face had turned mauve and her bosom rose and fell rapidly. The general looked at her fondly; perhaps, Bridges thought, the real warrior was the lady.

"Where did you fight?" the general demanded. His English was slow and heavily accented.

"I didn't."

"Not even Vietnam?"

Bridges shook his head: he was a big disappointment.

The general's wife was talking to Libby. "You don't eat enough," she said. "You would never exist in Russia. We eat to keep the cold out and the warm in."

Libby said, "I'm afraid I don't have much of an appetite."

"Russian men don't like thin girls," the general's wife announced, as if Libby was here to sample Soviet manhood. "They like everything big and strong. And we"—she stared hard at every Western weakling in the restaurant car—"we like strong men. Once my husband had his appendix out without an anesthetic. He had it removed at nine and by one o'clock he was eating a good lunch."

The general asked Bridges, "Which do you think is the best army in the world?"

"The Soviet?" Bridges speculated, grinning.

"Of course the Soviet. I mean after the Soviet."

"The French Foreign Legion?"

The general leaned across the table so that Bridges could smell the brandy on his breath. He spoke softly. "The Israelis. After the Red Star, they're the best fighting soldiers. I salute them. Everyone in Russia salutes them—except the Kremlin." He found some morsels of cheese on his plate and ate them. "Politicians? I shit on them."

"You could get into trouble saying things like that, I guess."

"Who from? The police?" The general picked up his fork and bent it in half. "That's what I would do to the police."

"Didn't Alexander III have a habit of doing that?" Bridges said, pointing at the fork.

"It was the same in Germany," the general went on, ignoring him. "If Hitler had listened to his generals he would have won the war. Instead he listened to the police—the Gestapo, the SS. Good soldiers," he added, "the Germans."

His wife said in Russian, "Be quiet. You've got a big mouth and you're drunk." She returned to Libby. "You should eat more bread and potatoes. Get some meat on you. Men don't like skin and bone." There were red blotches on her neck and the button at the foothills of her bosom had burst open.

Bridges excused himself for a moment and

walked down the corridor toward the bathroom. He closed the door of the restaurant car carefully behind him. Then he went into the compartment. Neither Stanley Wagstaff nor the Intourist girl was there.

He picked up Libby's holdall lying on her bunk and found the little keys. From under the bunks he took the white suitcase with the labels on it. He inserted one key; it opened with a genteel click. He rummaged through the clothes and took out the doll. He rattled it, then decapitated it by unscrewing the smiling, flaxen-haired head. He tilted the body so that the object inside fell into the palm of his hand. It was another smiling, flaxen-haired doll. He unscrewed that; then three more. Libby Chandler, he thought, you're cleverer than I thought. He searched the rest of the suitcase and the French holdall and found nothing. He replaced the keys and went back to the restaurant car.

They passed into the fifth day of their journey east of Krasnoyarsk. By the evening of that day they would be in Irkutsk, the Paris of Siberia. Outside the snow was falling as if it intended to stay. The engine gave a melancholy, melodious hoot, acknowledging the arrival of winter.

7.

The fifth imponderable in Viktor Pavlov's scheme of things occurred at 6:34 on the morning of the fifth day of the journey, about four miles east of Taishet.

Taishet lies north of the Mongolian border—and the Gobi Desert further south—and south of the Angara River which flows between the River Yenesei and Lake Baikal. It lies roughly on longitude 105°.

When the Great Siberian was first built Taishet merited little attention. A third-class station with a buffet, a feeding and medical station close by for pioneer colonists. The nearby village of Biruisa had 1,600 inhabitants, a wooden church of the Holy Trinity, and a school.

In the 1930's it achieved recognition of a kind

when the Russians decided to build a second railway in case the potential enemy—then the Japanese—decided to wreck the eastern sectors of the Trans-Siberian. The plan was to link Taishet to the east with 1,600 miles of track. Little is known of the project to Western observers except that, with slave labor, 434 miles of track was laid between Taishet to Bratsk, now the site of the world's largest hydroelectric power station, finishing at Ust-Kut, some 200 miles north of Lake Baikal. The little publicized railway, not marked on the latest Russian atlas, proved invaluable to Soviet geologists such as Anna Petrovna seeking diamonds in the Yakutsk Autonomous Republic.

As Train No. 2 began its descent in the direction of Nizneudinskaya, two hours and fifty minutes from Taishet, a faint seismic tremor shook the frozen tundra to the far north. It dislodged a few tribesmen's reindeer-skin huts, exposed a seam of gold soon covered by snow, and destroyed an old wooden church once erected in honor of the Archangel Michael and subsequently used as a storehouse for hides. It caused little consternation because such tremors are commonplace in Siberia and only occurrences such as the Tunguska Marvel which, on June 30, 1908, devastated 500 square miles causes alarm. (The marvel has been attributed to a meteor, nuclear energy, and the explosion of a spaceship from outer space.)

The tremor might have passed without comment, merely causing the granite, syenite, porphyry, diorite, and crystalline slate of the mountains to shiver a little. But, further south, one of the ripples found a weakness in an expanse of volcanic rock and split it open.

The chasm swallowed a couple of villages of gingerbread houses before fading, exhausted, just south of the Trans-Siberian Railway. But its force was sufficient to move the track a couple of feet, buckle a few rails, and rupture the bolts.

The Ukrainian saw the damage first. The brakes locked and the train skated to a halt just before it reached the damaged rail. The KGB fell from the carriages like insects knocked off by a gardener's spray. Suspecting an ambush, they drew their guns and scanned the bleak horizon. It was dawn—the time, like dusk, when even Siberia has a gentleness to it. The snow had stopped falling and the hills were soft and white, speared with pines; and, although the air was crisp, it had a milkiness to it as the sun rose.

Col. Razin strode up to the engine, long gray overcoat and sealskin boots over his pajamas. "What's happened?" he shouted.

Boris Demurin who wasn't sure what had happened pointed ahead. Six feet away the buckled track veered to the left.

"An earth tremor?"

Demurin nodded, scratching the gray fuzz of his hair.

Razin said, "You did well. I shall see that your action is relayed to the right quarters." He walked briskly away without speaking to the Ukrainian who shrugged philosophically. After all, it was the old man's last trip.

Razin hurried back to the special coach and knocked on the door of Yermakov's sleeper. The door opened. Yermakov was wearing a blue terry cloth dressing gown and he looked terrible, as if he'd been awake all night. His graying hair flopped over his forehead, the shadows under his eyes were mauve. "What's happened?" he asked.

Razin told him.

"What will happen now?" It wasn't often that he asked the questions.

"We'll send a man to Taishet to see if there's anyone capable of mending the track."

"Very well." Yermakov shut the door in Razin's face. He sat on the bedside chair trembling a little, thinking: It's an omen.

The sun rose, burnishing the snow-covered hills gold, finding jewels in the valleys. The tremor had caused a fire and, in the distance, the flames looked like red butterflies.

The passengers walked up and down beside the train.

Pavlov stood like a statue, hands thrust in the pockets of his overcoat, his hawkish face expressionless. He fed the incident into the computer of his brain and the answer came back with the first qualification: You must revise the timing. But how and for how long? The answer to the second depended on the length of the hold-up. To the first. . . . I'll have to get word to the Priest in Irkutsk. A phone or a telegraph office in Taishet? There was only one man who could go without raising suspicion—Semenov, the Policeman.

Pavlov went looking for the KGB officer with the white face and the scar beside his mouth. No time for elaborate caution: Semenov had to go now. He found him on the other side of the train, alone because the rest of the passengers had chosen the sunny side.

Semenov looked cautiously around before saying, "I thought you'd come round here. What the hell are we going to do?"

"You'll have to go to Taishet and get a message to the Priest. Tell him to find out how long we're delayed and then put back the plan the equivalent time."

Pavlov glanced up and down the length of the train but they were still alone.

Libby Chandler heard them talking through the half-open window of her sleeper. She, too, was alone, checking that the microfilm was safe behind the picture of Lenin on the wall. She knew enough Russian to understand what they were saying.

"You're sure we should still go through with it?" Semenov asked.

"We must. It's our only chance. Yermakov will never be as vulnerable again. We'll take him, just as planned, east of Chita."

Semenov fingered the scar at his mouth. "What reason can I give for going to Taishet?"

"Find one," Pavlov snapped. He thought about it. "They'll be sending a man there to get help. Tell them you know the town."

As Semenov walked away, feet crunching in the snow, Pavlov turned and stared up into the wondering face of Libby Chandler framed in the half-open window.

There was too much data in Pavlov's brain; it had become fallible like one of his electronic machines. She knows, he thought. She knows . . . knows.

But how much does she know? Pavlov didn't know how fluent she was in Russian. But I can't risk the possibility that she didn't understand. She would have to be eliminated. But if we kill her she'll be missed, there will be an outcry, Bridges will be onto it.

Pavlov paced up and down beside the train on the sunlit side. Occasionally he clapped his gloved hands together to indicate that he was taking exercise, getting warm.

The sun rose but the snow didn't melt, lying

softly and calmly waiting for the next fall. Pavlov looked into the blue sky and saw an eagle hovering, searching for prey.

He thought of the remorseless efficiency of the young Israeli insurgents in Beirut and wondered what they would do in this situation. This brought him no shame; they were in the fight together, the spirit of Masada; he was their representative in Russia, the second largest home of the Jews.

If she tells anyone, he thought, it will be Bridges. And Bridges will tell Razin to make sure that, for the rest of his life, he is a big fish in the small pond of Moscow's Western community.

Pavlov looked at the disembarked passengers. The children were playing in the snow; one family had lit a fire to roast a hare. The eagle hovered hungrily overhead.

Bridges was talking to the Tartar general and his wife and some other Russians. Libby Chandler was staring at the roasting hare; but she didn't look as if she was seeing anything.

If she *had* understood she was taking a long time passing on the information. There was one vague hope: she might sympathize with the cause: girls of that age like a cause. Pavlov shook his head; it was a risk he couldn't take. She would have to be silenced.

But don't let her talk now!

Pavlov was saved, although he didn't realize it, by Yermakov's decision to make an impromptu speech hastily prepared by his secretary who was violently anti-Semitic.

Yermakov looked totally ruthless and omnipotent standing there in the snow. The embodiment of the cult of personality which he swore to exorcize from the Kremlin. The tyranny of Stalin had been driven from the land but it had left its stigma on him; his presence chilled, particularly when he was at his most benevolent.

Razin beckoned and the passengers hurried forward, separated from Yermakov by a ring of uniformed militia and secret police.

Yermakov climbed on to the steps of his carriage, turned and faced the crowd. Once again he felt the power. Ghengis Khan, Kuchum, Marco Polo. Siberia, one tenth of the world's land masses, was his.

The sun was high and the air rang with the sound of the engineers' hammers against the warped track. In the distance tendrils of smoke rose from the fire which had spent itself in the snow.

They rigged up a microphone, and Yermakov spoke into it, holding the speech in one hand. It was a short heroic speech about Siberia and achievement. Halfway through it became more virulent, turning on the traitors who sought to undermine the achievement. Then on to the Zionists and Yermakov paused as if wondering about the wisdom of his text. His secretary had made it far too strong. He searched the crowd. There was only Bridges and half a dozen Soviet journalists present. Hesitating no longer, he launched into one of the strongest denunciations of Jewry heard in the Soviet Union since the era of his moustached mentor. He didn't agree with all of it but he was committed. He would attend to the secretary afterward.

Sickened with it, Libby Chandler set out for the green and white depths of the pinewood forest close by.

Bridges saw her go but couldn't follow because he was taking a note of the speech.

Pavlov saw her go and spoke urgently to the

Poacher. "Go and kill her," he said. "Make it look like an accident."

The Red Indian face of the Poacher registered pleasure. He preferred killing humans to animals, especially pretty girls with long blonde hair.

"If anyone asks," Pavlov said, "I'll tell them you've seen a wolf."

"A bitch," the Poacher said.

He caught up with her on the edge of the taiga. It was like entering a cathedral. The Poacher said in Russian: "You'll get lost in there by yourself." He pointed toward the train. "Mr. Bridges asked me to look after you."

"That's very kind of you," Libby said, glancing at the lean man with the big hands dressed in furs.

The Poacher pointed at some tracks. "Sable," he told Libby. And then at some others—"Mink."

"No bears?"

"Perhaps," the Poacher said. "Come, let's go a little further. We may see some wolves. But they won't attack us. They're cowards, wolves."

The silence was thick around them. There were no birds, no movement except for the occasional fall of snow from a branch. Sunlight and blue sky vanished beneath the ceiling, dark and woody beneath the branches.

The silence was so complete that Libby could hear the blood pulsing in her ears. "I think we should go back now," she said. She stopped beside a massive pine. Her face was aching with the cold.

"Just a little further." He took her arm and she noticed that he had taken his gloves off. The muscles on the balls of his thumbs were like small biceps. He noticed her gaze and said, "I have to kill ermine with these." He flexed his fingers. "I squeeze until they're dead. It's very sad."

"We must go back."

"No, we must stop here."

The snow and sunlight were a small glow of light in the distance. The cold entered her clothing and she knew that this man with the big hands was going to kill her.

"No!" She screamed but the scream lost itself in the silence. It was like crying out in deep green water. "No!" His grip tightened on her arm and one of the hands that squeezed ermine came up to her throat.

The harsh warning whistle of the engine, powered by air compression, tore through the forest.

His grip slackened. She tore herself free and ran, stumbling, slipping. He was behind her, but the mouth of light was growing larger.

Dimly, she could see the shape of the train. He was right behind her. Dear God, she prayed, Dear God. . . .

Behind her she heard a thump and a Russian oath. She turned her head as she ran. He was lying on the ground, struggling into a sitting position, a wire noose round his foot.

She stumbled on, laughing hysterically. The trapper trapped. She had reached the edge of the forest by the time he got free. She saw him loping behind as she burst from the trees into the arms of Harry Bridges.

If she's told Bridges, Pavlov thought, then it's all over. If she hasn't there's still a chance. They had lost eight hours and Semenov had phoned the Priest.

The fact that nothing had happened since the Poacher's attempt to kill Libby Chandler puzzled him. She would hardly conceal an attempted murder—unless, he mused, *she* had something to hide; unless getting to Nakhodka and Japan on schedule were more important than sentencing the Poacher to death.

They were approaching Zima, eight hours late. It was 9:30 P.M. Moscow time. Pavlov lay on his bunk, hands behind his head. The Poacher lay beneath him, brooding on his failure.

If the girl was so concerned about reaching Nakhodka on time, Pavlov thought, then it was just possible she wouldn't want her timing spoiled by communicating what she had overheard.

But why hadn't she told Bridges? If Bridges knew anything he would have told Razin. Bridges was that sort of man; he would never realize until it was too late that no one loves a traitor. Burgess, Philby, Maclean—they had all found out too late.

At this moment Libby Chandler was probably lying six inches away from him in the next compartment. With her blonde looks, her glacial beauty, she reminded Pavlov of Anna. But, unlike Anna, she was British and unpredictable and therefore he would have to kill her.

He waited until the train pulled out of Zima before going to the bathroom. It was dark outside, with black and white shapes flitting past the windows. Most of the passengers were in the restaurant car discussing the earth tremor, united by the experience.

He closed the door and removed some screws from the lock. He used the lavatory, washed his hands, combed his hair and returned to the compartment.

The Poacher said, "What have you been doing?"

"It doesn't matter," Pavlov said. The Poacher had his uses, but they were in his hands, not his brains.

He left the compartment door open and lay listening. The bathroom was one compartment away and he could hear people using it. Smoke from the samovar drifted along the corridor.

He heard three people use the lavatory. Beneath him the Poacher slept. Then he heard Libby Chandler and Bridges come into the compartment next door. He heard them talking, then the voices stopped for a while. Pavlov wondered if they were kissing or making hasty love before Wagstaff and the Intourist girl returned. The door of their compartment opened. Pavlov opened the door wider and saw Libby Chandler going to the bathroom.

He rolled off his bunk. The Poacher opened his eyes. Pavlov put his finger to his lips and went into the corridor. Then he slid the broken lock and let himself into the bathroom.

She was standing at the mirror brushing her hair. He clamped one hand round her mouth, twisting one arm behind her back. He glanced out of the window hoping the snow was deep so that the body would be buried.

She kicked back with her heel and bit his fingers. He released the pressure on her mouth just long enough for her to say, "I wondered when you were coming to see me."

He reapplied the gag and said, "If I take my hand away don't scream. If you do I'll kill you."

They looked at each other in the mirror; she nodded. He took his hand away.

"Now my arm," she said. "You're hurting me."

He let that go, too. He turned her round so

that they were facing each other. "Why did you think I would come to see you?"

"Because I heard what you were saying at Taishet."

"And?"

"If you think I'd tell anyone you're crazy."

He held her chin in one hand, staring into her eyes. "You wouldn't tell *anyone?*"

She shook her head.

"Not even Bridges?"

"Not even Bridges."

He took his hand away from her chin. "I must be crazy," he said. "I think I believe you." He touched the broken lock. "We can't talk here. Go back to your compartment and don't leave it until we reach Irkutsk. I can," he lied, "hear everything you say." He opened the door. "I'll see you in Irkutsk."

As he lay in his berth he wondered why he had believed Libby Chandler. Just before falling asleep he realized why: because he would have believed Anna.

8.

June 1973. The weather in Moscow was steamy with the temperature in the 80's. The vans selling *kvas* were out in the streets and ice cream was being sold by the ton. The men were in shirt-sleeves; the women wearing dresses with daisy and sunflower patterns made from a consignment that had just arrived in the capital; unlike the West, it was smart to wear the same material if it was new because it demonstrated your shopping and elbowing skill.

On this doomed Saturday, with the tender leaves on the birches wilting and the traffic streaming out to the forest, Viktor Pavlov and his wife decided to go to one of the river beaches.

They packed a hamper and Viktor drove the

black Volga out of the complex's parking lot, filled with Mercedes and Fords, and drove 30 miles to a bend of the Moscow River. Behind the sandy beach were pine and birch glades where families camped in orange tents. The big white river steamers glided past; the sun beat down on acres of tanning bodies. The summer was short, the winter long, and this tan would have to last; so they fried every bit of flesh, lying, sitting, standing against trees with their hands behind their necks wearing nose-shields made from *Pravda*.

Now was the time for Viktor and Anna to recapture their love—with the smell of pine, the sleepy water, the heat.

They stuck bottles of beer in the shallows, swam, and then lay in the sun listening to the rhythmic sound of table tennis balls, the strumming of a guitarist under the pines.

The sun had already brought a faint tan to Anna's alabaster body. Viktor, swarthy and matted, felt her warmth and moved closer to her. They held hands, lying on their backs, staring into the sky.

After a while she said, "It's good again, isn't it, Viktor?"

He said it was.

"Perhaps I should concentrate less on my work." She sat up, looking down into his face, pale hair falling over her eyes. "Perhaps you should too."

He spoke lazily, stroking her back. "Perhaps." He didn't commit himself because there was a lot to be done that had nothing to do with his work. "Our trouble," he said, "is that we've got too many brains between us."

She bent and kissed him. When she straightened up her expression was gentle. "What we should do," she said, "is have a third brain."

Viktor answered cautiously because he didn't want an argument this cloying, indolent day. When they got married they had agreed to have a child in five years time. "The child will be an infant prodigy," he replied. "A walking brain."

"When?" She stroked his chest and he felt his desire swell. "When, Viktor?"

"We agreed on five years."

"That was when we married."

"It isn't five years yet."

"We've both done well. We've got a beautiful apartment, a car. Why do we have to wait?"

He kissed her, not replying. Throughout his life Viktor Pavlov had put the cause first. If he ever came close to weakening—and he never acknowledged that he did—then it was now. Suddenly he understood the extent of his sacrifice.

He said, "I love you." His love was the most any man can hope for and yet he was going to discard it, a cold-blooded killing.

"You haven't answered my question," she said.

What wife really knows her husband? The adulterer, the pervert, the thief returning to her warm bed to bury his guilt between her breasts.

My child, he thought, would have Jewish blood. The progeny of a Jew and a Siberian princess producing a strain superior to any of Hitler's crazed Aryan dreams. Would the child be dark or fair? A dark girl, he reasoned, with lustrous black hair, or a boy with arctic eyes and blond hair.

"What are you thinking about?" She was still gazing down at him.

I'm going to betray you, he thought, staring into her blue eyes in which he could see flecks of sunlight. And my child: it would grow up with a stigma worse than any Jew, or mongrel-Jew, has ever known. He heard the children in the playground. "Did you know her father was Viktor Pavlov, the man who kidnapped Yermakov?"

He pulled Anna down to him, kissing her hard. Then he ran down to the river, past women sunbathing in brassieres, past a family secure and united, over a sandcastle, into the water, wading out with foam surging around his thighs, diving into the brown depths and swimming until his lungs ached. When he surfaced the beach lay behind him unchanged, children's voices reaching him across the water: a scene in which he had no part.

He swam slowly back, pulled the beer bottles from the shallows and returned to Anna. She laid their lunch on a tablecloth spread on the sand. Smoked sturgeon, green salad, new potatoes sprigged with parsley, black bread, a smoky cheese, Crimean champagne, and coffee.

She smiled at him as though, tacitly, they had reached a decision. Let us have this one day, he thought.

As he drank his beer Pavlov looked at his wife, seeing her oil-sleek limbs, her flat belly and full breasts in the black one-piece bathing costume with the fish-net at the waist. One day she would belong to another man; he pushed his plate away and uncorked the champagne.

In bed that night the sun and the beach were still with them. Grains of sand in the sheets and their bodies glowing. The window was open and the curtains moved in the gentle breeze.

She undressed in front of him as he lay beneath the sheet and he smiled as he saw the white shadows where her costume had been. It made a woman more defenseless, a lover not a sexual combatant. She was naked now, standing beside the bed, the patch of blonde hair near his face. He could smell her, taste her. My wife. Lover.

She slipped back the sheet and gazed at him erect. This was love and lust, he thought. The amalgam. Perfection. Wife and mistress. With a wife like this you never needed a whore. Other men thought: With a whore like this why have a wife?

And so much more. The sharing—sunsets, meals, movies, laughter. There was only ever one and it was a miracle if you found each other. No shame, no triumph in his hardness; no triumph, no supplication in her wetness.

She stooped and kissed his hardness. She went on kissing him, turning so that he could kiss her. Then again she turned, pausing above him, then sinking down so that he was deep inside her.

Now they reached a shuddering climax together, looking into each other's eyes, seeing the sex in each other's faces.

And it was only much later, when they lay in each other's arms, that they arrived at the preordained climax of this sensual day. The thunderstorm terminating the heat.

Her body was against his, her breath on his cheek when she said softly, "I know, Viktor."

"Know what?" The stars had assembled in the sky and, from a diplomat's apartment, they could hear tinny music crossing the space between the blocks.

"That you have Jewish blood," she said.

He was quiet for a few moments. He wasn't sure if he was shocked: it had always been a possibility. "So you found out," he said after a while. He reached for a cigarette and lit it. He lay still again, blowing the smoke at the ceiling. "How long have you known?" he asked.

"Only since yesterday."

"I see. Where does that leave us?"

She kissed him with a touch of desperation.

"What did you do?" he asked. "Trace my ancestry? Find my ritual murder kit in the bathroom?"

Even then everything might have been all right if she hadn't said, "I want you to know that it makes no difference."

He moved away from her, wishing he were dressed. "I'm glad," he said. He wanted to turn on her, grab her by the throat and shout, "Why the hell should it make any difference?" *It makes no difference. . . .* God! As if I were a rapist, a leper; the sort of remark a noble girl makes to an impotent lover.

She was scared now. Desperately seeking the right words. "I've got nothing against the Jews. . . ."

"That's very understanding of you." He swung himself out of the bed and pulled on his underclothes.

"Where are you going?"

"To wash," he said. "I think I should have a wash." He glanced at her scared, pale face. A part of him knew that she was sincere; that her words derived from the teachings of hatred from the first day she attended school. "Perhaps you should have a wash, too," he said, "having just made love to me."

She was starting to cry as he went into the bathroom. He took off his underclothes and had a shower, feeling the water like ice on his body. He could hear the music from the diplomat's party. American, British, French, German; getting drunk on tax-free liquor; trying to isolate the available secretaries and nannies as soon as possible because there was a shortage of girls, their small-talk strangled by the stilted language.

At this moment Pavlov wanted to be with Israelis. Walking down Dizengoff in Tel Aviv; he had read about this street, Israel's Piccadilly or Champs Elysées, and he wanted to mingle with the soldiers, the proud girls, the Jews who had returned home from the diaspora. To walk through the twisted streets of Jerusalem to the Eastern Wall. To drive across the desert. He saw himself in combat uniform, an Uzi submachine in his hands, racing up the stairs of an apartment block in Beirut; he saw the shock on the Palestinian's face as the bullets pumped into him.

He turned off the shower, knowing that he would never see any of these things.

He wrapped himself in a bath towel and went back into the bedroom. She had stopped crying and was sitting up in bed with the sheet pulled around her. "Viktor," she pleaded, "I want to explain."

"Explain then," he said, sitting on a chair.

"I know everything I say sounds wrong. But there's no other way to say it. You've got to understand that a lot of it sounds wrong because of what's inside you." She paused, searching for words. "Your Jewishness doesn't matter to me. Why should it? The Jews are as much a part of the Soviet Union as the Georgians, the Kazakhs, the Ukrainians, the Uzbeks. . . ."

"Except," Pavlov interrupted, "that a Georgian or a Kazakh has a somewhat better chance of getting a place at university than a Jew. Except that he doesn't get beaten up because he's a Ukrainian or an Uzbek."

She faltered, then strode on. "What I am trying to say is that we're all the same people. I'm a Siberian, you're a Jew. It doesn't matter, Viktor, it doesn't matter. All the hate is in the past. You should have told me when we met. It would. . . ."

". . . have made no difference."

"That's right," she said. "No difference. There's nothing wrong in that. It's what's inside you that makes it sound bad. It's as if you want to hold on to this hatred. To cultivate it."

"Look," Pavlov said, "I'm only ashamed of one thing. Do you know what that is?" She shook her head, staring at him. "That I'm not totally Jewish."

"Aren't you proud to be Russian?"

"Why should I be? What have the Russians ever done for the Jews except massacre them? Or send them to Siberia."

"I'm sorry," she said, "about you not being proud of being Russian. Not necessarily a Communist. Just a Russian."

My country, he wanted to say, is a long way from here on the shores of the Mediterranean. But I mustn't give too much away.

In the other block the party was livening up. Girls laughing, glass breaking. The younger guests would be getting bold and indiscreet now—to hell with the hidden microphones. Tomorrow their hangovers would be complicated by fear and worry.

He got his dressing gown from the wardrobe and slipped it on. "How did you find out?" he asked.

She said: "Gopnik—the Jewish professor you were talking to at the party that night."

"Ah." He sighed. "Professor David Gopnik." He tightened the belt of his dressing gown. "Caution, caution," he murmured. "How did you come to meet the professor? Or did he come to see you?"

"No," she told him. "I met him in a café near the Tretyakov Gallery." She hesitated. "I think he followed me there."

"Just to tell you that your husband was a Jew? Like some men tell a wife that their husband has got a mistress."

She reached for her cigarettes. She said, "No, it wasn't like that at all."

"What was it like then?"

"He's a very worried man. He wants to go to Israel and they won't let him."

"And you feel sorry for him?" Pavlov was astonished.

"I feel sorry for him because he wants to go. He doesn't understand. His mind is all figures and symbols. He can't see the truth."

"What did he want?" Pavlov asked harshly. "Apart from revealing my ancestry."

"He said you were involved with some sort of organization. He said you would ruin everything. He pleaded with me to ask you to abandon whatever you're doing." She got out of the bed and crossed the room, clutching the sheet to her breasts. She stood in front of him, looking down at him. "It's not true, is it, Viktor? Gopnik—he's crazy, isn't he?"

Pavlov stood up and paced the room. After a while he said, "It's true that I think the Jews should be allowed to return to their own country. The Universal Declaration of Human Rights. It's all there."

"But this is their country."

"A lot of them don't think so."

"Most of them do."

"Sixty percent of all immigrants to Israel are Russian. We helped to found Israel, now we are filling it."

"A Russian Jew."

"*We.*" The sheet fell away exposing her breasts; she pulled it up again. "We, Viktor. But you're Russian," she beseeched him.

165

"And a Zionist?"

Pavlov moved to the window, staring down at the foreign cars, the floodlit playground. The nights were short these brief summer months and already there was a rim of green on the horizon, dawn and sunset chasing each other. At the exit into Kutuzovsky he saw the sentry, and suddenly he thought: Perhaps I was allocated this apartment for a reason. Perhaps they wanted to keep me under surveillance like the Western diplomats and journalists.

"Zionism is treachery," Anna said. "They have been born, nurtured, educated here. Why should we let them leave?" She spoke eagerly. "You should come to Siberia with me, Viktor. Then you would see the spirit of Russia. We, too, make the desert bloom. Then you'd see it my way. Young people building cities in the ice. Earning good money—twice, three times, what they get in Moscow. The battle between man and nature—that's what they love. Such a great feeling working together, dancing, singing. The blue skies, the snow. . . ."

Pavlov turned from the window. "Are you sure you aren't more of a Siberian than a Soviet citizen? Aren't you finding your Israel to the east?"

She shook her head. "Moscow is my capital," she said with finality.

He could have argued with her. Siberians were famous for their independence. But it didn't matter.

"Will you come with me?" she asked. "I have to make a trip next week. We could stop at Lake Baikal. . . ."

He spoke slowly and brutally. "My promised land," he said, "is Israel. If Zionism is treachery then I am a traitor."

She shrank from him, moaned softly, and ran to

166

the lounge trailing the sheet behind her. He heard her lock the door.

It's over, he thought. I have committed my first murder.

Across the courtyard someone threw a plate out of the apartment where the party was being held; it smashed the headlamp of a new Mercedes owned by a German first secretary.

It wasn't difficult to find Gopnik. If he was in Moscow then he was attending the scientific conference at the Palace of Congress inside the Kremlin.

He found him during the morning recess in the coffee bar of the vast, glacial hall. He slid into a chair beside him and said, "Good morning, Professor."

Gopnik swung around, spilling some coffee. "Hello Viktor," he said, glancing uneasily around him. He seemed to have shrunk, looking more like a tortoise than before.

"How's the campaign going?" Pavlov asked. He ordered coffee. They were surrounded by scientists; pale faces, a preponderance of spectacles, shabby clothes, the brains of Soviet scientific progress.

"What campaign?" Gopnik peered at him anxiously.

"*The* campaign. The cause. The great escape."

"Please," Gopnik pleaded. "Not here. You never know." He acted like a fugitive. "I must see you, Viktor," he said.

"Must?"

"It's very important."

"So important that you've been in town five days and haven't bothered to look me up."

"I. . . ."

"Except, of course, that you've seen my wife."

"She told you, then."

"Yes," Pavlov said. "She told me."

"Tomorrow," Gopnik said. "By the space obelisk. Eleven o'clock." He swallowed his coffee and scuttled away from invisible pursuers.

The obelisk was a high, shining edifice with a space rocket perched on top probing the clouds, the whole structure sweeping upward like the prow of a ship. It was at the exhibition grounds where they had first talked, near the Ostankino TV tower.

Gopnik was waiting for him, his lightweight suit crumpled, sweat on his deceptively low forehead. They walked beside green banks cushioning the base of the obelisk.

Pavlov pointed at it. "Did Anna choose this spot —to remind me of heroic Soviet achievement?"

"No, it was my idea. I've never denied the Russians' achievements," he said anxiously.

"Neither have I." Pavlov quickened his pace. "Now tell me how the campaign's going."

"That's what I wanted to talk to you about," Gopnik said, puffing along beside him. "I've made five more applications since I saw you. Now, at last, there's hope."

"So," Pavlov remarked, "you've groveled five more times.

"The last time was at Lubyanka. With two members of the KGB. They interrogated me for six hours. Why had I indulged in anti-Soviet activities? Why didn't I like this country? Did I think everything was so much better in Israel? Did I know that under Article 7 of the RSFSR Criminal Code I was liable to punishment ranging from two years exile to seven years imprisonment plus five years exile? 'What for?' I asked. 'For anti-Soviet agitation and propaganda,' they replied." Gopnik staggered slightly and sat on a bench. "On and on it went without food or drink. I thought I was going to faint and had to stick my head between my knees. Then suddenly it was all over. They asked me—actually asked me—to tell my friends that there was nothing of an anti-Semitic character about the interrogation."

"And was there?" Pavlov wasn't sure what he felt for the man beside him. Pity, contempt—both.

"Nothing anti-Semitic," Gopnik said eagerly.

Above them, a TU 104 was beginning its descent into Sheremetyevo.

"They were pro-Jewish, were they?"

"Anti-Zionist," Gopnik mumbled. "Not anti-Jewish." He gazed up at the jet catching the sunlight on its fusilage. It became a symbol for him. "But at last there's a chance. I've got to see Madame Akulova at OVIR. So you see," he said, tugging at Pavlov's arm, "that's why I wanted to see you. If anything happens—you know, if there's any trouble—then they'll stop my visa. But I'm not just speaking on my own behalf. I know I'm a little pathetic. It's been so long. So many applications, so many interviews. I'm asking you for the sake of all the good, strong Jews who want to go back to their country. The ones who've kept on trying and kept their dignity, their pride. On their behalf I beseech you not to do anything that will wreck their dreams. They're doing it the only possible way." Gopnik wiped sweat from his forehead. "And we—they—are winning. Now they've dropped the education tax. . . ."

"Of course they have," Pavlov said. "Because the Americans threatened to cancel their new trade agreements if they didn't."

"Maybe that's true," Gopnik said. "What you forget is that America is only aware of our plight because of our campaigns. The whole world is only aware of it because of us."

"Caution, caution," Pavlov said. Had the Israelis who had stormed Beirut sought caution?

"So I beg you not to do anything that will wreck the dreams of 3 million Jews—certainly many, many thousands of them."

Pavlov took Gopnik's arm, feeling the damp material, the thin bone beneath the stringy bicep. "You told my wife I was Jewish. Why?"

Gopnik found a little of his old courage. "Does it matter? You're not ashamed, are you?"

Pavlov increased the pressure, feeling his thumb rotating on the bone. "No, Professor I'm not ashamed. But you should be." He released Gopnik's arm. "You also mentioned that I was a member of a secret organization. That I was plotting something. How did you know that, professor?"

Gopnik was flustered, his lower lip trembled. He swabbed his forehead again. "Didn't you mention something about it?"

The TU 104 was much lower—Gopnik stared at it hypnotized. He had presumed it was taking off; instead it was preparing to land on Russian soil.

Pavlov said quietly, "Your memory is at fault, professor. I merely said we must show the world that we have balls." He took hold of Gopnik's arm again. "Who told you, professor? Who said anything about a secret organization?"

"I can't remember," Gopnik said. "I only heard vaguely. Someone in the ordinary Jewish underground."

"Did they tell you what I was supposed to be plotting?"

Gopnik shook his head, spraying drops of sweat. Then he slumped forward, face ashen.

Pavlov pushed his head between his knees. In a more kindly voice he said, "Wait here. I'll get you a drink of water." He found a cardboard cup on the grass and filled it from a drinking fountain. Gopnik drank thirstily.

Pavlov said, "I'm sorry. I know what you've been through. God willing, you'll get to Israel."

He helped the prematurely old man back to his black Volga.

He thought: Don't worry—I'll avenge you.

That night Viktor Pavlov consulted the Penman about the leak. By a process of elimination they arrived at the only possible solution. Next day Alexei Mitin, known to the Zealots as the Poet, was knocked down by a car while walking along the Sadovaya Samotetchnaya and killed instantly.

9.

Viktor Pavlov's ration of imponderables ran out at 3:00 A.M. on the sixth day of his journey across Siberia. The train ran into Irkutsk exactly eight hours late at 2:42. With delays at the station and the shortage of cabs, it took him just under twenty minutes to reach the steel and concrete Central Hotel. He checked in and took his baggage to Room 250. He had understood that Anna would be waiting for him at Khabarovsk, 3,347 kilometres away. Instead she was waiting for him in Room 250. And, before either of them had spoken, he could see that she was pregnant.

10.

Irkutsk is the history, the soul and the spirit of Siberia. Larissa Prestina from Intourist, escorting her party round the city in a minibus, missed most of it.

Once Irkutsk was the mecca of the gold and tea barons. A wild city where Chinamen smuggled gold dust in corpses; where convicts, prostitutes and highwaymen prowled the wooden sidewalks. Before 1879 it was a maze of wooden huts; in July of that year fire broke out and, because most of the firemen were drunk and the hoses were rotten, three-quarters of the city was razed leaving 20,000 homeless. Wooden buildings were forbidden in the center of the city and a red fire engine was imported from England.

Larissa Prestina told her group that Irkutsk was

situated on 52° 17′ north latitude and 103° 16′ east longitude at a height of 1,455 feet on the right bank of the Angara. Stanley Wagstaff corrected the longitude—it was, he said, 104° 16′.

At night, on the streets where, in summer, dust lay inches thick, the highwaymen garroted their victims. By day they lassoed them from fast-moving sleighs. There was a murder a day and the police had to be bribed before attempting to catch the killers. When the gold-miners came into town they gave their fat bankrolls to whores, confidence tricksters, barmen, and cardsharps before returning to the mines.

An American in the Intourist party observed that there was a comparison with present-day New York. Larissa Prestina ignored him, pointing out the House of Soviets in the central square, with passing references to the three adjoining churches which were now a museum, a film studio, and a bakery.

The taverns were packed with gamblers playing vint and losing fortunes, high-kicking dancers, soldiers from the 3rd Siberian Army Corps, visiting gunmen, and drunks. To the cracked notes of honky-tonk pianos, worn-out burlesque acts from the Bowery, London, Paris, and Berlin performed their ravaged acts—baritones, fishing desperately for submerged notes, knife-throwers spearing their assistants, conjurors deceiving themselves, performing bears, dogs, and cats. In the gold barons' palaces, guarded by wolves, the nouveau riche threw parties in marbled halls hung with Gobelin tapestry; furnished with sandalwood and cedarwood and scattered with ashtrays made from gold nuggets. The parties went on for days with river excursions or sleigh races in the afternoon, boozing, eating, drinking, and fornicating at night until the hosts, fully clothed, went to sleep

*beneath their gold beds. Many of the hosts were
ex-convicts and some of their wives in their Parisian
gowns were murderesses.*

Larissa Prestina suggested a visit to the Irkutsk
Hydropower station on the Angara River.

*Lenin, Stalin, and Trotsky were exiled to this
area and in the city the White Russian leader Admiral
Kolchak was executed and his body shoved under
the ice on the river. Exhibits in an Irkutsk museum
include a sledge hammer with which the White Russians killed 31 Red hostages. Irkutsk was also the
home of Chekhov who praised the music, the gardens,
the museums, and even the hotels.*

Today the city is a storehouse of electricity, machinery, furs, timber, and minerals. And on the Intourist program for the evening was a visit to a musical comedy about the building of a power station.

Libby Chandler sat in the back of the mini-bus
beside Harry Bridges trying to persuade herself that
she wasn't double-crossing him. But what would he
do with the information? Make a story out of it for
his paper or betray Pavlov to the Russians? She still
wasn't sure about Bridges. They held hands in the
back of the small coach while Larissa Prestina talked
monotonously over her shoulder.

Libby had started the journey with one secret.
Now she had two. Like many criminals, she had a
compulsive desire to share her knowledge, to boast
about it. But she kept her secrets, wondering when
Pavlov was going to meet her. He's got to tell me
everything, she thought; I dictate the terms. Annette Meakin.

The microfilm was back inside the wooden doll.
A Nobel Peace prize, maybe. Then she thought:
What happens if the Pavlov Plan wrecks the Chandler

Plan? If they were stranded in Siberia, searched, body-checked. . . . Perhaps, she thought, I should tell Harry about the microfilm. She glanced at his lean, clever face beneath his fur hat. He would know what to do; if she told him this secret then, she reasoned, the other would be more intact. She squeezed his hand and he squeezed back. She would have to think about it. Maybe tonight. Because tonight she knew that they would make love and to hell with the crone on the landing outside.

Larissa Prestina was pointing out the scientific library of the university, a superb Corinthian-colonnaded mansion once the home of the governor-general. Larissa Prestina turned round and smiled. Actually smiled! "We call it the White House," she told them.

Stanley Wagstaff said, "There seems to be a lot of American influence round here."

The smile lingered. "Perhaps," she said, "the Americans took the name from Russia. Perhaps," she went on, addressing the American, a Harvard graduate traveling round the world before settling in real estate in Los Angeles, "you haven't heard the theory that America was discovered by the Siberians?"

The young American said he hadn't. Hadn't Columbus something to do with it? he asked.

"There is this theory," she continued, "that the United States of America was discovered by Siberians crossing the Bering Sea to Alaska and moving south. A lot of your Indian tribes bear a great resemblance to Siberian tribes."

The Harvard man said, "So you founded the United States *and* Israel."

"That's right," Larissa Prestina said, "both Moshe Dyan and Golda Meir are of Russian extraction."

176

The speech was to be made in a hall and relayed through loudspeakers to the crowds waiting outside in the crisp sunshine. Kirov Square had been cleaned of snow by the babushkas and only the rooftops, grass, and trees were still sugared white.

Pavlov joined the crowds around the fountain because they made it easy for him to shake off a shadow. Razin was suspicious and Razin would have him followed. Anna's presence wasn't generally known and she was resting in Room 250, four months pregnant.

The harsh voice boomed through the speakers. Achievement, heroism, the bumper wheat crop. The audience clapped and stamped. They mean it, Pavlov thought, they really mean it. Just as any electorate believes vote-catching promises because that's what they want to believe.

He edged toward the center of the crowd looking behind him for any movement. He couldn't see anything; but, if Razin was using one of his best men, he wouldn't. The crowd was thick, and Pavlov ducked suddenly, moving quickly at a crouch.

He surfaced a hundred yards away. If there was a shadow then he would report to Razin that Pavlov had taken evasive action. Why would an innocent man do that? If Pavlov was lucky he could get his business done quickly and let the shadow pick him up again near the Grand Hotel, sparing him the unpleasant task of reporting failure to Yury Razin.

One more dive, then he was away. He went down Karl Marx Street before heading, as before, for the wooden city. He skirted the blue, wooden synagogue which he had visited once in his student days. Irkutsk had the sixth largest Jewish community in the Soviet Union, and when he went to the synagogue there had been a group of black-shawled women in an anteroom mixing flour for the Passover matzos. The women weighed five kilos of flour, mixed it into a dough, and gave it to a man who flattened it. Pavlov had watched, fascinated, as the flattened dough was taken to another room and repeatedly put through rollers until it emerged tissue-thin. The tissue was cut into squares and thrust into a red-hot brick oven; after a few seconds it was pulled out, crisply baked. Pavlov had tasted some, still warm, and now he tasted it again as he strode past, keeping his distance.

He went straight to the wooden cottage where friends of the Priest lived. The Priest had been a member of the Russian Orthodox clergy; but he had rebelled; not so much against persecution, more against his own elders who crawled to the persecutors. They claimed it was the only way to keep some of their churches open: he saw religion in Russia as a crusade. Despite their different causes he and Viktor Pavolv were much the same sort of men. He wasn't fighting for the Jews: he was fighting for the right of man to worship whatever god he chooses.

He was getting old, with a gray-flecked, patriarchal beard, and in the process of his crusade, he had, like many church dignitaries before him, become a fanatic. But in a land where the young are brought up as atheists he found little support; so he searched and found Viktor Pavlov and Zionism. He was, he said, working for God, not the Jews.

The Priest was alone in the house.

Pavlov sat opposite him across a scrubbed, pinewood table.

"Has this house been watched?" Pavlov asked.

"No, my son." His eyes were deep-set, a little mad.

"Are you sure?"

"I wouldn't bring you here if I wasn't."

"Did the Prospector reach you?"

"He did." The Priest smiled beautifully. "Everything is going well. I told him where the guns were" —as if he were discussing altar candles.

"Did he have any trouble?"

"None." God was on their side—how could there be any trouble? "He told me there were KGB agents keeping watch on the helicopter. So he took a scheduled flight to Ulan-Ude. He will make the rest of the journey by road."

"And the men"—Pavlov leaned across the table —"are they assembling?"

"They are, my son. Nothing has been forgotten."

Pavlov was sweating; this holy calm was unnatural. "What about the timing? I gather the Policemen got through to you from Taishet about the hold-up."

"He did. But it doesn't matter. Your stay in Irkutsk will be a little shorter. You leave tomorrow morning at two minutes past nine in the morning as planned."

Pavlov leaned back in his chair. "I needn't have bothered to come round," he said, adding hastily, "You've performed miracles."

The Priest laughed. "I think you overestimate my spiritual powers."

Pavlov said: "You're sure everything is all right?"

"Quite sure, my son."

"Then I'd better be going." Pavlov stood up, then asked curiously, "Do you mind me asking one impertinent question?"

"I have no fear of any questions."

Pavlov said, "There's bound to be killing. What do you think about killing?"

The Priest stood up. The crusader with a flaming red cross on his breast. "Read your history books, my son," he said.

Pavlov let himself out the back way and headed toward the center of the city. With luck Yermakov would still be speaking. He was—threats to the Chinese paper-tigers across the border.

Pavlov crossed in front of the hall, letting himself be seen, then made for the Central Hotel. In the crowd he saw a man in a black coat eagerly pushing his way out. Pavlov lingered, giving him time to catch up.

Now, Harry Bridges thought ruefully, I have two stories. *English girl smuggles "another Pasternak" out of Russia,* and *Our own correspondent unmasks plot to assassinate Kremlin leader.*

The first story was all wrapped up in bed beside him. The second needed a lot of work, a lot of ferreting. And the only way to file it would be to get out of the country. And never to return. To hell with that, he thought.

He raised himself on one arm and smiled at the English girl lying naked beside him. "Strangers on a train," he remarked. "Wasn't there a movie called that?" He poured himself a measure of Scotch from the bottle beside the bed. "And where's the microfilm now?" There was no reason to bug an English girl tourist's room, but he had searched it anyway and it was clean.

"In the wooden doll."

"You should be in the CIA," he said. "It wasn't there yesterday."

"No," she said. "But it was the day before when the KGB came round. Then I switched it." She took the glass from his hand and had a drink. "I thought you might peep."

Harry Bridges, taught to question everything,

asked himself: If she didn't want me to find the microfilm yesterday why is she telling me about it today?

"What happened?" he asked.

"What do you mean, what happened?"

"Why are you telling me now?"

She hesitated and Bridges queried that, too. "Because I trust you more now."

"Because we've made love?"

"Not just that," she replied, feeling her way.

"What then?"

"Just being together today."

You're lying, he thought. Something's happened. Could it be anything to do with the killing in Novosibirsk? The shooting at Sverdlovsk? The plot, whatever it was, that Viktor Pavlov was involved in? "How can I help?" he asked, taking the drink back from her. "You've got it all worked out. The boat to Japan. The pick-up when you get there. What can I do? I'm staying here, remember?"

"I wanted to share it with someone. It was getting too much, keeping it to myself."

Like hell, Harry Bridges thought, switching the attack. "Why did you come tearing out of the forest like that?"

"I told you. I wandered too far and then heard the whistle. Would you like to be left alone in the middle of Siberia?"

Bridges admitted he wouldn't. His mind went on ferreting, all the old instincts rising from the dead. The effect of Siberia, maybe. There was only one way to banish them at this moment. He turned and kissed her breasts, started to make love to her again. This was also disturbing, the feeling he had for this beautiful, candid-eyed, double-crossing girl.

They had been to the musical comedy, laughing

in the wrong places, after he'd taken a fixed-time call from his London office and phoned a story on the speech, listening to the copytaker's sighs of boredom and sympathizing with him. Then they'd gone to a Georgian restaurant and eaten chicken Kiev with a vegetable said to be a kind of grass.

Back at the hotel they bribed the stony-faced watchdog on the landing with a bottle of Stolichnaya and went straight to bed.

As a lover, he found her a strange mixture of innocence and passion. Her body smelled of lemons and her eyes seemed to change color. Frightened, Harry Bridges realized that this act of sex was also an act of love.

He said, "So what happens now? You go to Japan, I stay here."

"I don't know, Harry," she said. "What happens?"

He felt her strength: it had once been his.

"Maybe," he said carefully, "I could make a trip to London."

"And meet the girl who smuggled an anti-Soviet manuscript out of Russia?" She looked sad as she said, "It wouldn't be good for your image, Harry."

So, he thought, she knows about me. He had sworn to make a decision by the time he reached Irkutsk. He decided to postpone it a day. There was plenty of time.

"'Maybe," he said, pouring more Scotch into the glass, "you could hand this manuscript over to your contact in Japan and come back to Moscow. There's no reason why anyone should know you're a smuggler."

She lay back, hands behind her head pulling up her breasts with the big, nuzzling nipples. "Harry," she said, "I'm not ashamed of what I'm doing."

He lit a cigarette and drew deeply on it. Then he asked: "What made you do it?"

"Annette Meakin," she said.

"What else?"

"Freedom," she said. "That old cliché."

"Don't be half-smart," he said.

"That speech he made at Taishet." She was counterattacking. "That must have been a good story for you?"

Sweet Jesus! Harry Bridges thought. If only we could love and marry the girl next door and be honest all our lives. "It was a good story," he agreed.

"And you sent it to your newspaper?"

He shook his head. "No."

"Why? Surely the attack on the Jews was a good story."

"We were warned off."

"We?"

"All the journalists on the train."

"But they're Communists. It was a scoop for you, wasn't it, Harry?"

"I suppose so," he said. He listened to his own hypocrisy. "But I couldn't have filed it from there. It would never have gotten through."

"So you'll file it when you get to the end of the line?"

"The end of the line," he said. "Don't make me laugh."

"But you will?" There was, he decided, a ferret brain inside that beautiful head.

He said: "No."

"Why?"

"Like I said, you should have been a journalist."

"Why, Harry?"

"Because," he said.

She took the glass, drinking and coughing a little because there wasn't any water with the whisky.

He appraised the room with its red plush and sticky varnish. He had made similar appraisals many times before. The shoddy Moscow flat compared with the lush Manhattan apartment. Did it matter if it gave comfort not qualified by knowledge of greater luxuries? The birthday present for your kid, a length of pipe with a wooden handle, did it matter if it compared unfavorably with a replica of an American self-loading Armalite AR 10 rifle? Did it hell, Harry Bridges thought, if it gave pleasure to your son. Happiness had nothing to do with refinements of civilization.

"You're very stubborn," she said.

"We're a good pair."

"Let's go down to the restaurant," she said.

"Will you come back to Russia?" he asked as they dressed.

"How can I? They'll know I smuggled the book."

"Don't tell anyone. Just hand it over and say you don't want any publicity. Then fly back to Moscow."

"I don't know," she said. "I would have to be sure there was something to come back to. I would have to be sure I was coming back to someone I admired."

In the hotel bedroom he had made his headquarters Col. Yury Razin considered the information brought to him by the crone. So Bridges and the English girl were sleeping together. He called for their dossiers and added the information, making a cross-reference to it. "Anything on their microphone?" he asked one of the two KGB officers who were also under scrutiny. The Mongolian-faced assistant shook his head.

"It wasn't connected," he said. "You told us to concentrate on Pavlov."

"Connect it," Razin said.

He took the list of passengers from a cardboard file and put a red cross against the name of Libby Chandler. The fact that she and Bridges were lovers wasn't in itself important. But Razin was always pleased to receive such information. It was all part of his survival kit.

"Like you," Harry Bridges said, "I have a secret." He poured more champagne.

"You have a wife and eight children?"

"No wives," Bridges told Libby. "I nearly got married once but her father shot himself." He decided he was a little drunk.

They were in the hotel restaurant. The tables had been cleared and the place was packed with boisterous Siberians.

"I am," Bridges told her solemnly, "onto a big story. Perhaps the biggest story of my life."

"Can you beat my manuscript? It could be another Zhivago."

Bridges nodded. "I can. An assassination maybe—the cause of many wars."

Libby put down her glass. "What are you talking about?"

"Don't you know?"

"I don't know anything about any assassinations."

In the middle of the room two jack-booted soldiers were doing a Cossack dance, squatting and kicking their legs out. Their colleagues clapped their hands and sang.

Bridges decided that Libby didn't know anything about an assassination; although he suspected that she knew something. Why had she suddenly decided to tell him about the microfilm?

"There's some sort of plot," he told her. "I don't know much about it. Except that it must concern Yermakov. I reckon it's timed for the next leg of the journey. Somewhere between here and Khabarovsk." He watched her closely, trying to determine if her surprise was genuine.

"What sort of plot?" she asked, eyes wide over the rim of the champagne glass.

"I don't know. Perhaps they are going to assassinate him."

"After that speech at Taishet—the one you didn't file—it can only benefit mankind."

"It won't make any difference to mankind. Someone else will take his place. Maybe someone a damned sight worse. In any case Yermakov has done a lot for the Soviet Union."

"Like Hitler did a lot for Germany?"

Bridges shook his head. "Look around. They're not doing too badly." One of the Cossack dancers fell on his back and was helped back to his table. "Look around Siberia—that's not doing badly either. Then," he said, "take a walk round Times Square at midnight. Or travel on the London underground at night."

"That's no argument," she said. "And you know it. . . ."

"I feel," he said, pouring more champagne, "that you're about to talk about freedom and democracy. They didn't do much for my old man."

"Your trauma," she said. "The monkey on your back. Your excuse for everything." They were silent for a while, then she said: "Do you know anything more about this . . . this plot?"

"Only that Viktor Pavlov's behind it." He thought he noticed something more than surprise in her expression.

"Anyway," she said brightly, "you'll have your scoop. I suppose you'll have to come to Japan to file it."

"I don't have a ticket or an exit visa."

"Then what are you going to do?"

"Nothing," Bridges told her. "I told you I was onto a big story. I didn't say I was going to write it."

There was contempt on her face. It gave him some sort of perverse pleasure. "Your father," she said, "would have been very proud of you."

Bridges stood up unsteadily. "Maybe I should warn the authorities. If I withhold information I am, after all, an accessory."

"Where are you going?"

"If you'll excuse me," he said, "I want to have a few words with an old contact."

He threaded his way through the tables and sat down beside Col. Yury Razin.

As Viktor Pavlov hasn't found me, Libby Chandler thought, then I must find him, to warn him.

She found him in the hotel lobby talking to the receptionist. She thought he looked like Tal, the chess player, briefly world champion. But, whereas Tal reserved his expression of deep intensity for chess, Pavlov wore it all the time.

He turned and said in a low voice: "I'm going for a walk. Perhaps you would like to accompany me? I'll meet you in ten minutes, outside the Museum of Regional History."

She went upstairs and dressed for the cold.

Pavlov was waiting outside the museum. Powdered snow was falling lightly. "Take my arm," he told her. "Make it look as if we're lovers."

She took his arm and they walked down a side street. "We can talk now," he said. "You were going to tell me why you wouldn't betray me. . . ."

Libby said, "I've come to warn you. Harry Bridges knows."

He didn't falter in his stride. "Really? Did you tell him?"

His attitude angered her. "If that's what you think we might as well go back to the hotel."

He put his hand on hers, protectively, like a lover. She thought: Perhaps he's going to kill me.

He said nothing, his silence forcing her to speak. "No, I didn't tell him. Someone else must have."

"Difficult to believe, Miss Chandler. You two are very close."

"Would I come out to warn you if I'd told him?"

They turned a corner and walked onto a wooden sidewalk. The powdered snow sparkled in the beams of light from the windows of the timber houses.

Pavlov was still considering her last remark. After a while he said no, he didn't think she would come out. "Unless you have a conscience and you didn't want me to think you'd betrayed me."

"I'm not as devious as that."

"No, perhaps not," he said, neither believing nor disbelieving.

"What are you going to do about it?"

"What I should do," he said, "is kill you and Harry Bridges."

"That wouldn't do any good. If Harry's going to betray you he'll have done it by now. I last saw him with Razin, the KGB man."

"Really. And how did you know our friend Col. Razin was in the KGB?"

"Because he questioned me in Novosibirsk."

"I see." They came to the Church of the Saviour. Libby stopped Pavlov at the entrance. They peered in and saw some old women, like bundles of clothes, kneeling on the floor. "Several of the Decembrists were buried here," Pavlov told her. "Princess Trubetskaya among them."

"Revolutionaries like you?"

"If you like. It's rather melodramatic though."

They walked on, his silence forcing her to ask, "What are you going to do about Harry Bridges?"

"There's nothing much I can do. It's up to Bridges. If he talks then the game's up—you're walking beside a dead man. But there's a chance he won't. In the first place he can't know much. In the second he won't *want* the Russians to know that he has any information. That would jeopardize his position in the Soviet Union. They would always suspect that he was biding his time to send it to his newspaper."

"Is he that much of a coward?" Her voice was sad.

"He's diplomatic," Pavlov answered.

They turned another corner. The lights of a main thoroughfare were ahead of them. Libby guessed that the walk was almost over. "So you trust me?"

"I don't know. You haven't explained why you didn't tell Razin."

"I heard Yermakov's speech at Taishet. Isn't that enough?"

"I suppose so." He took his hand away from hers. "I suppose I must trust you. If I didn't I would have killed you back there." He pointed behind them.

"You're Jewish, aren't you?"

He nodded, shaking snow from his fur hat. "Please don't say it doesn't make any difference."

"I wasn't going to. . . ."

"Another girl very much like you once did." He stopped suddenly and drew her into the shadows. "Good God!" Libby followed his gaze into the wide street ahead. Flanked by a dozen militia and men in dark overcoats, Vasily Yermakov was taking a walk in the streets of Irkutsk.

Anna had explained that she flew from Khabarovsk to Irkutsk because she couldn't keep the news from him any longer. She was having a baby and this would reunite them. She was sorry about the terrible row: it had been both their faults, she with her clumsy words, he with his perversity.

She didn't seem to doubt that they were together again, that anything could mar their love in this land of hers. She didn't mention his Jewishness—like a faithful wife not referring to the crime when her husband returns from prison, Pavlov thought.

Ruthlessness, he decided, lying on the bed beside her, with his son or daughter in her belly, was more difficult than he had imagined. She told him that the ceremony with Yermakov was still going to take place in Khabarovsk; but, because of the baby, the authorities had allowed her to come to Irkutsk. Then she drew his head to her swelling breasts and fell asleep while he lay awake. Finally, he too fell asleep, the dagger of guilt knifing his dreams. But even in those dreams he never wavered from his resolve.

Next morning—before he went to see the Priest —they drove along the 40-mile asphalt road to Lake Baikal. They arrived at dawn with a wild sunrise reflected on the waters of the world's deepest lake;

great obelisks and islands of red and orange on the calm waters that could be swept within seconds by massive waves that tossed the transparent fish on to the shore where they melted.

They went to the village of Listvyanka and stood hand in hand, remembering their honeymoon, awed by the lake.

"The history of Russia," Pavlov said, pointing at the water.

"The history of Siberia," Anna said.

When the Russians were fighting the Japanese in 1904 they tried to put a train across the ice, forgetting the warm springs underneath. The engine sank and was presumably still down there, crewed by the little pop-eyed, transparent *dracunculus*. At the beginning of the war troops were transported on the magnificent, elephantine ice-breaker Baikal built by the British; but it was always getting ice-bound; so the contractors worked desperately to complete the last link of the Great Siberian Railway—the loop round the toe of the lake. They blasted thirty-three tunnels through mountains plunging directly into the water; so hurriedly did they work, after the Japanese attack on Port Arthur, that the first train was derailed ten times. In the civil war that followed the October Revolution, whole families of refugees fleeing across Baikal were frozen to death on the ice or swallowed in fissures that opened up with a cannon roar.

Now the dawn silence enveloped Viktor Pavlov and his wife. They wandered down the lanes of Listvyanka among the wooden huts built by pioneer settlers, past a snow-covered sign bearing the warning Beware of Bears.

Anna had done a lot of research into Baikal and she took him to the Limnological Institute, talking as if they'd never parted, and showed him the relief map of Baikal. She told him that geologists thought Baikal was recently formed, part of the Great Rift that plunges down to East Africa. There was a theory, she said, that the lake wasn't always land-bound, which would explain the presence of its seals. Now the problem was pollution.

They tried to find the guest house where they had stayed on their honeymoon but it had gone out of business. Tourists no longer stayed in Listvyanka; they came from Irkutsk on the new 1250 h.p. hydrofoils and returned the same day. But the building was still there, deserted; they kissed outside it, lips warm on their cold faces. Pavlov looked for a fishing sail on the water, but there was none to be seen.

With despair cold inside him, resolve unchanged, he drove back to Irkutsk in the red Moscavich they had hired. He tried to think of a way to spare Anna, but his brain had no answer. How could he tell her to go to Khabarovsk by herself? What suspicions would it arouse in Razin's mind?

He dropped her at the Siberian Branch of the Institute of Curative Cosmetics of the Ministry of Public Health. "In other words," she grinned at him, "a beauty parlor." For twelve roubles you could have a massage, for twenty a paraffin mask, for eighty you could have freckles removed.

Pavlov went to see the Priest.

It was Yermakov's own idea to walk around Irkutsk. Razin was against it because the streets were dark and there were wild men abroad, descendants of revolutionaries, White Russians, murderers, and bandits.

But Yermakov was adamant. After his speech he sat in his state room in the center of the city exhausted. He had attacked the Chinese because the next leg of the journey took them alongside the Amur River and 1,892 miles of Chinese border. The speech depressed him because it was retrograde: for more than a century the Chinese and Russians had been contesting these border territories. The Black Crime of Blagoveshchensk—Cossack troops had been shot at from the Manchurian bank of the Amur and, in retaliation, they had taken thousands of innocent Chinese from their homes in Blagoveshchensk and drowned them in the river at bayonet point. That was seventy-three years ago and still they shot at each other across the Amur.

Yermakov gazed out of the window at the dusk settling on the city, the sun sliding away behind snow clouds. It gave a snugness to lighted rooms which he would never enjoy. What have I achieved? In whatever direction he looked there were camps filled with men whose only crime was disagreement. Was it so different from the days when convicts with split tongues worked the czars' gold and silver mines, branded, beheaded, or hung on hooks if they rebelled? When you could be exiled for begging, fighting, taking snuff, beating your wife, cutting down trees, or being idle.

Journeying across Siberia, Yermakov had been contemplating an amnesty for certain prisoners, a gesture to assuage his conscience. Paying off the creditors of the soul.

He watched some children playing on the sidewalk. He stared across the rooftops into snug rooms. He observed the outlines of apartment blocks. He remembered the crowd in the square, well-dressed and healthy. He thought of the Siberian oil wells of Samotlor which would produce 100 million tons of oil this year while the fuel crisis in the West worsened, the Komsomols building glacial cities in the tundra. He remembered his guns, his rockets, his atomic bombs. And, as the snow began to fall, he smiled. We are still on the ascent, he thought: America is on the decline. The prisoners in the camps are the casualties of victory. I have helped to lead Russia to these achievements. The melancholy was replaced by fierce happiness. It was then that he decided to walk among his people to reaffirm the sort of popularity that no young careerist motivated by selfish ambition could ever inspire.

As they walked Yermakov asked Razin, "Could Nixon walk alone in the streets of Washington without fear?"

Razin shook his head, watching the rooftops, the windows without lights, the dark side streets.

They walked for half an hour and Yermakov spoke to several passers-by and their children. They'll remember this for the rest of their lives, he thought, watching the children fondly as they raced away into the darkness.

They visited the old prison on the banks of the Ushakovka, where Admiral Kolchak had been executed by a firing squad in the headlights of a parked lorry before being pushed through the hole in the ice. Kolchak, Yermakov recalled, had "died like an Englishman"—whatever that meant. The visit to the prison chilled his exuberance.

They also visited the museum containing the materials Princess Trubetskaya wore in exile, Radichev's letters, convicts' fetters, bars from the old jail, whips used on the convicts, a photograph of a prisoner chained to a wheelbarrow. And a tattered Bolshevik flag.

Yermakov pointed at the flag. His eyes were moist. He said to Razin, "It's all been worthwhile, hasn't it, Comrade Razin?"

Razin said it had.

IN TRANSIT

The thaw in Novosibirsk lasted one day before winter set in. During that day a peasant walking along the banks of the Ob came across the body of a man wrapped in sacking. He phoned the police and, half an hour later, two yawning militia turned up and inspected the body without interest. One of them pointed to the mutilated neck and said "Looks like a wolf. They're getting hungry early this year." They phoned the morgue and an hour later—because there is no hurry in their business—two morticians arrived with their meat-wagon and took the body away. One of the miltiamen went through the dead man's personal effects; he found a thin wallet, a handkerchief, a ballpoint pen, car keys, loose change, a Moscow subway ticket—and an empty shoulder holster. The attitude of all three men changed. The senior of the two militiamen flipped through the contents of the wallet. He found a green card in a transparent plastic envelope, nodded at his colleague and said, "It's him." The second militiaman went to the phone. His colleague said to the morticians, "We'd better make a thorough job of it now." He went through the dead man's pockets again and, in the inside pocket of the overcoat, found an envelope with a Moscow address on it. On the other side, written in ballpoint ink, was the number 43. And the name Viktor Pavlov.

SECOND LEG

11.

The guns, ammunition, and grenades were stashed in a deserted railway station on a branch-line of the Trans-Siberian, 186 miles east of Chita, 4,033 miles from Moscow. In the prospecting days, when Americans, British, Germans, French, and Italians joined the gold rush, it was known as Panhandle and the wooden nameplate, in faded gold script, lay on top of the sacks of fertilizer covering the weapons.

The old ticket office, its wooden counter polished by gold roubles, was still intact and, outside the door, there was a brass bell covered with verdigris as thick as lichen. The platform had rotted but brass faucets from which passengers once drew boiled water were still attached to the outside wall. There were stumps of fencing around the garden and some fragments of fretwork hanging from the eaves.

The rails of the branch-line were still visible, two ribbons of rust in the snow. They wandered round a pine wood until they reached the main track of the Trans-Siberian; many years ago the track had been dismantled at the junction; overnight someone had replaced the missing links and oiled the points.

Halfway between the station and the main line stood an old black E-723 2-8-0 locomotive with a broken smokestack and a railed platform. Although it was decrepit, someone had been tending to it recently and there was coal on the tender.

"A little over a mile in the opposite direction to the main line stood the village which had been deserted during the rout of the White Russians and never repopulated. It contained a ruined church built in honor of St. Nicholas the Miracle Worker and the Martyr Saint Queen Alexandria to mark the coronation of the czar and his wife; a cemetery, a store which once sold liquor to the prospectors, exiles, and settlers who had been persuaded to go east and had done so at the rate of 52,000 a year with cheap rail fares, grants of 30 roubles, and gifts of 40 acres of permafrosted ground; the foundations of an inn and the ruins of a few log cabins.

Between the railway station and the village, hidden from the main line by the belt of pine trees, the rusty track passed over a deep ravine spanned by an iron bridge. On this single-span bridge, built into stone buttresses on either side of the ravine, the climax of the Pavlov plan was to be enacted: there above a wound in a white waste hedged by pine and banked by mountain foothills, between a deserted railway station and its ghost village, the most powerful man in the Soviet Union was to be held for ransom.

First the special carriage carrying Yermakov at the end of the Trans-Siberian express would be uncoupled after a false alarm had stopped the train; then Yermakov and guards would be swiftly and silently incapacitated; the main body of the train would continue on its way leaving behind the last coach which would be shunted along the branchline by the old E-723 2-8-0 locomotive; Yermakov would be held in the coach on the iron bridge already packed with dynamite until the Zealots' demands were met. If they weren't. . . .

It wasn't an ambitious bridge but it had style with its iron sides like the tips of two giant wheels and ornate buttresses, now ravaged; it had been built by Muscovite engineers, Italian stonemasons, and convicts, and they had managed to create dignity in the desolation. A few hundred yards away stood the crumbled workings of an abandoned gold mine. The mine had an open shaft and it took twenty seconds for a stone to hit water with a distant, silvery splash.

Far beyond the mountains, their haunches scattered with silver birch, lay the Autonomous Republic of Yakutsk and the Arctic. To the southwest lay the borders of Mongolia, the puppet of the Soviet Union, and, to the southeast, the Chinese border.

To the east, along the Amur River, lay the autonomous Jewish region of Birobidzhan, now in its death spasms, Khabarovsk, Vladivostok, and the Pacific linked with Europe by the world's longest continuous train ride.

All around lay the 4,833,496 square miles of Siberia.

The Prospector was there with his wolf; he was in charge of the weapons. Shiller, the Penman, had arrived from Moscow flying to Khabarovsk on a TU 114 turboprop and backtracking on a YAK - 40. He was in charge of this end of the operation until the arrival of Pavlov the Professional.

There were five other Zealots hiding in the ruins of the village—the Pilot, the Pederast, the Pupil, the Puppetmaker and the Planter who, through Semenov the Policeman, had managed to plant bugs in the KGB headquarters at Chita which would be handling all messages about the kidnap.

The Pupil, who was twenty-two, was in charge of the old locomotive. He was one of the Soviet Union's 3,500,000 railwaymen and the most suspect member of the Zealots because it was a good life being a railwayman in the Soviet Union with free medical service, pensions, and recognition of good work. One of his heroes was Boris Demurin.

Nevertheless the Pupil was a Jew, although it didn't show on his passport. He had a twin brother who worked as a laboratory assistant in the Scientific Research Institute of Clinical and Experimental Surgery in Moscow. His twin had been an active Zionist who had taken part in the hunger strike at the Central Telegraph Office. He had spent a lot of time at the 108th militia station and sobering-up station No. 9 and had been arrested twice under Article 122 of the Russian Republic Criminal Procedural Code. Finally, he had stolen some spirit from the laboratory and set fire to himself in Gorky Street. The Pupil had got to him too late and his hands were a mass of scar tissue from his efforts to beat out the flames.

The rest of the Zealots were not necessarily present for their professional capabilities. The Pilot flew An-12's for Aeroflot, the Puppetmaker made marionettes for a traveling show in Leningrad, the Pedarest operated outside the Bolshoi Ballet in Moscow and was a skilled assassin.

By the time the operation swung into action at 8:34 P.M. on the eighth day of the journey—the day after the train left Irkutsk—the Zealots would number thirteen.

12.

Stanley Wagstaff was arrested as Train No.2 was crossing the Primorski Mountains on its way to Sliudianka. It was nine o'clock in the evening and Stanley was standing in the corridor because he was interested in this stretch of track which had block signals and the steepest gradient anywhere on the railway; the line had been built in 1956 to avoid flood waters caused by the damming of the Angara.

He had notebook and pencil in his hand but he wasn't writing much because it was dark outside and snow was plastering the windows. He didn't mind because it felt good just standing there, feeling the smooth motion of the train; and, in any case, he had enough facts and figures in his notebook for three lectures in Manchester. His journey, he thought, would merit a few paragraphs in the Manchester *Evening News*.

The two KGB men were very polite. One took the notebook, the other searched him. They asked him to accompany them to a compartment in the special coach. Larissa Prestina was sitting in the compartment which was more like a cell. She looked very smug.

Stanley felt he should say, "I demand to see a lawyer." He almost laughed. He wasn't frightened —it was all part of the adventure and now he was worth more than just a few paragraphs in the *Evening News;* in fact, Stanley thought, I'll probably get national coverage.

He nodded at Larissa Prestina and asked: "What's this all about?"

The two KGB men sat opposite Stanley. The bunks had been removed from the compartment and it was furnished with a dark green metal table and four chairs. Between the two officers stood a table lamp with a brilliant glare. The third-degree, Stanley thought.

The officer with the Mongolian features said, "It has come to our notice through information laid by Comrade Larissa Prestina that you have been making notes of classified material relating to the deployment of Soviet troops."

"I don't know what you're talking about," Stanley said. He took a packet of Mannikins from his pocket and offered them round. The boyish-faced officer took one and slipped it into the breast pocket of his jacket. When will they start torturing me? Stanley wondered.

Larissa Prestina said, "Oh yes you do. I saw you take out your pad and make notes when we

passed a train loaded with guns. What's more"—
her voice broke with long-suppressed fury—"you
have spent the entire journey indulging in anti-
Soviet propaganda and mocking the achievements of
our glorious leaders."

"Bollocks," said Stanley Wagstaff.

The Mongolian KGB man opened the notebook
and perused it for a few moments. Finally he said,
"It won't take our code-breakers in Moscow long to
solve this."

"The best of British luck to them," Stanley
Wagstaff said.

"I'm sorry, but I don't seem to understand what
you say."

"Then scrape the wax out of your ears." How
long will it take before I break under interrogation?
he wondered. He had heard that they put electrodes
on your testicles until you told them everything they
wanted to know in one long, drawn-out scream.
The snag was he hadn't got anything to tell them
so the scream might be very long. The last entry,
he remembered, was a list of condemned 2-10-0's of
the Ea class standing in a railway graveyard .

Larissa Prestina turned to the two officers. "Are
you going to let this pig talk to you like that?"

"Calm yourself, Comrade. We must be sure of
our facts. Your wallet please." Stanley handed over
his pigskin wallet bearing a picture of Blackpool
Tower.

They laid the contents on the table. Driving
license with one endorsement for speeding in Sal-
ford, a photograph of his wife eating ice cream on
Scarborough sea front, the membership card of his
train-spotter's club, a photograph of Stephenson's
Locomotion on Darlington station, some flamboyant

Soviet postage stamps, coupons for buying food and drink and ten one-rouble notes.

The KGB men glanced at each other unhappily.

"We'd better tell Comrade Razin," one of them said in Russian.

"Comrade Razin said he mustn't be disturbed unless it's something to do with the security of the train."

They stared hard at Stanley Wagstaff: he didn't look much of a threat. And relations with Yury Razin had become delicate since he had realized they were communicating information to Yermakov. You would have thought that if you were cooperating with the most powerful man in the Soviet Union you were safe: the two officers were sufficiently experienced to know that this was far from the truth where Razin was concerned.

"Just the same, we'll have to tell him," one of them said. "He'd go crazy if we arrested a spy without telling him."

"Supposing he isn't a spy. That would be the end of us. This Wagstaff is the sort of shit who would make trouble. An international incident," he said, stuffing Stanley's papers back into his wallet.

"Of course he's a spy," Larissa Prestina said loudly. "Why else would he make notes of troop movements?"

"He says he's a train-spotter."

"A clever front," Larissa Prestina said.

"I'm hungry," Stanley said, knowing they would deprive him of food and water.

One of the officers went away, returning five minutes with black bread, red caviar, a rosy Kasakh apple, and a bottle of beer. He put the tray in front of Stanley and said, "Please eat. If there's anything more we can get you let us know."

Larissa Prestina sniffed.

"I'm afraid we'll have to keep you here for a while," the officer went on. "Let us know if there's anything you want."

They all left, locking the door from the outside.

The train rolled on smoothly through the night, reaching Ulan-Ude, where the Trans-Mongolian Railway branches off for Ulan-Bator and Peking, and beginning its descent through the Yablonovy Mountains to Chita where the aristocratic wives of the Decembrists once made their homes in Ladies Street.

The train was full of dreams except in one or two pockets of resistance. In the hard-class carriages, men in pajamas played cards through the night while Yakuti women from the north wearing furs and fine reindeer-skin boots, sipped Cognac and chewed cuts of ham, their Eskimo faces flushed with excitement.

Once there was a burst of cheering as the old chess-master, who had broken his journey at Novosibirsk and Irkutsk to play and lose several games, beat a young scientist planning Siberia's future at Akademgorodok. He was young and brilliant, moving quickly, slapping his pieces down on the board. Contemptuously, he accepted a sacrifice and lost the game in thirty-eight moves. He stared baffled at the board for some time before challenging the old man to a return game. But the old man, his eyes rheumy and his face like parchment, announced his retirement. He fell asleep smiling and died without waking from a heart attack.

In the kitchen of the dining car the Ukrainian

train-driver made love to the brown-uniformed waitress on a table beside a bowl of caviar; but it wasn't wholly successful because, with the cooks due in five minutes, he had to move quickly; and, when it was over, the waitress compared him unfavorably with southern lovers.

In the special coach Yermakov took two sleeping pills; but they had no effect. After sweating and moving restlessly for another hour he took a third, finally falling into a deep-black sleep.

Harry Bridges also had difficulty sleeping. With his talent for being in the right place at the right time he had seen Stanley Wagstaff taken away.

"What are you going to do?" Libby Chandler had asked at the time.

"What can I do?"

"You were action man himself in Irkutsk."

"I told you I didn't tell Razin anything."

"I'll do something for Stanley if you won't."

"What the hell can you do? Half the KGB are on this train."

"At least I can see him. He must be scared out of his wits, poor little man."

"You can try," Bridges told her. "They'll probably put you off at the next station."

"At least I'll have tried. "Or," she said thoughtfully, "I could round up all the Westerners on the train. Send a delegation along to demand his release." Annette Meakin took over. "Or we could even get him out by force."

"They're used to people trying force. In case you didn't know, they've got a machine-gun mounted at the end of the special coach."

"They wouldn't dare to use it."

"Want to bet?" Bridges asked.

"You know something," Libby said, looking up at him from her berth, "you're contemptible."

Bridges said, "I know it. It takes courage."

"Whatever happens I suppose you won't put any of this in your paper?"

"I might—British spy arrested on the Trans-Siberian."

"Stanley Wagstaff a spy?"

"Who knows," Bridges said. "Stranger things have happened."

"You don't honestly believe that?"

"No," Bridges admitted.

Libby said, "Can you please turn the other way. I'm going to get dressed and do something to help him."

Bridges sighed. "All right, I'll try and do something tomorrow. God knows what."

"You could see Razin. You seem to be on good terms with him."

"I'll see him," Bridges told her. "He might let me see Wagstaff."

The door opened and Larissa Prestina came in. She said to Bridges, "Please, could you go in the corridor while I undress."

It was dark in the compartment but Bridges went outside and waited. When he returned Libby Chandler was saying, "You reported him to the KGB, didn't you?"

"I did my duty," Larissa Prestina said. "He was making notes about troop movements."

"He was making notes about trains," Libby said. "And you know it."

"We shall see. The police have taken his camera and the film will be developed in Khabarovsk."

Bridges said: "He must be the first spy to use a Kodak Instamatic."

When the breathing of the two women indicated that they were asleep, Bridges remained awake. For a long time he had lived with his conscience; but he had never expected to be confronted with its embodiment in the shape of a twenty-two-year-old English girl.

In the next compartment Viktor Pavlov also lay awake. The Tartar general and his wife had left the train at Irkutsk and their places had been taken by an American research engineer and an executive of the Tokyo Gas Board collaborating with the Russians in developing gas fields around Yakutsk and beneath the sea bed around the island of Sakhalin. They slept peacefully while the Poacher snored.

When they arrived at Tankhoi, Pavlov checked to see that his wife was all right. The pregnancy was complicated and Anna had been given a compartment to herself with a nurse. Anna was asleep, her face content; the nurse put her fingers to her lips. Pavlov ignored her, kissed his wife's lips softly, and let himself out of the compartment.

Now he waited for sleep, knowing that it would become elusive, the more he thought about it. He thought about Birobidzhan, the Promised Land which Stalin had pretended to create in Siberia. *Evrieskaia avtonomnaia oblast*—a Jewish Autonomous Region. Created and destroyed in two waves of pogroms in 1937 and 1948. The street signs, he had been told, were still in Hebrew; there was little else Jewish about the place. They were due there on the ninth day of their journey; but Pavlov knew they would never make it.

He flirted with sleep; but he was trying too hard. Once, as he hesitated on the brink, he remembered an old Jew he had met near the synagogue in Moscow during his student days. The old man, wearing a threadbare black cloak, was half-crazed after years of trying to get a visa to visit parents in Israel, long-since dead. He still blessed the Hanukkah candles, he still danced the Simchat Torah; sometimes, even when there was snow on the ground, he believed himself to be in Jerusalem. He had spent much of his last years pleading with European and American Jewish tourists to give him prayer books for the synagogue, and one spring morning he mistook Pavlov for an American. He clutched Pavlov's arm and asked for a prayer book. Pavlov spoke kindly, looking around for evidence of surveillance, disengaged his arm and walked on. The old man shouted, "Why have you forgotten us?" Pavlov wanted to turn and shout back, "I haven't." Instead he walked on. Now the old man had returned, halfway across Siberia, and for a fleeting second of semiconsciousness, Pavlov wondered if he was really helping him; if he was helping any of them. Then he was awake again, listening to the steady rhythm of the wheels, and the doubt vanished.

He fell asleep just before dawn as a railwaywoman with a gold baton waved the train away from the platform at Petrovski-Zavod on the eighth day of the journey.

By that time Col. Yury Razin was shaving his thick beard, looking at himself with tired eyes. He ordered lemon tea, toast and a hard-boiled egg in his office. He spent the morning checking the reports on the new passengers, among them two North Vietnamese pilots returning to the Soviet Union for refresher courses; a French-Canadian forestry expert on an exchange visit from his country which bore so many similarities to Siberia; the usual Australians on their way home via Hong Kong; an Italian historian inspecting the bridges his country's masons had built at the turn of the century; a French specialist in tropical diseases in which the Far East of Siberia abounded; some Scandinavians trying to sell metal skis to the Siberians who used wooden cross-country skis; a lot of Soviet naval officers on their way to the closed city of Vladivostok.

Then he returned to the dossier on Viktor Pavlov, rereading it carefully, sipping lemon tea, frowning, and chain-smoking his American cigarettes.

At midday he went to see the *British spy* his two aides had captured. He thought their action might give him the opportunity to dispose of them.

Stanley Wagstaff greeted him stoically, awaiting a blow round the face with a leather glove; a fist in the teeth.

Razin sat opposite him and put Stanley's notebook on the table. "What?" he asked, offering Stanley his cigarettes, "are all these figures?"

Cautiously, Stanley accepted a cigarette and a light. Drugged?

"Well?" Razin looked at him patiently.

"They're the numbers of trains," Stanley Wagstaff said.

"This one?" Razin prodded a figure on the first page.

Stanley studied it. "That's the telephone number of Manchester Central Station."

Razin grinned, the heaviness lifting from his face. "That should be easy enough to trace." He flipped the pages. "And this?"

Stanley read the figures o-8-o. "A locomotive," he told Razin.

"But surely not on the Trans-Siberian, Mr. Wagstaff?"

Stanley looked at him suspiciously. "Hardly," he agreed, failing to discern any particular threat on the big, doggy face in front of him. "They were built in Germany and the Kolomna works started to make them in 1879. Eleven and a half ton axle weights," he recited.

"Beautiful old engines," Razin said.

A trick! "What," Stanley demanded, "do you know about old engines?"

"You'd be surprised what I know about, Mr. Wagstaff. The 0-8-0 had, I believe, one of those beautiful flask-shaped smokestacks."

"What's that then?" Stanley took the book and pointed at a number.

"Really, Mr. Wagstaff, I think I should be asking the questions. However. . . ." He studied the numbers 2,000 D.E., T.E.2. "I presume it's a reference to a 2000 hp. diesel electric Type TE-2 used on the Moscow belt line"

Stanley leaned back in his chair, awed. "You really are one of us."

"Even in my profession we are entitled to a hobby."

"Who would have thought it," Stanley said. "Wait till I tell them back in Manchester."

"If you ever get back to Manchester," Razin said mildly.

Tough and gentle; hot and cold. The old familiar treatment!

Razin retrieved the notebook and said, "After all, if you were spying, you would hardly fill the whole notebook with military data. I have no doubt that you are a railway enthusiast and I know that at least some of these numbers refer to locomotives. It doesn't mean to say all of them do." He stood up and stared through the reinforced glass in the window. "At a later stage I may have to ask you to sign a statement."

"Never!" Not even with the electrodes sparking away.

"We shall see. Meanwhile you must remain here. I'll keep this." Razin picked up the notebook. "I'll see that you have everything you want. A flask of vodka, perhaps? My own stock."

"No thank you," Stanley said. "I'd like a cup of tea, though, with milk and sugar."

"Very well," Razin said. "I'll come back to you later in the day."

He closed the door behind him. Stanley Wagstaff remained sitting at the table waiting for the poison gas to creep under the door.

When Razin got back to his office there was a message awaiting him from Harry Bridges. Could they meet in the dining car.

Why not? Razin thought. He could do with a Cognac with the tension pressing behind his eyes.

The usual waitress served them at the reserved table; Razin thought she looked edgier than usual. Perhaps the Ukrainian wasn't much of a lover. Too smart and too small, he speculated.

"Well, Mr. Bridges, what can I do for you?"

"Release Stanley Wagstaff," Bridges said sipping his brandy.

"So you know about that? I must hand it to you, Mr. Bridges—you're good at your job. News presents itself to you."

"I saw your men taking him away."

Good, Razin thought. Excellent. "And you want me to release him just like that."

"Stanley Wagstaff isn't a spy and you know it."

"An unlikely spy, I agree. But surely all good spies are unlikely."

"Not as unlikely as all that."

"I suppose," Razin said reflectively, "it would make a good story for you. If I allowed you to release it."

"Nothing fantastic. Not for an American newspaper."

The American engineer and the Japanese tried to sit at the table but Razin waved them away. They sat further down the dining car conversing in cubic feet.

Razin looked at Bridges carefully before asking, "What would your idea of a good story be?"

"The shooting at Sverdlovsk," Bridges replied.

"Apart from that."

"I haven't found anything better," Bridges said.

Noticing the hesitation, Razin said, "If you know anything, Mr. Bridges, I would advise you to be frank. For your own sake." He glanced at his watch: 7:56 and they were just drawing into Zubarievo. "Perhaps you would come and see me in an hour's time. It seemed to me that there was something you wanted to tell me in Irkutsk the other night."

The knuckles of Bridges' hands were white. "Okay," he said. "I've nothing to lose."

Razin finished his Cognac. "You might have a lot to lose if you aren't completely frank."

They were drawing out of the station when the boyish-faced aide came into the dining car, pushing past the waitresses.

"I think you'd better come back, Comrade Razin. There have been . . . developments."

Razin, who was feeling a little better, looked up with annoyance. "Can't they wait?"

The aide shook his head. "It's very important."

Razin said to Bridges: "Maybe you've exercised your talent for being around at the right time once again." He stood up.

Bridges said: "What about Wagstaff?"

"Patience, Mr. Bridges. You have no deadline to catch."

He strode off behind his junior officer.

The message had been received by telephone at Zubarievo. The body of Gavralin had been found on the bank of the Ob. His throat had apparently been torn out by a wolf. In one of his pockets police had found a slip of paper bearing Viktor Pavlov's name.

Razin swore. "Why didn't the idiots contact me on the radio?"

Razin was about to go and get Pavlov when one of the officers said, "There's something else, Comrade Razin. You have a visitor."

"He can wait."

"A very important visitor, Comrade Razin."

When Razin saw who the visitor was he postponed his visit to Pavlov for five minutes.

Ten minutes to go. Viktor Pavlov said to the Poacher, "Is everything ready?"

The Poacher nodded. "Everything's ready." He lay on the bottom bunk. Pavlov sat at the table facing the door. The American and the Japanese were in the dining car.

Pavlov sat very still. He glanced at his watch. "Nine minutes," he said.

Outside dusk was approaching and the snow was falling lightly but steadily.

Pavlov was lighting a cigarette when the door opened and Razin burst in, gun in hand.

"Stand up," he said, "and turn around, hands behind your neck."

The Poacher hit him in the crotch and Razin folded, retching.

Behind Razin the boyish-faced KGB officer went for his automatic. But Pavlov reached him first across Razin's crouching body. He got him by the throat, slamming his head against the door.

As he did so the Poacher chopped at the back of Razin's neck. Razin hit the floor, face down, dropping his pistol.

With one hand Pavlov shut the door, holding the KGB man's throat with the other. But, despite his schoolboy face, he had a thick skull. He shook his head and drove his knee into Pavlov's groin. But, in the confined space, there wasn't much force behind it. Pavlov hit him low in the belly. The KGB man shoved the palm of his hand under Pavlov's chin, pushing upward, trying to break his neck. Pavlov stumbled backward, hooking his foot around the man's legs. The KGB man slid down the wall. Pavlov broke away from the outstretched hand and hit him across the throat with the blade of his hand. The man gave an ugly rasping cough and sat down, head lolling.

Pavlov took the pistol from the Poacher. "Is he dead?" he asked, pointing at Razin.

The Poacher shook his head.

Pavlov looked at his watch again. Eight minutes. "I'll look after these two. You go to the dining car and make sure the American and the Japanese don't come back."

"How can I do that?"

"Talk. Keep talking. We're almost there."

The Poacher let himself out of the door and Pavlov locked it. From the Poacher's bag he took some cord with which the Poacher tied up animals; Pavlov tied up Razin and his assistant and put them in two of the berths, one above the other.

He sat down at the table, gun in hand. Sweat trickled down his face and his groin ached. He hoped the emergency had left the bugging system unattended.

His watch ticked loudly. Five minutes. A surplus of imponderables now.

The Poacher passed Harry Bridges in the corridor and went into the dining car. The American and the Japanese were sitting there, deep in cubic feet.

The Poacher sat at their table and said, "Can I get you gentlemen a drink?"

The American, tall and crew-cut like a White House aide, looked at him with surprise. The Poacher had hardly spoken until now. "No thanks," he said in Russian, "we were just going back to the compartment."

"I insist," the Poacher said. "Russo-American friendship." His smile was fierce.

"And Japanese friendship?" The Japanese, gray-haired and delicate, smiled.

"Of course," the Poacher said, beckoning the waitress.

The American shrugged. "Very well. A very quick one. My friend and I have some work to do. . . ."

The waitress brought a carafe of brandy and the Poacher poured generous measures. Then he began to talk about Siberia, its history and legends.

Had they heard the famous story that illustrated the size of Siberia? Without waiting for an answer the Poacher told them about the six virgins from

Kamchatka invited to St. Petersburg by the Empress Elizabeth Petrovna. Their escorts were two officers of the Imperial Guard. Just before they reached Irkutsk each of the girls gave birth. More trustworthy escorts were found and the six girls continued on their way to the capital. But by the time they got there each had given birth to half-brothers and sisters to their first-born.

The Poacher guffawed. He glanced at the American's wristwatch. Three minutes.

The American said: "Yes, I had heard that story." He swallowed his brandy, adding, "Now we must. . ."

The Poacher switched to the Japanese. "This will interest you," he said wildly. Most people think World War II started in Europe, eh?"

The American said, "Where did it start—Siberia?"

The Poacher nodded vigorously. "It really started on July 29, 1938, when the Japanese attacked Vladivostock."

The Japanese's smile faded. "How very interesting," he observed.

The Poacher looked apologetic.

Two minutes.

"Just one more story which you must hear. It illustrates how romantic the Siberian people are. You should always remember that when you're doing business with them."

"I really don't think. . . ." the American began.

"Two swans," the Poacher said desperately. "The starlings of Siberia. A hunter shot one of them. Its mate mourned all night and then, at dawn, flew as high as it could and dropped like a stone to its death. Russians often cry when they hear that story."

"You don't look as if you're crying," the American observed, standing up.

One minute.

The Poacher made an expansive gesture and knocked the rest of the brandy over the Japanese's neat dark suit.

Razin choked and vomited. He spoke with an effort, his face twisted with pain. "You won't get away with this," he said.

Pavlov said, "Tell me one thing. How did you find out?"

"A friend of yours boarded the train at Ulan-Ude. He came to visit me."

Pavlov leaned forward, pointing the pistol. "Who?"

"Professor David Gopnik," Razin said.

At that moment the train stopped.

13.

There were red lights on the track and two men, their outlines blurred by falling snow, swinging lanterns.

Boris Demurin applied the brakes, swearing. "What now?" he asked. "Isn't one earthquake enough for my last journey?"

The train stopped, throbbing gently. "You stay here," Demurin said to the Ukrainian. "I'll go and find out what's happened."

"Just as you like," the Ukrainian said. You wouldn't get interruptions like this on the Moscow-Leningrad line, he thought.

Demurin climbed down and walked toward the swinging lights. As he did so a man with the graceful movements of a ballet dancer and, in the gap of his

Balaclava helmet, the eyes of a man who enjoyed killing, climbed into the locomotive from the opposite side carrying a submachine gun. He said to the Ukrainian and the third member of the crew: "Anyone who moves gets it." He looked as if he hoped they would move. "When I give the order, get this train going."

In his compartment Viktor Pavlov stuffed a handkerchief in Razin's mouth. He looked at the KGB assistant. No need for handkerchieves—he was dead.

He put on his heavy overcoat and fur hat, let himself out of the compartment, locked it and dropped from the train on to the snow.

Harry Bridges saw him go and said to Libby Chandler, "This is it." He snatched his coat and hat from the peg.

Libby said, "I'm going with you."

"You stay here," Bridges snapped.

She put on her fur hat and coat, tucking her long blonde hair beneath the collar. "I said I'm going with you."

"What about your precious microfilm?"

She unscrewed the doll's head and slipped the package into her pocket.

The Peasant and the Painter killed the two uniformed militiamen at the entrance to the special carriage, shooting them in the chest and head with pistols fitted with silencers supplied by Semenov the Policeman.

They waited for a moment until the attack from outside began.

Meanwhile the Poacher dropped into the snow on the other side of the track and loped, with his hunter's stealthy stride, to the end of the train. He hauled himself up and peered through the last window. The militiaman manning the machine gun was staring out of the opposite window, trying to see what was happening. The Poacher hung there, waiting, snow caking his fur clothing; he had spent most of his life waiting like this.

The Zealots, all masked with Balaclavas, waited behind a nest of bushes until most of the KGB had alighted from the special coach. A hand wiped the condensation from a window and they saw Yermakov's face staring into the dusk.

Somewhere a whistle blew.

Four Zealots ran swiftly and silently to the carriage at the end of the train.

The Pupil and the Puppetmaker dealt with the coupling and switched the points while the Planter tossed a gas grenade into the coach.

The militiaman manning the machine gun swung the barrel as the Poacher came through the rear door. The Poacher put his two big hands round the man's throat, fingers on the windpipe, and squeezed. Just like killing ermine, he thought.

So far there had been no noise except the thud of the silenced pistols. Snow and dusk made confusing patterns of everything and the passengers lining the corridor stared perplexedly through the windows, not daring to get out until permission was given.

The Pupil worked expertly with his scarred hands until the coupling parted. He nodded to the Puppetmaker who blew his whistle twice.

The Planter, gas mask over his face, stood over the unconscious bodies of Yermakov and his secretary.

From behind the bushes a whistle sounded three times.

The Pederast jerked his submachine gun. "Get the train moving." he told the Ukrainian and his mate.

The red lights were doused and Train No. 2

inched forward, gathering speed. Leaving the special carriage behind at the point where the old branchline made its diversion to Panhandle station, the iron bridge, and ruined stations beyond.

Standing in the falling snow beside Shiller the Penman, Viktor Pavlov stared at the departing train. The faces at the windows were blurs, but the shape of one was familiar, pale with an aureole of blonde hair. He raised his hand and waved, but there was no response. He lowered his hand and, as the train disappeared into the veil of snow, turned on his heel to attend to the business at hand.

The Pupil and the Puppetmaker drove an old Army truck beside the branch-line to the waiting locomotive. E-723 had got steam up, wheezing impatiently as the two men climbed on to the worn footplate. The Pupil handled the brass levers of the old relic with love while the Puppetmaker shoveled coal into the furnace.

"How long have we got?" the Puppetmaker asked. He was a middle-aged man with tapering fingers and short sight.

"The next train's due on the main line in five minutes," the Pupil told him. He pulled a lever, the pistons began to move pushing the wheels round in reverse. But the wheels didn't grip. "Shit," the Pupil said. "The rails—they're iced up."

He switched the lever and the engine moved forward, protesting. They progressed 50 yards, then stopped. The Pupil shoved the controls into reverse again. "Come on my old beauty," he whispered, and when the wheels continued to slip, shouted, "Move you mother-lover." The engine moved. It gathered speed, throwing clouds of steam and plumes of sparks into the white-and-purple dusk. By the time they reached the main line the KGB men who had jumped from the train had been herded together by three Zealots masked with Balaclavas. The Pupil noticed a girl with them, and an old man.

The Pupil braked, backing the engine and tender onto the main line. He and the Puppetmaker jumped down and coupled it to the special coach. The prisoners were marched into the tender at gunpoint, Shiller and another gunman taking up positions on the footplate.

In the distance the Pupil heard the rumble of an approaching train. He climbed back on to the footplate with the Puppetmaker, grabbing the controls. The engine groaned but didn't move. "More steam," the Pupil shouted. "I need more steam."

They could hear the approaching train clearly now.

The Puppetmaker shoveled coal into the furnace. The Pupil pleaded, cajoled, soot-rimmed eyes gleaming behind his Balaclava. "Move you son of a whore," he screamed. The engine and tender moved, pulling the special coach behind them.

They had just rounded the pine trees on the branch-line when the freight train bound for Khabarovsk rumbled past on the main line with its long snake of wagons.

Near Panhandle station one of the KGB men tried to make a break for it. He jumped on to the side of the tender and dived for the ground. Shiller hit him with a bullet from his AK 47 assault rifle in mid-air, his scream drowned by the noise of the laboring engine.

The engine stopped outside the station and the prisoners—KGB officers, Boris Demurin, Harry Bridges, and Libby Chandler—were marched into the waiting room where the weapons had been hidden. It was dark now, the snowflakes like moths in the glow from the engine's furnace. The Pupil drove on to the iron bridge, uncoupled the special coach containing the unconscious Yermakov and two Zealots, and left it for the night above the dark wound of the ravine.

The Puppetmaker joined the Planter and the Poacher in the special coach while the Pupil drove the engine to the outskirts of the village. He climbed down, circled E-723, and patted its hot black body. Then he began to walk back to the station. He had got halfway when the boiler blew up, the explosion momentarily lighting the countryside, throwing its echoes into the mountains.

Pavlov boarded the special coach and took in the scene. Yermakov was sitting on the satin-covered chair in his deluxe sleeper, his head slumped forward. He was conscious but his face was gray and there was a blue tinge to his lips.

"He'll be all right," said the Physician, a young doctor from Vladiovstok studying the problems of rejection in transplants. "Unless there's anything wrong with his heart that I haven't detected." He put the stethoscope to Yermakov's chest. "It sounds all right. Just a little sleepy from the gas, like its owner."

Pavlov pointed at the corpses. He told the Poacher: "Throw them down the mineshaft and clean up the mess."

The Poacher slung a body over his shoulder as if it were an animal he had shot.

"Is the radio working?"

The Planter said it was. "We could also bug the railway station to hear what they're talking about."

The Planter was a small neat man who held his head like a bird listening for danger.

"We don't have to," Pavlov said. "We've got men there." He went into the office, striding up and down it. A wind had sprung up and the bridge seemed to sway slightly. "There's only one thing we haven't decided—what to do with the prisoners."

The Poacher returned and suggested: "Kill them." He and the Pedarest were competitors in killing.

Pavlov shook his head. "There's no point. They can't do anything. No sense in wasting ammunition. In any case, we'll have the whole Red Army here tomorrow." He sat down on the swivel chair by the desk. "We don't want to appear too cold-blooded either. They might think we've killed him"—pointing at Yermakov—"and send the troops in."

"What about the girl?" The Poacher's hands moved convulsively.

"What about her?"

The Poacher shrugged. "I thought perhaps you wanted me to finish the job I started at Taishet. . . ."

"Your brains," Pavlov said, "are in your hands. The Jews want the sympathy of the world, not the hatred."

The wind gained strength brushing the snow from the windows.

Pavlov went on: "We've also got to decide who is going to stay. The Pupil has finished his job, so have some of the others." Pavlov lit a cigarette and stared at the Zealots. "Whoever stays has only got a slim chance of escaping. You realize that?"

They nodded, watching him closely.

"We all agreed that we were prepared to die?" Again they nodded.

"Whatever happens, I'm a doomed man. So I stay. The Prospector is also a marked man after the killing in Novosibirsk. That's two of us. I need two more to stay to the end. I need the Pederast when he returns from the train because he's the best marksman we have. I need the Planter for the radio. Shiller, of course, will stay. The rest of you haven't been identified. If you move out now you stand a chance—no more—of getting away before the troops arrive."

No one spoke.

"Very well, I leave it to you." Pavlov stood up and went back to the sleeping compartment.

Yermakov raised his head and regarded him through glazed eyes. "Who are you?" he asked in a slurred voice. "Where's Razin?"

The Physician said, "It's no good talking to him for a couple of hours. In fact it would be better to leave it till dawn."

Pavlov said, "Very well. The troops will get here during the night. But they won't know what the hell to do. The first thing we'll see at dawn is a helicopter." He turned to the Planter. "Can you get through to Shilka?"

The Planter nodded. "It's the best equipment I've ever handled."

"Then send a message in one hour's time to the local KGB. Just as we rehearsed it. Tell them we're holding Yermakov as a hostage against the immediate release to Israel of eleven Jews." He remembered Gopnik's treachery. "No, ten Jews. Tell them we'll supply the names later. Tell them that if any attempt is made to attack—if one tear gas bomb is lobbed—then we'll kill Yermakov and they'll be answerable."

The Planter consulted his wristwatch. "I'll send the message at 10:30."

The Poacher walked down the corridor past the

open door, carrying another corpse over his shoulder, staggering a little under its weight.

Pavlov said, "Tomorrow we'll get you"—looking at Yermakov slumped in the chair—"to sign a few documents." He turned to the Puppetmaker. "Have you checked all the Aeroflot timetables?"

The Puppetmaker said: "Everything is synchronized—provided our timetable goes according to plan."

"It will," Pavlov said tersely. "It's taken my whole life to plan." He went into the corridor, tapping on the door of the cell. "What's in there?"

"We don't know," the Planter said. "We can't unlock it."

"Are you out of your minds?" Pavlov drew his pistol.

The Planter mumbled, "There wasn't time. You came just as. . . ."

Pavlov shot away the lock and Stanley Wagstaff fell into the corridor.

There were 30 degrees of frost outside and blades of cold came through the gaps in the boarded-up windows. The Painter stood in the ticket office, the barrel of his submachine gun poking through the pay box. Shiller and the Prospector sat on a bench opposite the prisoners—five secret policemen, Boris Demurin, Harry Bridges, and Libby Chandler. In one corner of the station, roped under the door to an iron shoe-scraper outside, sat the Prospector's wolf.

"What are we going to do?" Libby asked, shivering violently.

"Get a fire going," Bridges told her.

He stood up and the Prospector's gun jerked. Bridges told him what he was going to do; the

Prospector nodded without altering the aim of his submachine gun.

Under the sacks where the arms had been hidden, Bridges found some old posters that cracked when he handled them. An advertisement for a company with offices in Yinka Street, Moscow, manufacturing Glycerin Soap, Glycerin Powder and Petrol Soap—"the great helper in the unfortunate case of hairs falling off." The salesman, Bridges reflected, must have realized the futility of selling soap to the pioneers of Panhandle and dumped his inducements. On the wall were tattered posters issued by Gustav List Ltd. of Moscow, who made steam pumps and fire engines, and an advertisement from Keller and Co., 92 Obdodny Canal, St. Petersburg, who distilled rectified spirits and table wines. Underneath some lusty miner had drawn a sketch of a woman with her legs open. The *graffiti* underneath indicated what he proposed to do with her when he reached the fleshpots of Irkutsk.

Bridges stuffed the posters into the rusty stove in the middle of the room. Under the sacks he found some rotting planks, broke them with a soft crack and shoved them over the paper. He pointed to the bench on which Shiller and the Prospector were sitting. "Now that." When they moved he jumped on the middle of it and broke it in two. He put the pieces into the boiler and lit it. Smoke billowed into the room and a rat ran out of the boiler.

Libby watched it without visible emotion. "Now what?" she asked.

"What do you suggest?" Bridges sat beside her on the sacks. "Wait for the next train?"

"We've got to escape."

"Sure," Bridges said. "Sure." He took his overcoat off and put it round her shoulders. "Can you give me one good reason why? We don't want to get help. This is what you wanted to happen, isn't it? Those are your heroes out there. The only possible reason for wanting to escape," he said, beginning to shiver, "is to freeze to death."

Libby said, "I don't want your coat. I can take care of myself."

"Keep it."

She kept it, surprised by the authority in his voice. The wind had risen playing wild music through the eaves. A ridge of snow crept under the door and the musty air smelled of kerosene from the oil lamps.

"If we stay here we'll see the action," Bridges said. "Besides, what about the guy waiting for his package in Japan? You don't want to jeopardize that, do you?"

"I suppose not."

"Let's sit tight. They'll realize what's happened when the Trans-Siberian gets to Shilka. Christ knows what will happen then."

"Another scoop," Libby said, "which you won't send to your newspaper."

The Pederast returned at 2:35 on the ninth day. He bypassed the station to reach the bridge from the far side, noting the black bulge of the explosives bound to the girders. It had stopped snowing and the wind was driving the clouds over the slice of moon. The Pederast walked along the bridge with dainty steps as if he were walking a tightrope. He could see the outlines of the old pit-head and he fancied he could hear the clanking of convicts' chains.

He answered the Planter's challenge and climbed into the carriage.

"Well?" Pavlov was sitting in the swivel chair. Shiller who had joined him from the station sat on the other side of the desk. He looked sullen, the Pederast thought, missing the authority he had wielded before Pavlov's arrival.

"Everything went as planned. The train stopped at Shilka. No one knew anything had happened. I fixed the driver and his mate. . . . Clubbed them with the gun," he explained. "Then I ran for it. The car was parked there. I drove back, and here I am." He smiled and only the Poacher scowled. *My rival,* the Pederast thought. *He likes to kill, too; but with his hands, like the crude oaf he is.*

The Poacher said: "Did you kill them?"

"Did I kill who?"

"The driver and his mate."

"I don't think so. Does it matter? What's another death?" He noticed Stanley Wagstaff sitting groggily in the corner. "Who the hell's that?"

"Mr. Stanley Wagstaff," Shiller told him. "Our courier."

Stanley was holding a Press conference at the Savoy Hotel, London. *"I was their courier,"* he told the reporters, watching them scribble in their notebooks.

"What do you mean—courier?"

Pavlov said, "We need someone to carry the message. Mr. Wagstaff has consented to take it for us." He looked at his watch. "The troops will be here at first light—possibly before. Mr. Wagstaff had better get some sleep—the gas came through under the door of the cell."

Shiller handed Stanley his notebook. "Here, we found this in the control room. If you are a spy make good use of it."

"Thank you," Stanley said. *He told the reporters, "I took the details of Russian troops on their way to fight the Chinks. . . ." The Foreign Office repre-*

*sentative at his side dug him in the ribs. "I'm sorry,"
he told the journalists, "that was off the record."*

"The first lot will come back by train," Shiller
said. "It's the obvious way. . . ."

Pavlov interrupted him. "It doesn't matter how
they come. They daren't do anything."

Shiller said, "They didn't mind killing Beria.
They didn't mind exiling Malenkov. They didn't
mind sacking Krushchev."

"Yermakov," Pavlov said, "is different. How
would the Nazis have reacted if Hitler had been
held hostage—just for the release of ten Jews?"

"I suppose you're right," Shiller admitted reluctantly. "I hope you're right."

Pavlov said, "If you want to quit you can. There's
nothing stopping you. Within ten days you could be
back working for *Pravda* as if nothing had happened.
In fact," Pavlov said, "you could be writing an article
about the kidnap. Except," he added, "that nothing
will ever appear in the Soviet press about it." He
drummed his fingers on the desk. "Although a lot
could appear in the world press."

Shiller looked suspicious. "What do you mean?"

"I mean Mr. Harry Bridges," Pavlov said.

"Bridges? He wouldn't report a drunk in Red
Square. I'm a journalist. I know Mr. Bridges."

"You did know Mr. Bridges," Pavlov said.
"Things have changed. Mr. Bridges is in love."

They were interrupted by a snore from Stanley
Wagstaff. They picked him up and laid him gently
on the floor of the cell.

14.

First light. The sun rose behind the white mountains filling their folds with pink shadows; there were tendrils of mist curled round the peaks but these would soon be gone. All the sounds of the taiga were sealed by the snow.

From the east came a faint insect noise. The men in the carriage shielded their eyes but they could see nothing.

You could see the depth of the ravine now. A sheer drop of 2,000 feet down to the bed of a dried-up river whose waters had been diverted by the builders of the Trans-Siberian.

As the sun rose higher the snow on the plain took on a pink tinge. A twist of blue smoke issued from the chimney of the railway station.

Now the layout was plain: pine trees hiding the whole scene from the main line, the branch-line forming a loop after the Panhandle station in the direction of the village with the bridge in the middle. There had once been a pathway from the station to the village—like the string of the bow formed by the rail track—and station and bridge were clearly visible from each other.

Two companies of troops were packed into four hard-class carriages on another branch-line eight miles down the Trans-Siberian awaiting further orders from Brigade H.Q. at Chita.

The men in the carriage strained their eyes until Pavlov pointed and said, "There it is." The insect took the shape of a helicopter. It circled the bridge a couple of times, then slanted down so that they could see the pilot and observer staring down.

Shiller said: "We don't want him landing too near the bridge. We've got to assert ourselves."

Pavlov said, "Give me the Very pistol." He opened a window and fired into the sky. The shell exploded in bright pink flame which hung for a few minutes like a second sun.

The helicopter veered away at a sharp angle before going into circuit again, a marker for the reinforcements on their way.

Pavlov shut the window and went down the corridor to the sleeper. Yermakov was sitting up in bed watched by the Planter with a Thompson submachine gun with a folding butt, a relic of American aid to Russia in World War II. Yermakov looked up as Pavlov came in. He looked full of menace and authority —or as full as an unshaven, dishevelled man being held at gunpoint can look. He said, "You're all Jews?"

Pavlov nodded. "A few half-castes."

"You're more ambitious than I gave you credit for."

"Thank you," Pavlov said.

"Now release me. If you don't you'll all be dead within a couple of hours."

"If we did we'd all be dead within an hour."

"What do you want?"

Pavlov sat in the chair. To the Planter he said, "Get us some coffee from the larder."

"Do you want the gun?" the Planter asked, head cocked inquisitively.

"It won't be necessary. Close the door as you go out."

Yermakov said, "I want to shave and clean myself up." There was no hint of fear in his voice.

"After we've had coffee and a talk."

Yermakov swung his legs off the bed. His eyes were bloodshot; but he looked no better or worse than he did most mornings. He said, "You're quite mad. You're aware of that, I suppose?" He found his tie on the bed and began to knot it.

"A case for compulsory psychiatric treatment? There are many crazy Jews according to the Kremlin."

"But you *are* crazy."

"And the others aren't?"

Yermakov shrugged. "I know a madman when I see one."

"A fanatic, perhaps. Are the Black Septembrists mad? Are the Israeli guerillas mad when they ride into Beirut knowing that some of them will die?"

"I've lived and worked with madmen," Yermakov said. "I know."

"But who," Pavlov asked, "is sane?" He watched the helicopter circling. "Your troops will be here any minute," he said. "I want to explain our demands."

"Requests," Yermakov corrected him, pulling the knot of his tie.

The door opened and the Planter came in with two cups of coffee. Pavlov told him to fetch the briefcase, which Shiller had brought with him.

They sipped their coffee, watching each other through the steam, until the Planter returned. Pavlov dismissed him and took a sheaf of papers from the case.

Pavlov said, "I have here the names and addresses of ten Jews I want released. I want them out of the country within forty-eight hours."

"It can't be done," Yermakov said.

"Yes it can. We've worked out the routes from each city they live in. Moscow, Leningrad, Kiev. . . . They can all be on planes tomorrow to London, Stockholm, and Vienna. All it needs is your authority transmitted through the KGB to OVIR. After all," Pavlov said, "you don't usually give the Jews much time to get out when you've finally made up your minds."

Yermakov blew on his coffee and drank it thirstily. When he had finished he wiped his mouth and said, "Why should we be considerate to deserters?"

"Not deserters, Comrade Yermakov. Men and women who want to return to their homeland."

"Deserters, Comrade Pavlov." Yermakov paused. "You *are* Viktor Pavlov, mathematical genius and husband of Anna Petrovna, heroine of the Soviet Union, aren't you?" When Pavlov nodded Yermakov remarked, "Then Razin was right." He ran a metal comb through his hair. "No, Comrade Pavlov," he went on, "the Jews who want to leave are traitors. We let them go because they have no place in the Soviet Union. Tell me, do all the Jews want to leave America and Britain and go to Israel?"

"Many of them."

"Only a small minority."

"What are you trying to prove?"

"Merely that there is always a minority of dissidents who want to leave the country that has nurtured them, educated them, trained them. It's just the same in the Soviet Union."

"Not quite," Pavlov told him. "You don't get called a dirty *kike* or *sheeny* in Britain or America."

Yermakov raised his hand. "Please, Comrade Pavlov, don't be naïve. I find naïveté repugnant—innocence blighted by stupidity. Are you trying to tell me there's no anti-Semitism in the West? Are you trying to tell me the way the Negroes are treated in the United States or the Pakistanis in Britain is better than the way we treat the Jews?"

Pavlov smiled faintly. "You don't have any coloreds in the Soviet Union. I seem to remember that African students at Moscow University weren't too happy with their treatment." He lit a cigarette. "What I am trying to tell you is that the Jews in the West are free—free, Comrade Yermakov—to follow the destiny they choose." His tone became more brisk. "But we're not here for dialectics. I want your signature on these documents sanctioning the release of these ten men."

Yermakov took the documents and studied them. "Are you sure they all *want* to leave?"

"Quite sure. They have all made applications and been refused for the usual reasons—lack of references from their employers, lack of money to buy themselves out, lack of authorization from relatives."

"Who are these men?" Yermakov's tone was sardonic. "They must have brains or we would have been only too happy to get rid of them."

Pavlov said, "It doesn't matter who they are. They are just Jews who want to go home."

"I'm not a fool, Comrade Pavlov—not naïve. They must be very special, these men." He put the papers beside him on the bed. "Tell me one thing," he said, "did your wife know anything about this?"

"Nothing!"

"I'm glad. But you must remember that, while you hold me, your wife is still in the Soviet Union." He leaned forward, his features benevolent. "Would you be prepared to let your wife die for your cause? Your wife for ten Jews?"

Pavlov stood up. He didn't answer. "You have three hours in which to make up your mind."

"And if I refuse?"

"Then we blow the bridge," Pavlov said.

Several Zealots including the Pupil, the Poacher and the Physician left during the night, heading for distant villages on cross-country skis. The Painter left the station in the early hours of the morning and headed west, leaving the Prospector in charge. At dawn the Prospector also left the station with his wolf, leaving the prisoners unguarded, barring the door behind him and running across the snow to the bridge. There were now five Zealots left—Pavlov, the Prospector, the Penman, the Planter, and the Pedarest; all the rest had quit.

Bridges, assuming command, knocked the boards from a window, climbed out and opened the door for the rest of the prisoners. They stood breathing the iced air, watching the helicopter flying up from the east.

The KGB men stood in a huddle, banging their hands together, trying to reach a decision. One of them pointed at the snow and picked up an automatic pistol dropped during the night.

Boris Demurin leaned against the wall, his unshaven face bewildered. All night he had sat on the sacks, shaking his head and asking: "Why did it have to happen to me? My last trip. Why didn't they wait?"

Bridges gave him a cigarette and said: "You know the Trans-Siberian inside out. Where does this branch-line lead to?"

"I don't know," Demurin mumbled. "Leave me alone."

Bridges grasped the front of his blouse. "Pull yourself together. You must know where it goes to."

Demurin pushed his hand away. "It goes nowhere. A deserted village. All ruins. Then on to other deserted villages, other ruins." He lit a cigarette with gnarled, shaking hands. "They could have waited. I didn't want anything to go wrong." He peered along the snow-covered track, his shoulders lifting a little. "I remember it here when they used to bring the gold out on the old, wood-burning freights. We used to have a lot of flyers in those days. *Brodyagi* and settlers who used to jump on to the tops of the coaches. It was always adventure in those days. Bandits raiding the trains, students at the controls derailing the engines. . . ."

Bridges said, "We're not short on adventure right now."

Demurin's shoulders slumped again. "They've ruined me. Ruined everything. The past, the future."

Bridges handed him the pack of cigarettes, saying to Libby, "Let's go to the village." He took her arm and they started off toward the pine trees.

The senior KGB officer shouted after them. "Stay here. No one leaves." He was the one with the Mongolian features.

Bridges stopped, turning. "We're leaving."

The KGB officer pointed the automatic. "Come back. The authorities will be here soon."

"What authorities? You're the authorities. Shoot me and you'll have another international incident on your hands—on top of this mess." Bridges gestured around. "Shoot me or the girl and you'll be back at Lubyanka—in the cells." He took Libby's arm again. "Come on."

They walked on.

"Will they shoot?" Libby asked, fingers tight on his arm.

"They might. But I doubt it."

"I can feel him taking aim now."

"This is the way they shoot them in Lubyanka. You walk down a white-tiled corridor and get a bullet in the back."

They reached the pine trees. Bridges turned round. The policemen were following a hundred yards behind.

"If you're in the secret police," Bridges said, "you exist through fear. When you lose your authority it works the other way. They're scared."

"But they're still behind us."

"Follow my leader," Bridges said. He put his hand over hers.

They took the short cut to the village, past the pit-head, the loop of track, and the iron bridge to their right.

"A beautiful bridge for blowing," Bridges remarked. "Maybe that's what they're going to do."

Behind them the five KGB men stopped.

"Perhaps they're going to rush it," Libby Chandler suggested.

"Only if they're related to Japanese suicide pilots."

The five men walked toward the bridge, black crows against the snow.

The rear door of the carriage opened and the muzzle of the Gruyanov machine gun popped out like a bird's tongue. Someone waved a red flag.

The five black figures marched on and the Gruyanov opened up with its barking cough throwing up a line of snow plumes ten feet in front of them. They faltered. Another burst nearer, the explosions cannoning off the mountains. The five turned and walked back to the wood.

"They were brave," Libby said. She was shivering and her fingers were still tight on his arm.

"Come on," Bridges said, "before they have a go at us."

They ran for the shelter of the pit-head. Beside it stood the wreck of an old wooden machine for getting gold from tailings. Between the pit-head and the railway stood a conical hill of slag. The abandoned place was deceptive in the snow, as though life was merely in deep freeze. They investigated the remains of a shed beside the broken wheels and arms of machinery. Snow had piled into the shed but above its line someone long ago had carved a message.

Libby examined it. "My Russian doesn't run to it," she said. "What does it say?"

Bridges read slowly. "We came to find gold. Instead we found. . . ."

"What?"

"Not in front of an English rose."

"What does it say?"

"Shit," Bridges told her. He kicked the snow around. "Someone's been here before us." His foot found a soft object and he picked it up. It was a new fur *shapka*.

Bridges looked down the shaft. He dropped a

246

stone down it and, after a long pause, they heard a splash.

"I reckon they dumped the bodies down there," Bridges said. Libby leaned against him. "Come on," he said, "not even Miss Meakin encountered anything like this."

When they reached the village the sun was climbing the sky but the snow wasn't melting. They investigated the store and found that someone had been living there recently. "Some of the hijackers," Bridges said. He leaned on the battered counter while Libby gazed out of the door at the wooden church, its dome lying in the porch like an onion husk.

Libby turned. "What are they trying to do, Harry?"

"Viktor Pavlov is a Jew. I figure they're all Jews, or at least they've got Jewish blood in them. They must be holding Yermakov for ransom. As they're Jews the price must be the release of Jews. They couldn't hope to hold out while all the Jews who've applied for exit visas get out. So I think they must be demanding the release of certain key men. It would be very interesting to find out who," he added thoughtfully.

"But they can't escape from the bridge."

"They could demand a safe passage. Although the safety factor would be zero."

"So they're committing suicide."

"Madmen often do. And Pavlov's as crazy as they come."

"Harry," she said.

"Yes?"

"I knew this was going to happen."

"What do you mean you knew?"

She told him about the conversation she had overheard between Pavlov and Semenov.

"Did Pavlov know you overheard him?"

She nodded. "He saw me."

"Then you're lucky to be alive."

"I promised not to tell you."

"A wise decision," Bridges said. "I might have told Razin."

"No you wouldn't," she said. "You knew there was a plot of some sort but you didn't tell him that night in Irkutsk."

"I didn't know enough. All I knew was that Pavlov and the guy they call the Prospector killed a man back in Novosibirsk."

He told her about the killing and the shooting at Sverdlovsk. "Stories happen to me," he said. "Like this one."

"Will you send it to your newspaper?"

"It would never get out."

"Then the only solution is to take it out."

"Without an exit visa?"

"You're hedging," she said sadly.

"You're still looking for a man to admire?"

"Tell me a woman who isn't."

"Not all that many find them. They're pretty scarce."

"Yes," she said, "I know."

He took her arm and they walked round the decayed village. At the far end they found a small wooden building without a roof and silver birch crowding its walls. Bridges climbed the steps and rubbed the snow away from above the frame of the door. "Well I'll be damned," he exclaimed. "Do you know what this was? A Jewish prayer house."

"Do you know what those are," Libby said pointing to some tracks in the snow.

"A bear by the look of it," Bridges told her. "We

have two choices: stay here and get eaten by a bear or go back to the KGB."

"The KGB won't eat us," Libby said.

The Red Army solved their dilemma. They came into the village, dressed in white combat gear, carrying AK 47 assault rifles. A platoon of hooded, weather-toughened soldiers commanded by a lieutenant with pistol drawn.

They took Bridges and Libby back to the station where there was considerable activity. Troops were clearing the snow and erecting reindeer-skin tents. They had lit fires and the smoke smelled of autumn.

Bridges and Libby were greeted by a major in uniform—long belted overcoat, leather boots, gray fur hat. His face was polished and healthy, his eyes ice-blue. "Ah," he said in perfect English, "the wanderers returned. What were you doing—prospecting?" He stared approvingly at Libby. "English?" he asked; and, when she nodded, he said, "I lived in London for a long time. My father was in the Soviet Embassy. I liked it there very much."

Libby said, "I had a flat in Kensington not far from the embassy."

The major smiled, directing all his attention to Libby. "We're a long way from Kensington now." He frowned. "I should lock you up in the station. But if you give me your word you won't try and escape you can stay out here. Not," he added, "that there's much point in escaping." Reluctantly, he turned to Bridges. "You're American, I believe. Do you give me your word you won't try and escape?"

"Sure."

The major looked doubtful. The word of a pretty English girl was one thing: the word of Harry Bridges was another. "Very well," he said after a pause, "I'll take you at your word." He returned to Libby. "We'll have some coffee going soon. Perhaps you'd like to join me? We're under orders not to do anything at all." He gazed ruefully at the carriage perched on the bridge. "Just one shell. . . . But they're very clever," he went on. "How would you feel," he said to Bridges, "if it was the president of the United States up there? They can demand almost anything. But, of course, they'll get killed in the end." To Libby he said, "You look like a Siberian girl, except that they're inclined to be a little plumper than you." He smiled showing a lot of white teeth. "You have a very good figure."

Bridges laughed. "Annette Meakin never had it so good," he said.

They could smell the coffee and they were suddenly very hungry. "Come this way," the major said.

They went into the station. Two orderlies wearing belted tunics snapped to attention. They had made a table out of ammunition boxes and there was black bread, soused fish, fruit, and coffee on them.

"What are you going to do?" Bridges asked as they ate and drank their coffee.

"Wait," the major said. "The decision won't be mine. I suppose," he said, crumbling a slice of black bread, "it will be his," pointing toward the bridge.

"Have you any idea what they want?"

"Your guess is as good as mine. A Jewish exodus, perhaps."

"Maybe," Bridges agreed. "It's kind of sad, though. They're doing more harm than good. The Kremlin was beginning to soften up. These are the last sort of heroes the Jews want. I don't even know whether it will help world opinion. Although I suppose it might—most people admire the Israeli commandoes."

The major poured them more coffee and said,

"But surely, Mr. Bridges, the world needn't know anything about it."

Bridges and the major appraised each other. Bridges was about to reply when the droning they had vaguely been aware of developed into a clattering roar. They went outside and saw a helicopter blotting out the sun. It circled the station, tilted away, then began its descent on the opposite side of the station to the bridge. It sank down gently, its blades throwing up the snow. The major walked toward it, buttoning his coat in case there were any generals on board.

The first passenger to alight was Col. Yury Razin. Neither he nor the major saluted. Army and secret police—the old wary confrontation.

There was a dressing on Razin's neck and his walk was stiff. They greeted each other politely.

Razin said, "Has there been any communication yet?"

"Nothing. We calculate there are about six men in the carriage. They fired a couple of bursts with the Gruyanov at your men." The major smiled faintly. "None of them was hit. What's the plan, colonel?"

"There isn't one," Razin said shortly. "We'll have to wait and see what they want. They sent a radio message to Shilka warning us that if we made any move they'd kill Yermakov. They've packed the bridge with explosives."

"They're smart," the major said, leaving the implication hanging between them that they had outsmarted Razin.

"Is it smart to commit suicide?"

"Terrorists do it every day."

"How have you deployed your men?"

"I've deployed them," the major said flatly. You didn't disclose military information to a policeman.

"How, major?"

"Does it matter?"

Razin's hand strayed to the dressing on the back of his neck. He touched it and winced. He addressed the major coldly, "General Rudenko is flying in from Irkutsk. I spoke to him on the phone this morning."

The major said, "Then I'll tell General Rudenko when he arrives."

"Several members of the presidium are flying out, too."

The major smiled. "Some of your superiors from Moscow as well, Comrade Razin?"

Razin spoke softly. "You're a fool, major, to mix words with me."

"So be it." The major clicked his heels and gave a mocking salute. "I'm breakfasting in the railway station. Please be my guest." He turned on his heel and walked away.

Razin stared after him reflectively. Too young to have learned how to survive. The pain throbbed in his neck and groin. And I am now facing my supreme test.

He signaled to the occupants of the helicopter. The local KGB chief alighted first, followed by Professor David Gopnik and Anna Petrovna, Heroine of the Soviet Union.

15.

"I told you to destroy it." Pavlov stared at the wolf curled up at the end of the carriage. Without total obedience flaws appeared in any military stratagem. So far the plan had gone well, despite the excess of imponderables: a minor infraction like this could ruin everything. "I should have you disciplined," he told the Prospector.

"This isn't the army," the Prospector said, his eyes resentful in his shaggy features. "We're all together in this. We all die together."

"You have a chance," Pavlov said. "If they accept the terms." A pulse beat on his temple. "They release the ten scientists and we hand Yermakov over. Then I offer to stand trial and inevitable execution in exchange for the safe conduct of you and the others."

"Do you think there's a chance they'll accept?" the Planter asked. Now the Pupil was gone he was the weakest link, taking nips of vodka in the bathroom.

Shiller said, "Your desire to die is very commendable."

"Do you doubt my courage?"

"No," Shiller said, "it's not your courage I doubt."

Pavlov ignored him, staring down at the bed of the ravine far below. Not my courage, he thought, my sanity. Something was happening to the computer inside his skull: figures whirled and clicked but the answers were all wrong. As if too much had been fed into it. He took a phial from his pocket and swallowed one of the capsules prescribed long ago when the figures spun too quickly, too brilliantly, so that his pulse-rate stepped up and the adrenalin flowed fast in his veins. They weren't tranquilizers, the doctor had assured him: just a therapy for genius.

He glanced at his wristwatch. They would have Yermakov's decision in two hours. Maybe less. First he had to send a message to the railway station. "Get me a pen and paper," he said to the Planter and, as the Planter stood up, "a bottle of brandy and a glass at the same time." He was aware that Shiller was staring at him.

The wolf twitched and whimpered in its dreams, tearing out another throat.

Pavlov wrote, "To whom it may concern." Then he stopped, staring at the white Kremlin notepaper. He poured himself a shot of Armenian brandy and swallowed it. Tension was swelling inside his head as if a balloon were inflating.

He swiveled from side to side in the leather chair. What had happened to Anna? Did she now know the truth about him? There was, he decided, a faint chance that she didn't. The authorities would be trying to stop any news of the kidnap leaking out. A wave of emotion assailed him. Anna, what have I done to you? He poured himself a generous measure of brandy and pushed the bottle away.

He took the binoculars from the rack and focused them on the station. Five minutes earlier a helicopter had landed behind it; a group of people had gone into the wooden shack but he had only been able to identify Razin. Now he saw Bridges and Libby Chandler standing at the doorway. What would Bridges do with this story? he wondered. Kill it like he'd killed so many stories before? Pavlov not only wanted to get the ten human components of a nuclear bomb out of Russia: he wanted to get the news of his feat out as well. Even if I am dead by the time it reaches the West.

The Planter went into the bathroom. When he came out he looked happier.

Pavlov stared at the sheet of paper, but no words came.

"Having trouble?" Shiller asked.

He wants to take over, Pavlov thought. He's got the scent in his nostrils. He picked up the ball-point pen and began to write; explaining the position, explaining that there would be a message from Yermakov at 2:00 P.M., reiterating that they mustn't take any action until then; if they did . . . Pavlov's thoughts moved to the explosives packed beneath the bridge. The detonating equipment stood at the end of the carriage, by the wolf. He felt like a man scared of heights enticed to the brink of a precipice by the death wish. He fought the compulsion.

"What's the matter?" Shiller asked. "Have you finished it?"

"Finished," Pavlov said, signing the message. "Get Wagstaff."

Shiller went to the cell and knocked on the door. "Time to begin your courier duties," Shiller said as Stanley came out. "You'd better carry a white flag or something."

"And I would like someone to take my photograph," Stanley said. "The newspapers will want one."

Yermakov read the documents through again. They were foolproof. The exact addresses of each Jew. Their anticipated movements today and tomorrow. The departure and ETA's of Aeroflot international flights and, in the case of Jews living away from big cities, the times of domestic flights. Once the planes took off each Jew would be in a Western capital within four hours. At the first reading of the document Yermakov had thought it possible to bluff Pavlov into believing that the ten Jews had been released; but that had been taken care of. In each of the capitals Zionist organizations had been instructed to put fixed-time calls into Moscow. When the calls were received radio messages would be transmitted from Moscow to Siberia; not until the last confirmation had been received on the radio in the special carriage would Yermakov be released.

He still had an hour. Sixty minutes of total honesty with himself. The foreboding, now it had concrete form, had vanished. There were only two possible decisions: Capitulation in which case he would lose face; Defiance in which case he would die.

Yermakov didn't want to die and saw no shame in it. Perhaps it would still be possible to emerge a hero after the release of the Jews. It needed some political thought—scheming, manipulating, delegating uneasy responsibility. The maneuvers of all the world's leaders. In Britain they "reshuffled the cabinet" to get rid of incompetents and dangerous careerists. In America they operated beneath an umbrella of zealous endeavor until the umbrella suddenly collapsed and there was Watergate. We're all the same, he thought, we leaders of men. There was no dishonor in it; all that mattered was what you did with the power you obtained through these methods.

He was surprised by the clarity of his brain after the long nights of doubt. It was as if this forgotten place in Siberia had always been his destination. He poured himself a glass of Narzan, tasting the clean effervescence in his mouth, and stared at the ruff of mountains sharp against the blue sky. What have *I* done with my power? The camps, the interrogations, the executions crowded behind him; but they were no longer guilt; they were a foothold on which the blood had long since dried. Out of the confusion of suffering the Soviet Union had emerged, more stable than any country in the West; more stable, perhaps, than any country in the world.

The question was: Which is the more important for Russia—my continuing leadership in exchange for ten Jews, or my martyrdom? He was still deliberating this when Pavlov came in. "Well?" Pavlov asked.

"I believe I have forty-five more minutes until your ultimatum expires."

Pavlov looked at him curiously. Reluctantly, he conceded respect.

"I should like to wash and shave," Yermakov said. It was almost an order.

"Certainly," Pavlov said. "But you'd better be quick."

"Perhaps I've already made my decision." Yermakov stood up. "In a way, Comrade Pavlov, I admire you. The tragedy is that you're doing your people a great disservice. You see," he said, "you're not a leader of men."

Pavlov led him to the bathroom, leaving the door open, watching Yermakov smooth shaving cream into his stubble, using the safety razor with a steady hand. Yermakov washed his face and hands and said: "And now, Comrade Pavlov, a change of clothes."

As they returned to the sleeper Shiller the Penman observed, "I wonder which of you is really in charge of the situation?"

"Would you please remain outside while I change," Yermakov said to Pavlov.

Pavlov hesitated before agreeing.

Yermakov selected a white shirt and maroon tie which his wife had given him before he left Moscow. His family, he reflected, hadn't entered into his deliberations. Except that they were citizens of the Soviet Union and were therefore embraced in everything he did. It had always been that way and his wife understood. He knotted the tie carefully before selecting a charcoal gray suit from the built-in wardrobe.

Pavlov knocked on the door. "Are you ready?"

"Ready, Comrade Pavlov," Yermakov replied.

From the window of the sleeper Pavlov saw a solitary figure approaching across the snow. The courier returning. He told Yermakov that he would

leave him alone for another five minutes. Then he
went to meet the courier. But it was a substitute:
David Gopnik for Stanley Wagstaff.

"I should kill you," Pavlov said.

"Why don't you then?"

"I wouldn't waste a bullet. A Jew betraying a
Jew!"

"You're betraying every Jew in Russia."

Gopnik and Pavlov faced each other across the
desk. Gopnik didn't seem to care any more.

Pavlov asked, "Why did you do it?"

"Razin knew already. Something about a body
in Novosibirsk."

"And you confirmed it for him. . . ."

"I was going to Khabarovsk. I heard you were
on the train. I knew it wasn't a coincidence. I knew
I had to stop you."

"Why?" Pavlov asked, knowing the answer.

"I told you—because you're destroying everything the Jews, the Democratic movement, is working for."

"Working on their knees," Pavlov said contemptuously. "Why don't they stand up and fight?"

"Because that's not the way. You know that as
well as I do. They have a central committee, they
meet in secret, they're getting the Jews out of Russia. It's working. Why ruin it?" His voice was without emotion, he was like an officer who has sur-
rendered to the enemy.

"Why did they send you here?" Pavlov asked,
again knowing the answer. "To plead, to grovel?"

Gopnik pinched the bridge of his nose. "Of
course. They've made me an offer. You might as
well know—it makes no difference. I didn't get my

exit visa from OVIR. I was told I might get one in three months. Razin has told me that if I persuade you to stop this crazy scheme then I can go now. If I fail then I'll never go. I don't really think I care any more," Gopnik said softly. "I'm only here to plead on behalf of 3 million people."

Pavlov said, "You're here to plead on behalf of yourself." But he knew it wasn't true.

"Believe what you like." Gopnik's face was gray and there was sweat on his narrow forehead. "But I'll tell you this: you're not concerned with the Jews. You're only concerned with Viktor Pavlov, glory-seeker. This is the Pavlov Crusade; it has nothing to do with the Jewish exodus. Viktor Pavlov, hero, martyr, half-Jew. Too scared to admit his Jewishness in case it interfered with the making of a hero. You sneer at the rest of us. Caution, caution. It's you who are the coward, Viktor Pavlov. The very worst kind. Willing to sacrifice anyone or anything on the altar of your vanity."

Pavlov leaned across the desk and hit Gopnik with the back of his hand. Gopnik slipped sideways hitting his head against the window. Shiller watched with interest. Gopnik straightened up; blood was oozing from his nose but he didn't bother to wipe it away; it reached his lips and he licked them.

"Don't tarnish the portrait of a hero," Gopnik said. There were four white marks across his cheek where Pavlov's fingers had landed.

Pavlov stared at him with disgust. "I'm sorry," he said.

Gopnik shrugged. "It doesn't matter."

Shiller brought the bottle of brandy over to the desk. "Another drink, Viktor? You seem a little overwrought."

"When I want a drink," Pavlov said, "I'll ask for

it." He turned to Gopnik. "I'm sorry I hit you. Nothing more. I've no intention of abandoning what I'm doing. And I think Israel should count itself lucky that you won't be going there. It can do without people like you."

The blood was beginning to congeal on Gopnik's face. He spoke quietly. "Believe you me, Viktor Pavlov, Israel can do without men like you. It wants men, not madmen." The weals on his face had turned pink. "Could it be that you see yourself as an Israeli commando? A hero in a combat jacket with an Uzi submachine gun under his arm? Forget it, Viktor. They wouldn't send a man like you to clean the latrines." At last he took a handkerchief from his pocket and dabbed at the blood. "You shouldn't have bothered with Israel," he said. "You should have gone to Hollywood. You would have been a star. . . ."

Pavlov stood up. "Go back to Razin," he said. "Tell him that nothing has changed. Tell him to send Wagstaff back. Tell him your mission has failed."

"I never thought it would succeed. Just remember, hero, that you could be plunging Soviet Jewry back into the Black Years. . . ."

"Get out," Viktor Pavlov said. "If you hadn't betrayed me I would have arranged for you to be out of Russia within forty-eight hours."

From the window he watched Gopnik walking slowly across the snow to the group of figures outside the station. He thought it would have been kinder to have shot him.

The sky still had a polish but it was bruising over the mountains; there was snow dust in the air and the sun had a dark glow to it as if there was fog around.

The message was garbled at first because the technicians were having trouble with the electric megaphone. The words were like melting ice slithering across the no-man's-land between the station and the bridge.

Finally Pavlov recognized Razin's voice. "If you can hear me wave a flag."

Pavlov told Shiller, "Wave a flag."

"Do we care what they have to say?"

"Wave the flag."

"Very well," Shiller said. "If that's the way you want it."

The technicians fixed the megaphone and Razin's voice reached them with frozen clarity. "Viktor Pavlov, you are not the only one holding a hostage. We have your wife."

Nothing more. Just a sharp click.

Shiller said: "Quite an opponent, that Razin. What are you going to do?"

"Do?" Pavlov turned away so that Shiller couldn't see the expression on his face. "Do? We're proceeding as planned, of course."

"But your wife. . . ."

"One person," Pavlov said. "Just one person." Remembering that she was pregnant and it was two people.

After that the messages came at intervals as Razin applied everything he had learned about psychological torture: you don't begin a course with a prolonged application of agony, you apply doses of increasing strength at regular intervals so that the pressure derives from anticipation.

The next message said, "Viktor Pavlov, your wife is bearing up well."

From what? Pavlov poured himself a brandy and paced the corridor. There were fifteen minutes left before his ultimatum expired. Would they torture a pregnant woman? Anna, what have I done to you?

"Viktor Pavlov, your wife is not feeling well. She is asking for you."

A miscarriage? Pavlov poured himself more brandy and Shiller said, "Don't drink too much of that stuff—this is the one day in your life you've got to stay sober."

"Are you trying to say I'm drunk most other days?"

"I'm just advising you not to drink too much today." Shiller picked up the bottle and studied its level. "This threat to your wife. I know how you must feel. . . . Would you like me to take over?"

"No," Pavlov said abruptly. Not after a lifetime of planning for this one day. He waited for the next message.

"Viktor Pavlov, the deadline for your ultimatum expires at 2:00. Our deadline expires at 1:55. If you have not released your hostage by then. . . ." There was a pause. ". . . . I can no longer guarantee the safe custody of your wife."

"An odd way of putting it," Shiller remarked.

"Because they daren't kill her," Pavlov said. Yes, that's it, he told himself, they daren't go through with it. He went to the sleeper. "Have you signed yet?"

"Not yet," Yermakov told him. "Plenty of time yet." He looked very composed, sitting at the table staring at the darkening sky. "Col. Razin has put you on the spot, eh?"

"It will make no difference."

"You're a hard man."

"I'm what Russia has made me."

"And you're proud of your hardness, Comrade Pavlov. But, believe me, no one will remember you as a hero. If you're remembered at all it will be as the man who allowed his wife to die for an insane cause. Not much glory there, Comrade."

"If you've made your decision why don't you sign now?"

"I didn't say I *was* going to sign. I said I had made my decision."

They heard the click of the megaphone and then a woman's voice, "Viktor, it's me, Anna, your wife. Please, Viktor, for my sake, for the sake of Russia, give up this crazy scheme. You're not well. Everyone here understands that. They've promised me that none of you will come to any harm if you abandon it. Please, Viktor, for us, for the baby. . . ." A sob reaching Pavlov across the snow. "They say you have only a few minutes to make up your mind. Then—" she didn't finish the sentence—"Viktor, I love you. . . ."

Pavlov tried to light a cigarette but his hands were shaking too much. He went into the corridor as Razin's voice replaced Anna's.

"Viktor Pavlov if your hostage is not released now you will hear a single shot. I don't have to tell you the target for the bullet."

"Well?" Shiller asked.

"We proceed as planned."

Shiller and the other Zealots watched Pavlov curiously. He went to the cell where Stanley Wagstaff had been locked up and closed the door behind him. He prayed as an atheist prays just before death. *If I forget you, O Jerusalem. . . .* He asked the God he had failed to worship to forgive him. He wept without tears.

A minute later there was a knock on the door. Shiller said, "The Englishman's returned."

"Send him in," Pavlov said.

Stanley Wagstaff came in and Pavlov grabbed him by the lapels. "What's happening? What are they doing to her?"

Stanley Wagstaff said, "We don't know. They've taken her down to the pit-head."

"Are they going to kill her?"

"I don't know," Stanley Wagstaff said. "We only know what you've heard."

Pavlov pushed him away. "Wait outside," he said.

At 1:55 they heard a single shot.

At 1:56 Yermakov signed the documents and Stanley Wagstaff took them back across the snow.

16.

Two men tried to reach the bridge during the next twenty-four hours of waiting while messages authorizing immediate exit visas for the ten Jews were relayed to various cities in the Soviet Union.

The first was Boris Demurin. His motive was obscure. Unknown elements had conspired to wreck the triumphant climax to his career. He had been drinking vodka brought by the troops for most of the day. At six in the evening, with snow pouring steadily from the sky, obscuring the bridge, he decided to die heroically: it was the only thing left for him. Vaguely, without much hope, he thought he might kill the gangsters in the special coach; forty years ago, he remembered, a train driver had fought a gun-battle with four bandits, killing three before getting a bullet between the eyes. They had erected a monument to the driver. Why not a monument, here in the heart of Siberia, for Boris Demurin?

He stuffed the bottle of vodka inside his blouse and tied down the ear-flaps of his *shapka*. No one took much notice of him—an ancient, drunken train-driver. Why should they? The two soldiers standing guard outside the station asked him where he was going. "For a piss," Demurin told them. "Watch you don't trip over it," one of them said. "You piss icicles out here."

But Demurin didn't feel cold. He wore his felt boots, worn fur gloves, thick blouse, and trousers stuffed with paper. The cold was his friend, the breath of Siberia. There were scars on his face from frostbite which had nipped him many years ago; but now, if he felt the familiar numbness, he rubbed the skin with snow and the blood started to circulate again.

Almost immediately he was lost, lurching away from the track, snow caking his face and covering his eyes. He pawed it away with gloved hands and took a long swig of vodka. He wasn't scared; the pioneer railwaymen had faced worse than this—building camps in blizzards, awakened at night by the crack of bolts on the track snapping in the cold. Boris Demurin, pioneer, marched groggily on hearing the wail and thunder of an old 0-6-6-0 Mallet, hearing the clank of convicts' chains.

He stumbled, falling into a drift; got to his feet grinning. Taking another swig of vodka, he thought: The Trans-Siberian, the railway they said we couldn't build. The British, the Americans, all sneering. Until it was done and suddenly Russia was a power, a menace, a threat to their trade, linking east with west.

How many derailments had there been? How many bridges had collapsed? How many deaths? How many sacrifices?

When Boris Demurin was in Moscow he often visited the Armory Museum inside the Kremlin, to see the collection of eggs created by Peter Carl Fabergé. One egg in particular—the Great Siberian Easter Egg made in 1900. It was fashioned from green, blue, and yellow enamel with the route of the railway traced in silver. If you touched the Imperial eagle surmounting it, the top came off to reveal a scale model of a train about one foot long, five cars and a gold and platinum engine with a ruby for a light; if you wound it with a gold key the engine pulled the coaches.

That's the sort of monument I would like, Boris Demurin thought. Hero of the Soviet Union. Why not? He was in the pine wood now, all sound muffled by the snow. If I meet a bear, he thought, I'll dance with it. His face ached with the cold but he rejoiced with it.

Where the hell was the bridge?

He veered to the right before resting on a log. The snow wasn't falling so thickly now, the foliage of the trees taking most of it. There was a burning pain in one of his legs and, when he struck out from the pine wood into the thick snow, he limped. Eventually he came to the pit-head where they had taken Pavlov's wife. Whatever had happened there, the snow had covered the evidence. He rested in the hut remembering that the track ran alongside it. He took another nip of vodka before setting out again, dragging his leg behind him. He stumbled against metal, cleared away the snow, and saw the rusty line. Was the bridge ahead or behind him? He shook his head, it was as if his skull was full of snow. He touched his cheek with his gloved hand, but all sensation had gone from it. To hell with it, he thought: it took more than a touch of frostbite to deter a pioneer.

Clutching the almost empty bottle to his chest, he set off along the line. The snow was a white wall and thus he almost walked into the wrecked hulk looming in front of him. Boris Demurin stared at it in disbelief. He brushed some of the snow away. It was the E 723 2-8-0. The boiler had burst and the engine's body was splayed into flaps and daggers of torn metal. Demurin had once driven one of these engines and it seemed to him as if it had been brought to him wounded.

The footplate was still intact and he climbed on to it, brushing the snow from the controls. He put the bottle to his lips but it was empty. Flinging the bottle away, he leaned out and gazed down the track, seeing it straight and gleaming new, seeing smoke and cinders fly past; the track, he knew, led to the beginning of the end.

He took off his fur *shapka* and stayed like that, the snow settling on his hair. That was how they found him.

The second man to make for the bridge was Harry Bridges.

Before he went he told Libby what he was going to do. She told him he was crazy and he agreed with her.

They were huddled together in a corner of the station watched by one soldier sitting beside the incandescent stove with a submachine gun on his knees. They had tested him with English and decided he didn't know any; just the same they talked in whispers. Stanley Wagstaff and Gopnik had been taken to a tent.

"I knew I'd have to make a decision on this journey," Bridges told her. "I've just made it. Time I was a reporter again."

She held his hand under the gray army blanket. "You'll never make it. It's pitch dark and snowing. You'll get lost. If you don't you'll either get shot by the troops or Pavlov's men."

"Can you imagine it? An interview with Yermakov while he's being held hostage?"

"Yes," Libby Chandler said, "I can imagine it. But you'll never live to write it."

"You're talking like I've been thinking." He stroked her arm and her breasts beneath the blanket. "I thought you wanted someone to admire."

"I want someone alive to admire."

"I'll survive," Bridges said. "I always do."

She held his hand to her breast. "Why do you have to do it, Harry?"

"Because everything you said about me was right. Now they've killed Pavlov's wife . . . I have to go. I have to do something."

"You don't know that they killed her. We only heard the shot."

"That's something I could do. Find out if they did. Take the news to Pavlov. Here"—he felt in the pocket of his overcoat—"take this back. Just in case. . . ." He slipped her the microfilm under the blanket.

"Don't go, Harry," she said. "Please don't go."

"I'll come back. It's not as dangerous as you think. They aren't geared to security. Only a madman would try to escape."

"But what about the madmen on the bridge?"

"I figure Pavlov will want the news spread.

Heroes don't like to die unsung. Not his breed of hero."

"If they realize who you are they might shoot you before you get there."

"They can't see too much in the snow," Bridges assured her. "I'll be able to see them but they won't be able to see me."

"What are you trying to prove, Harry? You told me you wouldn't be able to get the story out."

"There's always a way," he said. "I once knew a guy who filed a whole story in five-word takes. He was in a city where they were censoring all phone calls. His office got each of their bureaus all over the world to put calls into him. Each time they came on he got five words over before the operator cut him off. Each bureau then filed the five words back to the head office and there was a complete story."

"It would be more difficult," Libby Chandler remarked, "to get a story out of jail."

Bridges said, "Kiss me. If you kiss me just as I get up to go it will look as if I'm not returning."

She kissed him, clinging to him.

He smiled at her. "Dinner in London? I'll take you to some of the pubs in Fleet Street. Then maybe New York. I'll take you out to Bear Mountain. . . ."

"I love you," she said.

He left her and spoke to the guard who shrugged, pointing to the door. Bridges used the same pretext as Demurin; but this time one of the soldiers went with him behind the station. The soldier, not expecting anyone to try and escape in the middle of Siberia in the dark in a blizzard, selected his own tree and began to urinate. Bridges edged away in the darkness, then ran. He heard a shout but it was gagged by the snow. Then he was away. He made for the tent where Razin had set up his H.Q.

It was heavily guarded but he thought he heard a woman's voice. He skirted the camp ringed with Gruyanovs and Katyusha rocket launchers, heading in the direction of the pit-head, hoping then to cut sharp right to the bridge which was directly opposite the trees.

He pulled the fur flaps of his hat over his ears, tying the laces under his chin. He buttoned his coat up to his neck, stuck his gloved hands in his pocket, thanked God for the sealskin boots bought in Montreal. The snow poured steadily down; he thought the chances of reaching the bridge were remote.

By the time he reached the pine wood the cold had found its way inside his clothes. He stopped just inside the wood and rubbed snow into his face. After a few minutes his cheeks began to burn. You saved your face that time, he thought. His fingers ached and there were tears of ice at the corners of his eyes. Now all he had to do was turn right and he was bound to reach the track, provided he kept going in a straight line.

He set out again, head bowed into the snow, a blind man. After ten minutes he began to wonder if he had kept in a straight line. If he hadn't then he could be walking into the barrels of the Red Army guns. He peered at his luminous watch; it was fifteen minutes since he left the wood. No tracks, no bridge. The cold was reaching his feet through the sealskin and the collar of his coat was iced up from his breath. His face was going numb again and he rubbed more snow in it; this time it took longer to thaw. He remembered a girl friend in Moscow whose legs still bore the purple scars of frost-bite.

He was whispering to himself, reassuring himself. He found he was scared of the black snow-flying night which could bury you. Here lies Harry Bridges, one-time journalist, part-time defector. He stumbled on until he noticed that the ground in front of him fell away. He took another step forward. "Jesus!" he exclaimed. He was staring into the ravine spanned by the bridge. He backed away, like a dog scared of a cat. To his right he saw a yellow glow. He moved toward it until the outline of the carriage on the bridge became clear.

He approached the carriage from the end that wasn't protected by the Gruyanov. The lights stabbed the darkness until the snow cut them off. He slipped several times on the rails buried by the snow before he finally reached the carriage. He hauled himself up to the first door and banged on the window.

He saw a face peering through the window. Then the door opened and Bridges stared into the barrel of a pistol.

They gave him coffee and brandy and rubbed his face. "Like bringing back a man from the dead to hang him," Shiller remarked.

Bridges sipped his coffee, choked over his brandy. "I once covered a story like that," he said. "The former Turkish prime minister. Took an overdose of drugs. They got a stomach pump to him, then executed him."

"What do you want?" Pavlov asked. "Not another courier from Razin?"

Bridges shook his head. His cheeks were glowing again and his feet ached as the blood began to circulate. "No requests from Razin. I assigned myself this story."

Pavlov said, "Anna. Is she alive?"

"I don't know," Bridges said. "She might be. I

heard a woman's voice in Razin's tent." He saw the hope on Pavlov's face and was happy.

Shiller said contemptuously: "Assigned yourself a story? You wouldn't report a traffic offense if you thought it would get you into trouble."

"Times have changed," Bridges said.

Shiller said, "It's some kind of a trick."

The Pederast said, "We should kill him." He looked hopefully at Pavlov.

"Look at it this way," Bridges said, reaching for the brandy bottle. "Would I have risked escaping and wandering through a blizzard by myself if I wasn't after a story? What harm can I do? You're all doomed and you know it. You might as well take me on trust. There's just a chance that I can let the world know what you've done."

They looked at him doubtfully until Pavlov said: "He's right—he can't do any harm."

"And," said Shiller softly, "he could make sure of your place in the history books."

"The world should know what we've done," Pavlov said. "The world should know what we've done for Israel."

"What exactly have you done for Israel?" Bridges asked.

"I'll let you know," Pavlov told him, "when we get confirmation."

Bridges peeled off his *shapka* and gloves, showering snow on to the floor. "I'd like to see your hostage."

Pavlov shrugged. "Why not?"

They went to the sleeper where Yermakov was sitting at the table drinking Narzan water and writing letters on Kremlin notepaper. He didn't look up.

Pavlov said, "A visitor for you."

Yermakov finished a sentence before looking up.

Bridges noted that his eyes were clearer, that he wore authority like a favorite suit. "Who are you?"

"An American journalist."

"Bridges?"

"That's right," Bridges replied with surprise.

"And you want to interview me?"

Bridges nodded.

"It usually takes three months of applications."

"I know," Bridges agreed. "And then we don't get the interview."

"You are a resourceful man," Yermakov said. "Not the man I was led to believe you were."

Whatever else he might be, Bridges thought, he is a leader. He looked like a man who had just fought and won some sort of battle, not a man held at gunpoint over an explosive charge that would distribute his body over the ravine with one downward plunge of the detonator.

Yermakov folded the letter. "To my family," he explained. "In case anything goes wrong. . . ." He glanced at his watch. "It's getting late. I only grant interviews in the morning. Try again after these lunatics have served me breakfast." He turned his back: the audience was over.

"And now," Pavlov said when they were outside, "I propose to lock you up in the cell. You can start writing your story. God knows how you can ever get it out of Russia, though."

"There is a way," Bridges said.

It stopped snowing at three in the morning. Five minutes later the carriage was illuminated with a glaring white light. Slitting his eyes together, the Pederast killed the searchlight with one shot from his AK 47.

17.

The major was cheerful. He brought hard-boiled eggs from the field kitchen and an orderly brought coffee, bread, and fruit. Libby guessed he chose his meal times so that he could be alone with her. She asked him what was happening and he gave her some vague, cheerful answers. The worse the situation the chirpier he became. He asked her where Bridges had gone and when she said she didn't know he replied, "It can only be there"—pointing toward the bridge.

"Do you think he made it?"

The major sliced off the top of his egg. "Perhaps. Who knows?" He dug into the egg with a plastic teaspoon. "Are you very fond of Mr. Bridges?"

"I respect him."

"Then you've changed your ideas."

"You're very observant."

"I'm sensitive to atmosphere. Especially when it is the atmosphere surrounding a beautiful woman."

"You did say your father was in the diplomatic corps?"

The major grinned, eyes bright blue and healthy. "I'm a Siberian. We're romantic people. Siberia is full of romance and sorrow. Did you ever hear the story of the French engineer's daughter who became engaged to a Russian at Krasnoyarsk?"

Libby said she hadn't. She tried to eat but the bread was dry in her mouth. She sipped her coffee, staring through the open doorway toward the bridge.

"Her father built a bridge for the Great Siberian Railway there. She was given a set or earrings made from Siberian diamonds as a wedding present. The wedding was arranged for the same day as the opening of the bridge. But, to wear the earrings, she had to have her ears pierced. She got an infection and died on her wedding day. It is said that every true Siberian weeps when he passes over that bridge."

Watching him through the steam from her coffee, Libby thought it unlikely that the major had ever wept in his life. She asked what had happened to Pavlov's wife.

The major was vague. "She has been dealt with," he said. "That's all I can tell you. Perhaps Colonel Razin will enlighten you. He's in charge of security." He implied that this accounted for the lack of security.

"What happens now?" Libby asked.

"We wait. There's nothing else to do. It would seem that Comrade Yermakov has no wish to be a martyr. Why should he? He's worth ten Jews. A hundred, a thousand. . . . Why should we keep them here, anyway? Clothing them, feeding them. I think we should let them all go. Send 3 million Russian Jews to Israel. How would Israel like that?"

"Are you anti-Semitic?"

"Of course not." The major decapitated his second egg. "I'm pro-Russian, that's all. As a matter of fact I'm pro-Israeli, too." He didn't bother to lower his voice. "As a soldier I must be. Since when has the world seen such a fine army? And why?—because they're fighting for their existence. I would be proud to fight with the Israelis."

"Then why are you against the Jews who want to leave Russia for Israel?"

"Because they're Russians," the major said shortly, peeling an apple with a clasp knife. "But let's talk of other things," he said, quartering the apple and handing the segments to Libby. "It's very pleasant, you and I being alone here together."

"You, me, and about 500 soldiers."

"Together in this building," the major went on. "Think of its history. The romance of gold. The greeds and passions that existed here as the men waited to get back to civilization. As men arrived hoping for their pot of gold only to find that the seam had been worked out." He poured them more coffee. "Perhaps you will return to Russia when you've finished this trip? Perhaps we could meet in Moscow or Leningrad? I can always save my leave. . . ."

"Perhaps," Libby said. "Anything's possible."

The major sighed. "But you're in love with Bridges. The Americans. . . . They seem to be our rivals in everything." He summoned the orderly and said something in Russian which Libby didn't understand. The orderly left the station building.

The major said: "There will be a lot of saluting later today. A lot of very important gentlemen are coming from Moscow, including"—the thought seemed to please him—"Colonel Razin's superior officer. Although," he added meditatively, "I expect Razin is a match for him. He has survived a long time. But he's got a lot to talk himself out of this time." He finished his coffee and lit a cigarette. "If it wasn't for his sort, Germany would rule the world today. If they'd let the generals handle the war they would have won it."

The orderly returned carrying a pair of gray Zeiss field binoculars. "The spoils of war," the major commented. He took them to the doorway and stared through them toward the bridge, rotating the focusing mechanism. "Ah," he said, "there is our beloved leader eating a hearty breakfast. I must say I admire that man." He continued to stare through the field glasses, looking not unlike Rommel. "Here." He beckoned Libby. "You have a look."

Libby took the field glasses but at first the carriage was a blur. "Here." The major came to her aid, putting his arms around her from behind, fiddling with the focus. "Now try." He stayed with his arms round her. "Try the last compartment," he advised. Libby panned along the carriage until she found Bridges standing at the window.

The major withdrew his arms. He grinned saying, "I think I've just canceled a date in Leningrad."

Libby kissed him happily. "You're very sweet," she said.

The two helicopters arrived at 10:00 carrying ten men in civilian uniform—long, dark coats with square shoulders, gray scarves, *shapkas*. Even their faces had a uniformity about them: flinty, wary, composed. The men from the Kremlin climbed down from the helicopters, standing together beneath the lazy blades, as if they were waiting to take their places on the platform in Red Square. Among them was the young careerist threatening Yermakov's authority. They were escorted to a long white snow tent equipped with field stoves, insulated against the cold.

General Rudinko and the major went to one tent, and Anatoly Baranov and Razin went to another.

"Well?" said Anatoly Baranov, unofficial head of the KGB. "What explanation have you to offer?"

"I don't have an explanation," Razin said calmly. "I can give you an account of what happened."

An orderly brought lemon tea which he placed on the packing case between the two men. Razin appraised his superior: lanky body, bony head, pale eyes, a monocle would have suited him, he thought. Razin knew that he was now fighting for his career, possibly his life. He was fortified by the knowledge that Baranov was a little scared of him—his relationship with Yermakov, his past association with Beria whose name still engendered fear.

Baranov sipped his tea, crooking his little finger. "I think an explanation is more in order, Comrade Razin. Although I can't see any possible excuses for this . . . this debacle."

"Perhaps when you've heard what I have to say. . . ."

"I'm waiting, Comrade Razin."

"Are the Jews being released?"

Baronov nodded. "We had no choice—thanks to your handling of the affair."

"In that case Yermakov will walk out alive."

"Can you guarantee that? What's to prevent them killing him after they've achieved their object?"

"A lot," Razin said, rationing his information so that, subtly, he dominated the conversation.

Baranov drummed his fingers impatiently on the packing case. "Please continue, Comrade Razin. So far you've said nothing that impresses me."

"They won't kill him," Razin said, "because we shall broadcast a message to them threatening that, if any harm comes to Comrade Yermakov, then exit visas for every Jew wanting to leave Russia will be stopped. Then they would be traitors to their cause rather than heroes." Razin's hand strayed to the bruise on his neck.

Baranov stood up and strode around the tent, hands behind his back. "Very well, I accept that Comrade Yermakov will probably be released. Now let's hear your explanation—your account—of why you let this disastrous situation arise."

Razin allowed a smile to crease his face; Baranov noticed it and frowned. "I allowed it to happen," Razin said slowly and deliberately, "because you authorized the presence of Viktor Pavlov on the train. You, Comrade Baranov, authorized a ticket for a mongrel Jew on the same train as Comrade Yermakov."

Baranov turned on his heel, muscles working in his jaw. "Don't try and threaten me."

"That's your interpretation," Razin said. He almost felt sorry for this lanky, ruthless man who had never fully learned the rules of survival. Rule No. 1: Never aspire to the top because the fall is precipitous, often fatal. Far better to be a gray eminence.

He went on, "I have the document bearing your signature. The signature taking full responsibility for what has happened."

Baranov sat down abruptly, his face gray. "Do you have the document with you?"

"Of course not."

"I authorized the ticket on the instructions of certain members of the presidium."

You fool, Razin thought. He said, "Do you think they will admit that?"

Baranov's expression showed he didn't believe any such thing.

"Anyway," Razin said, "I'm happy that you've arrived to take command of this . . . this debacle. I hope to learn a lot from your techniques."

He strode out into the sunlight leaving Baranov hunched over the packing case. The sun was bright, the sky was blue, and snow dust was suspended in the air like gossamer.

There is just a chance, Razin thought, that I shall survive once again. He had one more weapon: the tape of the conversation on the train in which Yermakov instructed him to take no action against Bridges or Pavlov. It was even possible that Yermakov would appreciate the initiative of a man prepared to bug the desk of a Kremlin leader. Razin had one fear: that, as a result of the "debacle," he would get Baranov's job.

He picked up the megaphone and warned Pavlov and his men that if any harm befell Yermakov no more exit visas would be issued to any Jews.

From her handbag Libby Chandler took a hand mirror. She slipped it into the pocket of her coat and approached the two white-clad soldiers at the door making the same request which Demurin and Bridges had made before her. The guards nodded—

they had taken advice on this eventuality—they took her handbag containing all her papers and let her retire to a cluster of bushes to one side of the station.

Libby reached the bushes, breathing deeply of the pure sharp air. Taking the mirror from her handbag, she began to flash it in the direction of the bridge, hoping Bridges had been a Boy Scout. She had briefly been a Girl Guide and she frowned trying to send the message HARRY ARE YOU ALL RIGHT MY LOVE QUERY.

She stepped out from behind the bushes so that he would be able to see her through binoculars. Nothing happened for a few minutes. She was about to transmit again when the flashing began in the compartment where she had seen him. She thought it said AM FINE MISS——She had trouble deciphering the next word which she thought would be YOU. Instead it began with an M. MY KIN? Perhaps it was some sort of code—he wanted a message relayed to someone in America. A wife? MY KIN? Then she understood: MEAKIN. She smiled, wishing she were with him.

Razin said "Who's Miss Meakin?"

Libby swung round guiltily. Then she said, "You never give up, do you?"

"Never," Razin agreed. But there was a smile on his heavy features.

She told him about Annette Meakin.

"You have a lot in common with her," he said when she had finished. He shook his large head. "You British . . . I sometimes wish we were on the same side." He took her arm. "Shall we return to the station?"

They walked back, feet sinking deep in the snow.

"It would seem," he said, "that Mr. Bridges has undergone a change of heart. He's acting like a man again. . . ."

Libby interrupted. "He was never a coward."

"I didn't say he was. Just misguided. He would have found a retreat here but never a home. That's what they all find when they escape to Moscow. No one admires a defector. In fact," Razin said thoughtfully, "you could say that Mr. Bridges was a courageous man even to contemplate staying here because he knew what it would be like. He knew the Philbys and the Macleans: he knew what sort of hell they have created for themselves."

"What will happen to him?" Libby asked.

"Ah." Razin patted her hand. "I can't answer that. There are more important people around than myself." He didn't sound as if he believed it. "He will be fairly treated. That's all I can promise you." They were almost at the station. "But, more important, what will happen to you?"

"I shall go to Japan."

"And await the arrival of Bridges? It might be a long wait, Miss Chandler." He paused. "That is, if we allow you to continue your journey."

"You can't stop me," Libby said. She stopped, pulling her arm away. "I'm a British subject and all my papers are in order."

"I doubt it. In the first place your visa is only valid for your journey across Siberia. By the time you reach Nakhodka that will have expired. We would be perfectly within our rights in detaining you."

Libby turned on him angrily. "It isn't my fault that I've been delayed because you allowed Yermakov to be kidnapped."

Razin shrugged. "Not your fault, I agree. But

you see, Miss Chandler, the Soviet authorities won't want the world to know about this bizarre episode. Now there are only three people who can leak the information—Bridges, Stanley Wagstaff, and yourself. Bridges can be taken care of quite easily. Wagstaff can be detained on suspicion of spying. That leaves you. What are we to do?"

"If you keep me in Russia there will be protests at international level. . . ."

"We've survived many such protests," Razin interrupted. "They don't bother us too much. No country goes to war over one missing person. What happens? Maybe Britain expels a few diplomats. We do the same. The world loses interest. The two countries continue as before because they need each other." Razin opened the door of the station and ushered Libby inside. "Sometimes, of course, it emerges that the missing people have met with an accident. No one can argue. Especially," Razin said, removing the smile from his face, "in the middle of Siberia."

He closed the door behind him.

Libby sat down trembling. In her pocket she felt the microfilm. If they wanted an excuse to detain her there it was.

18.

The eagle hovered above the bridge watching the activity below curiously. It had been flying for two hours, its great wings splayed out and turned up, yellow talons trailing beneath its square tail. During the blizzard it had rested under a ledge in the mountains where only a powdering of snow reached it; then, when the sun rose, it had taken off, soaring and gliding exultantly in its blue kingdom. Now it floated, looking for prey, diverted by the movements of humans in an area where it usually found vermin.

Several of the humans watched it, finding their own symbolism in its flight.

Bridges stopped writing in his notebook to watch the eagle. He wanted to write what he wished, unshackelled, uncensored; he was contemptuous of the Harry Bridges who had ever thought otherwise. He sat down again with the notebook, writing with a ball-point, linking his words together with sprawling loops. *Dateline: Panhandle, Somewhere in Siberia. For forty-eight hours Zionist extremists held hostage. . . .*

He sucked the tip of the pen to make the ink run smoothly. Yermakov had refused him an interview, but it didn't matter. He was here, the only journalist. What was it they used to say? Reporting is 90 percent luck, 10 percent knowing what to do with it. The story had been delivered to him; now he had to work on his luck. As he wrote he paused occasionally, thinking of Libby Chandler; when he did so the eagle soared away to a white, clapboard house overlooking the Hudson.

In another compartment Vasily Yermakov also watched the eagle. It took him across the snow to the station, back along the long ribbon of track to Moscow, to his family—to the Kremlin where, he thought, the knives would be out. Vasily Yermakov—hero or coward? How could a man who had bartered his life for ten Jews command respect?

Yermakov had no doubt about the outcome of the in-fighting. He would survive. Only if he *was* a coward would his enemy and his followers triumph. But Siberia and the threat of death had worked a therapy on him. The specters of the night had retreated: the future was clear-cut. Siberia, Yermakov thought, is what I have achieved, Russia's future as glittering as its diamonds.

From the tent he shared with David Gopnik Stanley Wagstaff watched the eagle. He flew with it from the labor camp in Siberia where he expected to serve a sentence of about three years to a press conference in Manchester. *"Photographers first, please. I will give you a short account of my experiences and then answer your questions."* He hoped the camp would be close to the railway.

For David Gopnik the eagle flew from the bright blue sky into the gentle light of a synagogue. He heard the singing of the cantor and choir, saw the rabbi holding the Scroll of Law pass by. He took his place beside the old men in their prayer shawls, read from his prayer book, gazed upon the Ark. Over the years he would continue to campaign for his release; a hundred applications maybe, until he was as old as the autumn-faced worshippers. His campaign was a word of a verse of a chapter of a book of suffering; it was merely that it hadn't been ordained that he should live in the era when suffering and patience finally triumphed. He was filled with melancholy that wasn't far removed from peace. David Gopnik knew that the synagogue was his Jerusalem.

Viktor Pavlov's wife observed the eagle and it was her son who would live in Siberia and never be told that he had Jewish blood in his veins.

Col. Yury Razin shielded his eyes to watch the eagle dive and level out above the bridge. A bird of prey that had mastered the laws of survival. He grinned fiercely.

For Libby Chandler the eagle flew east, across the ocean to Japan, across more oceans and continents, on and on, until she found Harry Bridges waiting for her.

Viktor Pavlov noticed the eagle as it dived for its prey. He followed its descent until it vanished behind the pine trees.

19.

It was the tenth day since the Trans-Siberian left Moscow station. The first radio message came through at 11:15 P.M. A nuclear physicist named Mikhail Altman had arrived safely in Vienna from Moscow on a TU 134 Flight SU 081 at 5:00 P.M.

The Planter took the news to Pavlov who was sitting at the desk staring into the night. It was very still outside and the sky was deep with stars. Pavlov hardly reacted; he looked very strange, the Planter thought, eyes staring at some distant, invisible object, a vein throbbing at his temple.

The Planter ticked Altman's name on the list spread on the desk in front of Pavlov. "Only nine to go," he said. "By midday tomorrow the whole operation should be over." He consulted his wristwatch. "Just over twelve hours."

Pavlov looked at him with bloodshot eyes. "Do you want to die?" he asked.

The Planter began to tremble. "No. But I'm prepared to—for the cause."

"I'm prepared to die."

"None of us has ever doubted that."

"Then you think it is all worthwhile?"

He's looking for reassurance, the Planter realized with astonishment. "Of course," he said, trying to control the breathlessness in his voice. "Otherwise we wouldn't be here. We are sacrificing ourselves. . . ."

"This is what I propose to do. When we receive the last confirmation on the radio you and the other three can leave. I'll hold Yermakov until 2 o'clock as agreed. That will give you two hours. A chance, nothing more."

"Very well. I'll take that chance." The Planter's voice faltered. "I'm not as much of a hero as I thought I was."

Pouring himself some brandy, Pavlov said, "At least you're not insane. A crazy half-breed. If only I had been wholly Jewish. But then," Pavlov said thoughtfully, "neither you nor I might have been here."

"I don't understand you," the Planter said. He wondered if Shiller should take over. "You're not making sense."

"Perhaps Gopnik was right. Perhaps I am betraying the Jews of Russia."

The Planter shook his head desperately. "Don't say that, Viktor. Not now. Not when everything is beginning to work out. . . ."

"Gopnik said they would cancel all the exit visas. . . ."

The Planter looked relieved. "They'll never do that. America won't cooperate if they do. They need American aid."

"Supposing," Pavlov went on, "the Israelis already have the atom bomb. There have been rumors. . . ."

"There have also been rumors that they have the cure for cancer. You don't believe that, do you?"

"I don't know what I believe," Pavlov said.

He reminded the Planter of an incurably sick man questioning the life behind him. The Planter said quietly, "If you talk like this then you're betraying *us.*"

"Everything is betrayal," Pavlov said. "We all betray each other in some way or another."

The Planter guessed he was thinking of his wife and told him, "I think she's alive. Bridges said he thought he heard a woman's voice. Who else could it be?"

"Perhaps it would have been better for her to die."

The Planter removed the brandy bottle. "You're drinking too much. Like me."

"Perhaps. What docs it matter. You might as well die drunk as sober."

The Planter decided to consult Shiller.

At 1:00 A.M. on the eleventh day they received a message from Geneva. Two scientists had arrived safely from Leningrad.

Shiller stood over Pavlov and said, "I'm taking over."

"You always wanted to," Pavlov said, looking up from the swivel chair. "You've left it a bit late."

"You're not in a fit state to continue," Shiller said contemptuously. "You've lost your nerve."

"Have I?" Pavlov rubbed the pulse on his temple, trying to quiet it. "Is there anything wrong with being a coward? Only cowards can be brave, Shiller."

"There's a difference in being a coward and losing your nerve. A coward can still lead men but a man who's lost his nerve can't."

"So what are you going to do? Take away my general's stars? Lock me in the cell with Bridges? Throw me in the ravine?" He shook his head. "It's you who haven't the nerve. If you had you would have challenged my leadership years ago. Not wait until you think I'm drunk, sick. . . ."

"I have the courage to die."

"Many cowards commit suicide."

Shiller's hand moved toward the pistol in his belt but Pavlov fired first from the automatic he had been holding under the briefcase on his lap. The bullet threw Shiller against the door of the compartment where Bridges was imprisoned. He slid down the door into a sitting position, his muddy features a ruin of blood and bone.

The explosion filled the carriage, forcing needles of pain into Pavlov's eardrums. He swung round in the swivel chair as Yermakov, the Planter, the Prospector, and the Pederast came into the corridor. "Be warned," Pavlov shouted. "That goes for all of you." He waved the automatic at the Pederast. "Get rid of that"—pointing at Shiller's body—"and keep away from the Gruyanov."

Bridges shouted, "What the hell's going on?"

No one answered him.

The Pederast said, "You should have let me do that." There was disappointment in his voice. He opened a door and pushed Shiller's body toward it; then he stood back and, with one foot, pushed the corpse into the ravine. They waited for the sound of the body hitting the ground; but they heard nothing.

It was as if Shiller had dispatched into a bottomless well. Or hell, Pavlov thought.

In his sleeping bag in the tent he shared with Baranov, Razin heard the shot.

Baranov sat up awkwardly. "What was that?"

"I should imagine," Razin said, "that the thieves are falling out."

By 11:00, with one hour to go, messages had been received confirming the arrival of nine scientists in various European capitals. None of the radio operators transmitting the messages—nor the scientists themselves—knew the circumstances of the Soviet change-of-heart; nor did they know why they had to confirm arrival. Each scientist was told to meet at a certain table in the Dan Hotel, Tel Aviv, at 11:30 A.M. on Thursday, November 1. They knew each other, Pavlov had reasoned, and when they met they would realize that, together, they were the human elements of a nuclear bomb; Israel's warhead of the future gathered around a single hotel table.

Pavlov sat with his back to the window, automatic on the desk beside him. He hadn't eaten and his head ached. He had been awake all night and, despite the imminence of death, his eyes were heavy with sleep. Once or twice his head jerked forward; but he awoke immediately, hand reaching for the gun. But no one seemed to be trying to overcome him; there wasn't much point any more.

At 11:10 Pavlov told the Planter to send a message over the radio to Shilka for immediate transmission to the field headquarters beside the railway station. "Tell them," Pavlov said, "that Comrade Vasily

Yermakov will walk free from the carriage at 2:00 provided three men are granted free passage from the coach at 12:00. If I hear any shots then I'll blow the bridge." Pavlov glanced at the detonator. "Tell them this only applies when I've received the last message from"—he consulted the list—"from London."

The Planter went to the radio and sent the message.

Ten minutes later they heard a voice over the megaphone. A new voice. "All right, Pavlov, we agree to your demands."

"So," Pavlov said, weighing the automatic in his hand, "you stand half a chance. If you can make it back to Irkutsk the Priest may be able to help you. You have," he went on, "about the same chance as the *brodyagi* in the old days. Except that they were helped by the peasants. Even then they usually gave themselves up—or fell asleep in the snow. The winter is your friend and your enemy. It will hamper pursuit but it may take your life. Don't go north—the cold will take the flesh off you." Pointing across the ravine, he went on, "Don't head that way. They've got troops there, too. You can just see them through the binoculars. You can try for the coast, if you like, and stow away on a fishing boat. Your chances are minimal. Finally," Pavlov said, "pray for snow. You've only got a two-hour start. Should any of you reach Moscow contact Semenov the Policeman—he'll fix you up with papers."

The effort to speak had exhausted Pavlov. He rested his head on his hand, feeling his eyelids sag over his eyes.

The Prospector said to the other two, "Stay with me. I know Siberia as much as any man can ever know it. I can survive. Me and the dog." The wolf wagged its tail, showing its teeth. "He has already saved us once," the Prospector said.

Pavlov thought: There's something I've forgotten. His computer had completely seized up; times, figures, schedules spinning wildly. Then he remembered: Bridges. "Bring the American to me," he said.

When Bridges appeared he asked: "Have you written your story?"

"Most of it. Except that I don't know the end."

"Show it to me."

"A good newspaperman never allows his copy to be vetted."

"Give it to me."

Bridges shook his head.

"You used not to have such scruples."

"Times have changed."

Pavlov made a weary gesture. "I suppose it doesn't matter. You can hardly distort what's happened here."

Bridges, astonished at the change in Pavlov, said, "No distortion. Just as it happened."

"How have you described me?"

"Does it matter?"

"A condemned man's wish."

"How do you want to be described? Guerilla? Freedom fighter? Terrorist? They all amount to the same thing. It just depends which side's doing the describing."

"How about commando?" Pavlov smiled. "Yes, commando. I would like that. Zionist commando."

"Okay," Bridges told him. "Commando it is." He wrote in his notebook.

"We've both changed, eh, Mr. Bridges?"

"I guess so."

"You for the better, me. . . ." Pavlov pushed

aside the automatic; no one was going to shoot him now. "God," he said, "I feel tired."

"Just one thing," Bridges said. "How do you figure I'm going to get out of here to send the story?"

"I hadn't thought of that," Pavlov said.

"You'd better send another message on the radio."

Pavlov called the Planter. "Send another message to Shilka. Tell them Bridges, the American correspondent, will be coming across in ten minutes."

"Thanks," Bridges said. When the ten minutes were up he put on his coat and fur hat and extended his hand. "What do I say? Good luck? All the best?"

"Don't say anything," Pavlov told him. "Just go —while you can."

Bridges walked along the bridge on to the far side of the ravine. The day was bright again with the sky shedding a few flakes of snow. He fancied he saw the muzzles of the Gruyanovs moving outside the railway station. He walked toward them thinking that one burst would solve the problem of what to do with the story.

When he was 100 yards from the guns in their nests of packed snow Libby broke free from the guards and ran toward him, crying and laughing, her long blonde hair flowing behind her. He took her in his arms, feeling her cold cheeks against his. "Oh Harry," she said. "Oh Harry."

He kissed her, loved her. Behind them he saw Razin approaching. He slipped the notebook into her coat pocket with the microfilm. "Listen," he whispered. "I've only got a couple of seconds. I've slipped the story into your pocket. When you get to Japan put a call into my New York office. Tell them what happened then phone the story. It's our only chance. There's no ending to it but you'll know that soon enough. You'll have to write the ending." He kissed her again. "Promise me that you'll send the story whatever happens?"

"I promise," she said. "I promise."

"You see," he said, "a good newspaperman can always find a way to get a story out." And, as Razin came up to them he said: "I love you. Always remember that. I'll get out soon. Don't be afraid. . . ."

Razin said: "I think you'd better come with me, Mr. Bridges, and let me know what's happening over there."

It was 11:50 and the last confirmation from London still hadn't come. Pavlov, the Planter, and the Prospector waited in the control room; the Pederast stayed with the Gruyanov, fingers playing with the trigger as he mowed down an imaginary line of advancing soldiers, a smile on his pale, ravaged face; Yermakov stood at the other end of the corridor, smoking one of his cardboard-tipped cigarettes, wearing a neatly pressed gray suit, white shirt, and maroon tie. The wolf, feeling the tension, raised its head and howled; the Prospector spoke to it gently and it sat down, ears flattened.

The Planter said, "We should have heard from them half an hour ago."

"They'll come through," Pavlov told him. His eyes had a yellowish tinge to them; there was stubble on his chin and he smelled like an alcoholic. "They have to. This is the most important one."

The scientist was Academician Leonid Tseytlin. Russia's most brilliant young nuclear physicist, he had been lecturing at the cosmodrome at Baikonur, the launching pad for the first man into space, Yuri Gagarin, and the first woman, Valentina Tereshkova, when the authority for his release had been sent. The

Zealots had routed him by domestic flights to Moscow's Vnukova airport and then to Sheremetyevo to pick up a BEA Trident to Heathrow. At Heathrow he would be taken to an office in Mayfair for the final act—the safe arrival transmission to Siberia via Moscow and Irkutsk.

The Prospector said, "Maybe his flight was delayed."

"We allowed for that," Pavlov snapped. "If Sheremetyevo was closed then the whole operation was put back twenty-four hours. But the others took off. Why not Tseytlin?"

"Engine trouble?" the Planter suggested.

"Then BEA would have flown out another aircraft," Pavlov said.

The Pederast sauntered up. "Perhaps," he said, "he's been hijacked." He smiled and walked back to his gun.

Pavlov said to the Planter: "Try again."

The Planter fiddled with the controls, hands trembling. "Nothing," he said after a while. "Maybe we should leave it now. After all, nine of them have got out. That's enough, surely."

"Ten," Pavlov said. "It has to be ten. If we don't hear from London then we blow the bridge."

Yermakov joined them. He had slept, bathed, dressed with care: the general from headquarters visiting battle-weary troops. "I thought," he said, "you had made allowances for every eventuality."

"Don't worry," Pavlov said, "you've got nothing to be scared of."

"But you have, Comrade Pavlov."

It was 11:58. Snow was still flaking gently from the sky; but you could see the railway station, the troops dug in, the group of men in dark coats standing behind them.

At 11:59 the message came through. Tseytlin had arrived. There had been bad weather at Heathrow and the Trident had been diverted to Manchester.

The Planter buried his face in his hands and began to laugh. The Prospector called the wolf. The Pederast stayed at the machine gun looking reflectively at Yermakov.

Pavlov said, "Victory." He passed his hand over the stubble on his chin; his lips were trembling and he was trying to smile. He turned away from the others. "Victory," he repeated. He turned back, muscles on his jaw working. "Thank you," he said. He shook each of their hands. "Now you can go. Good luck."

The Pederast spoke from behind the machine gun. "Why don't we kill him?"

Pavlov walked down the corridor toward him. "Yermakov goes free."

"Why? We've won. All ten of them are free. Why let him go back?"

Yermakov stood impassively in the corridor. Pavlov had his automatic in his hand. "Yermakov goes free," he repeated. "That was the bargain. We Israelis are men of honor. If we kill Yermakov then there is no honor, no victory."

"No fine epitaph for Viktor Pavlov," the Pederast said. "Honor? What's honor? It's something I've never known," he said softly.

Pavlov raised the automatic and the Pederast said, "Go ahead and kill me. It's the only experience I've never had." He swung the barrel of the Gruyanov. "But I promise you this—we'll share the experience."

The Prospector began to shout at him, profanely, obscenely. The Pederast looked at him with surprise, then shouted back, matching every obscenity, his voice rising to a shriek. The Prospector whistled softly and the wolf took the Pederast knocking him aside from the machine gun. His teeth were at the Pederast's throat when the Prospector whistled again and the wolf stood back.

"You see," the Prospector said, "I was right to bring the wolf. I had to make him shout at me," he explained, "otherwise the dog wouldn't have known who to go for. He might even have gone for you. . . ." he said to Pavlov.

The Prospector pulled the Pederast to his feet. There were blue and red marks at his throat. "Come on," the Prospector said. "It's time to go." He turned and saluted Pavlov. "You did it," he said. "You were the one."

The three of them climbed down from the carriage making their way along the bridge leaving Pavlov and Yermakov alone together.

General Rudinko was an archetypal Soviet general: big and square, inclined to corpulence, a soldier's soldier who styled himself on Rommel. He had been posted to Egypt to help the Arabs restore their fire-power wrecked by the Israelis during the Six Day War and had stayed there until Sadat ejected his Soviet advisers. He wasn't sure where his personal affinities lay in the Middle East.

He pointed toward the bridge and said to the major, "There they go."

The major nodded and gave an order to the Army photographer with a long lense like a bazooka. The photographer squeezed the pistol grip three times. "For Razin's rogues' gallery," the major said.

300

"Just in case we lose any of them."

"Is that likely, major?"

"I don't think so. They can't get far." He gestured toward six white-hooded scouts. "They'll let them get as far as the pine trees and then take up the trail. There's an old Jewish prayer house in the village. I've got men hidden all round it just in case any of them feel they should pray."

"I would," the general said, "if I were them." He consulted his watch. "We've got one hour and three-quarters before Pavlov releases Yermakov."

"Perhaps Comrade Yermakov will make a break for it. There are only two of them now."

"Why should he? Pavlov's got the weapons. Why risk being killed if you're going to be released. After all," General Rudinko said, "the man's a politician"—as if that explained everything. "Is everything ready for the moment he reaches the station?"

"It's ready," the major said. "But I don't hold out much hope."

The general frowned, defeat only existed to be turned into victory. "We want Pavlov alive."

The major said, "We have a platoon deployed on the opposite bank of the ravine. Two of them have found cover behind some boulders on the brink. They've got a machine gun with them. According to Gopnik, the detonator's at the end of the coach near the Gruyanov. If they can get a quick burst in then they can destroy it before Pavlov has a chance to blow himself up. But in any case," the major said brightly, "I should imagine he will shoot himself before we have a chance to take him."

The general remembered the shattered evidence of Israeli aggression in the Middle East. "He's a brave man," he murmured. "They all are. Worthy opponents, major."

The major grinned. "Don't let Razin hear you say that."

"To hell with Razin," Rudinko observed. "Let's go and have some coffee with our Western friends. A pretty girl that, eh major?"

"With respect, sir," the major said, "that's one victory you'll never win."

They reached the pit-head, the three men and a wolf. Here they paused. "It's useless," the Pederast said, feeling his throat. "Why don't we just give ourselves up? Shoot each other. Dive into the pit-shaft."

The Planter said, "They'll put a helicopter up soon. Then we have no chance."

"We have a chance," the Prospector said, eyes blue and alert in his shaggy face despite his fatigue. "There's always a chance in Siberia. But you must make friends with it."

"Siberia isn't my sort of friend," the Pederast said. The teeth bruises on his throat were swollen with blood trapped below the skin.

The Prospector ignored him. "Most people prepare themselves to die when they're lost in the taiga. They're beaten before they start. But you must use what Siberia has to offer. It has many weapons and you must accept them. Like falling snow," he added, staring into the sky at the sparse Christmas flakes fluttering in the breeze. "If it falls harder it will soon cover our tracks."

"So what?" the Pederast asked.

"We must go on because they'll be watching us with field glasses. Then we'll cut back into the pine wood and hide there till it's dark." He shielded his eyes and stared toward the station. "They've already

ent some scouts after us. But they're clumsy. I can
ose them."

"And then what?" the Planter asked.

"Then we come back here and pray that the
now covers our footprints." He peered down the
mine shaft. "You two wait here. There are some old
steps down the side. I think they lead to a gallery."

The Pederast said, "You do what you like. I'm
going it alone." He grinned. "Have fun down your
mineshaft." Then he was gone, heading for the village.

He passed the delapidated shop where he had
stayed with the others and walked on till he came
to a small wooden building flanked with birch trees.
Someone had brushed away the snow above the door
and he could still read that it was a Jewish prayer
house. He decided to pray for the first time in
twenty years; the first time since his father, who had
fought for the Red Army in the siege of Leningrad,
had been taken away at 1 A.M. and thrown into a
labor camp where he had died. He went through
the broken doorway where he was immediately taken
by two soldiers wearing snow combat uniforms before he had a chance to draw his pistol.

The Planter waited for fifteen minutes until the
Prospector reappeared 50 feet down the shaft and
began to climb the steps. When he reached the top
he told the Planter, "It's all right. There is a gallery
down there. Provided we don't freeze to death we
can hide there. The troops will be searching for
us much farther on. Come on, my friend."

They made for the pine trees, plunging through
the great pillars of the trees. "Now," the Prospector
said, "pray for snow."

"And what do we do when we get out of the
shaft?"

"We do exactly what the old pioneers used to

do when they hadn't any roubles to buy a train ticket. We become flyers. We jump on a train and steal a ride."

Viktor Pavlov and Vasily Yermakov faced each other across the desk, a half-empty bottle of brandy between them. Pavlov offered his hostage a glass but Yermakov refused: he didn't want to smell of alcohol when he faced the other members of the presidium, particularly the young upstart. They would say he had to fortify himself with brandy; and, by the time they got back to Moscow, they would be whispering that he was drunk as Nikita Khrushchev used to be. He fetched a bottle of Narzan water, filled a glass and sat down opposite Pavlov. He thought, I could take him now if I wanted to. His glance strayed to the automatic on the desk. But what was the point? A struggle, the gun going off as they wrestled on the floor. . . . No, I will walk out of this coach like a statesman, smiling as if I were greeting the American president at Sheremetyevo airport.

"So," Pavlov said, "in ten minutes you will be a free man. If," he added, "anyone is free in the Soviet Union."

"If anyone is free anywhere in the world. Is a man free in the West when he has a family, a mortgage, and he has to crawl to his employer for fear of losing his job—losing everything? Is the American free who is conscripted into an army to fight a war he knows nothing about? Are the students of France free as they fall bleeding from the police clubs? Is the British government free when it's held to ransom by a handful of strike pickets? Are the Irish free as they kill each other in Belfast?" Yermakov leaned cross the desk, stabbing with his finger. "No, Comrade Razin, freedom is a luxury of the past. It is merely that the Russian people realized this first."

"In the West," Pavlov said, "the people are free to leave." His voice was husky, the pupils of his eyes unnaturally dilated. But, now it was all over, he had steadied himself, as Yermakov had done. What was done was done; no more doubts; victory was his—the means had justified the ends.

Yermakov said: "I will tell you this. The difference between democracy and socialism is merely this: In a Socialist state we hide our dirty wash, in a democracy they air it."

"And I'll tell you this," Pavlov said. "The difference between a democracy and a Socialist state is that in a democracy a man is allowed to keep his soul. . . ."

Yermakov stood up. "Very shortly," he said, "you will be in a position, according to your faith, to give the ultimate judgment on that." He swallowed the rest of his mineral water. "And now I'll get my coat. You are, I presume, allowing me to go?"

"Of course."

Yermakov returned, buttoning his coat, adjusting his *shapka*. He glanced at his watch. 1:59. He stuck out his hand. "You are an outstanding man. I wish you had been on the right side."

Yermakov made his way along the bridge then turned right across the snow toward the railway station. As he drew near they began to clap and cheer. Yermakov adjusted the smile on his face as the dark-coated men from the Kremlin stepped forward to wring his hand and slap him on the back. As a survivor of long-standing, he had heard such applause before. It reminded him of distant gunfire—the prelude to a battle.

From the coach Viktor Pavlov saw them bring
Anna to the front of the crowd. But she didn
wave. For a moment she was his life, the crusad
behind him. His brain cleared and certain figures be
gan to settle into an inarguable equation. Viktor Pa
vlov didn't want to know the answer. He took a las
long drink of brandy, fighting to keep it in his stom
ach. *The Masada Complex.* He walked to the en
of the carriage and tossed the bottle out the door
hearing it break against the side of the ravine. A
that moment a machine gun opened up from behind
a clump of boulders with a deep bark. The bullet
slammed into the woodwork around him, shattering
the windows. He grabbed the Gruyanov and fire
back. He thought he saw a body fall. Another clutch
of bullets whipped into the carriage and he thought
They're trying to get the detonator. He let go o
the machine gun. As he stood up, a bullet caugh
him in the chest throwing him against the wall. The
blood pumped steadily from his chest. More bullet.
hit the carriage, grouping around the detonator
With his hand to his chest, Viktor Pavlov made
his way through the streets of Beirut with an Uz
submachine gun under his arm. . . .

The explosion sent blast-waves loaded with snow
over the crowd outside the railway station; they
ducked their heads as the tortured air pushed at
their faces. The explosion chased its way around the
mountains before finding an exit and losing itself in
Siberia. The bridge snapped in the middle, breaking
the back of the coach. It seemed to fall in slow
motion beneath a mushroom of smoke and snow
veined with flame. Bridge and coach disappeared
and for a long time there was silence.

ARRIVAL

The Trans-Siberian pulled out of Shilka at 9:19 P.M. on the twelfth day. Libby Chandler shared a compartment with a sailor bound for Vladivostok who snored, a New Zealander who talked enthusiastically of being bathed by a Geisha girl immediately on arrival in Japan, and a Scottish schoolmistress with relatives in Hong Kong.

When they arrived at Ksenievskaya at 4:32 on the thirteenth day two men, one with very shaggy features, the other with an inquisitive, bird-like face, were found half-frozen on the roof of the train. They were chased away by sleepy railway officials: such escapades were the stuff of Siberia and who were they to hand them over to the police?

On the fourteenth day, after passing through the mock Jewish settlement of Birobidzan, the train finally pulled into Khabarovsk, the city named after Yerofei Khabarov who, in the seventeenth century, helped to tame the natives by pillage and torture.

Today Khabarovsk is the biggest city on the Pacific side of Irkutsk, 5,289 miles by rail from Moscow. It throbs with industry and is the junction for foreign travelers going east on the Trans-Siberian. Here they board a train which has air-conditioning and better-looking girl attendants; it takes them 456 miles to the port of Nakhodka where they embark by boat for Japan.

Travelers spend the night at the Khabarovsk Hotel and that's where Libby found Colonel Yury Razin waiting for her in her room. He greeted her cordially and waved her to a chair as if it were his room.

Libby said, "Get out."

Razin held up his hand. "Give me three minutes. All right?"

Libby sat down abruptly, feeling sick. "What do you want? Haven't you done enough?"

"Quite enough," Razin said. "But I admire you and I want to give you a few words of advice. Listen carefully. As you know, we are at great pains to stop our . . . our shared experience being recounted in the West. Now"—he studied her face—"I presume Bridges gave you some sort of story to send to his newspaper. Am I right?"

She didn't reply and he went on, "This is the position. We're holding Mr. Wagstaff for a few months. When we finally release him the story will be so old that it will have lost its impact. And no one will take him seriously anyway. Bridges can't leave without an exit visa and we shall ensure that he cannot make any contact with his office—or contact with nyone who might be able to get his report out of the ountry. That, Miss Chandler, leaves you."

Razin stood up and went to the door. "I want to ell you this. If you do as you're told and don't transit Bridges's story then perhaps one day you will be ble to meet him again. If you transmit it then Bridges s a dead man." He closed the door gently behind im.

THE ODESSA FILE *by* FREDERICK FORSYTH,
author of THE DAY OF THE JACKAL

The life-and-death hunt for a notorious Nazi criminal
unfolds against a background of international espionage
and clandestine arms deals, involving rockets designed in
Germany, built in Egypt, and equipped with warheads of
nuclear waste and bubonic plague. Who is behind it all?
Odessa. Who or what is Odessa? You'll find out in *The
Odessa File* . . .

'In the hands of Frederick Forsyth the documentary thriller
achieves its most sophisticated form—Mr. Forsyth has
produced both a brilliant entertainment and a disquieting
book.' *The Guardian*

552 09436 6 — **50p** Ta65

THE TERMINAL MAN *by* MICHAEL CRICHTON

The Terminal Man is a novel of breathtaking suspense
and alarming implications; its theme—mind control. A
thrilling combination of science and fantasy, it is the story
of the first operation linking a human brain and a computer.

'Michael Crichton uses literary techniques similar to those
developed in his earlier novel *The Andromeda Strain**;
but here greater impact is achieved. This is a fast, exciting
novel that with its diagrams, graphs X-ray charts and computer printout, has all the credibility of a detailed case history or a brilliant piece of reportage. —*Sunday Times*

Also published by Corgi Books

552 09192 8 — **40p** T66

A SELECTED LIST OF FINE NOVELS THAT APPEAR IN CORGI

All these books are available at your bookshop or newsagent: or can be ordered direc from the publisher. Just tick the titles you want and fill in the form below.

CORGI BOOKS, Cash Sales Department, P.O. Box 11, Falmouth, Cornwall.
Please send cheque or postal order, no currency. **U.K. and Eire** send 15p for first bo
plus 5p per copy for each additional book ordered to a maximum charge of 50p
cover the cost of postage and packing. **Overseas Customers and B.F.P.O.** allow 2
for first book and 10p per copy for each additional book.

NAME (Block letters) ....

ADDRESS ....

(Aug. 75) .... O

While every effort is made to keep prices low, it is sometimes necessary to increa prices at short notice. Corgi Books reserve the right to show new retail prices on cove which may differ from those previously advertised in the text or elsewhere.